Praise for Tim Hemlin's first Neil Marshall mystery, *If Wishes Were Horses*...

"A welcome new voice in the mystery field."
—EARL EMERSON

"A very promising, quite smart, launch to a new series...a Southern-fried tale blessed by an unconventional cast of characters."
—*Publishers Weekly*

"Tim Hemlin is a thoroughbred among mystery authors. This debut novel serves up down-home characters and a delicious, fast-paced plot that readers will want to devour in a single sitting."
—DEBORAH ADAMS

"Tim Hemlin's *If Wishes Were Horses*... is one of the most entertaining first mysteries I've read in several years, and aspiring writer Neil Marshall is the most engaging amateur sleuth to come along since Jeff Abbott's Jordan Poteet. This novel is so good I'd like it even if it weren't set in Texas."

—BILL CRIDER

Please turn to the back of the book for an interview with Tim Hemlin.

By Tim Hemlin
Published by Ballantine Books:

IF WISHES WERE HORSES . . .
A WHISPER OF RAGE
PEOPLE IN GLASS HOUSES
A CATERED CHRISTMAS

A CATERED CHRISTMAS

Tim Hemlin

BALLANTINE BOOKS • NEW YORK

A Ballantine Book
Published by The Ballantine Publishing Group
Copyright © 1998 by Tim Hemlin

All rights reserved under International and Pan-American Copyright Conventions. Published in the United States by The Ballantine Publishing Group, a division of Random House, Inc., New York, and simultaneously in Canada by Random House of Canada Limited, Toronto.

www.randomhouse.com/BB/

Library of Congress Catalog Card Number: 98-96314

ISBN 0-345-42001-2

Manufactured in the United States of America

First Edition: December 1998

10 9 8 7 6 5 4 3 2 1

To Valerie

Acknowledgments

A special thanks to my editor, Malinda Lo, for her enthusiasm and hard work on the manuscript. There's no doubt she went over each and every word. Also I'm grateful as usual to Joe Blades for his continued support and for hooking me up with Malinda. A heartfelt thanks goes to my agent, Kimberley Cameron, whose energy and positive attitude are definitely contagious. A tip of the hat to Dale Pinkerton, graduate of the Colorado School of Mines, for answering my many questions about mining. Finally, if not for my wife's tough critiques, my parents' encouragement, and my children's continued support, completing this book would've been next to impossible.

How many observe Christ's birthday! How few, his precepts!
O! 'tis easier to keep holidays than commandments.
—BENJAMIN FRANKLIN

Prologue

The Christmas party buzzed with joy, but the cheer hit rock bottom with me. Drinks were flowing liberally, hors d'oeuvres were being consumed in gluttonous proportions. I took a turn at carving the leg of lamb on the silver butler's cart, slicing bite-sized portions onto silver-dollar rolls and serving them with dabs of jalapeño jelly.

"Well, look here," Richard Wentworth, the host, exclaimed from beneath six or seven double Scotches. "We've got the head man on the floor."

I smiled, preparing the choicest piece of lamb I could find.

"Neil Marshall," Wentworth continued, "you ever met the governor?"

"Haven't had the pleasure," I replied, though I recognized the man standing next to him as being the ex-president's son.

"Governor Bush, this here's Neil Marshall, chef for the best damn catering company in Houston," Wentworth proclaimed.

"Pleasure to meet you," the governor said, stretching out a hand. I switched meat fork and knife to my left hand to accept his shake.

"Likewise," I said, though I hadn't voted for the man.

"You put on a good show," the governor stated. "Maybe sometime you could come to Austin."

"I'd love to."

He smiled. I nodded, and the two men wandered off toward the male quartet that had positioned themselves on the winding stairwell to sing carols. A twenty-foot tree *flanked their right, stretching up to the balcony on the second floor.*

"God rest ye merry gentlemen. . . ." burst forth. I grabbed Booker Atwell to take over for me at the lamb station and walked around the large estate myself to monitor the other food stations.

Richard Wentworth's huge antebellum mansion was a bastion of wealth in the exclusive River Oaks section of Houston. Interior designers had loaded the estate with holiday decorations. Garland wound up the banister. Poinsettias were everywhere. A large wreath donned the front door and, outside, lights that wrapped the length of the porch shone brighter than those on a used-car lot. I drifted, in charge this evening, only caring because it was another job. Another job.

I perused the crudité trays and the cheese and pâté displays in the game room. The dessert buffet in the breakfast room was still healthily stocked. The seafood center downstairs—piled high with boiled shrimp, fried shrimp, fried oysters, oysters on the half shell, and crab legs—was a popular spot. There were more wreaths with red ribbons and silver and gold baubles along the walls. Mistletoe hung above the entrance, occasionally causing a traffic jam. The oyster shuckers were working a mile a minute. The fryers were cooking batch after batch. The bartender in the corner was working up a sweat. Plenty of red sauce, tartar sauce, lemon wedges, and crackers lined the tables. Everything was running smoothly.

Couldn't be better.

Back upstairs, the quartet wound into "White Christmas" as the guests chattered and laughed. In the dining room the creamed wild mushrooms with petite toasts were running low, so I cornered Candace Littlefield to replenish the dish. I also directed her to check the tamales and spicy chicken drummettes. Then I told one of the temporaries on tonight's staff—a hotel-and-restaurant student from the University of Houston whose name escaped me—to tidy the honey-baked-ham display he was working on. Like the lamb, it was a manned station, sliced and served on mini–corn muffins with Dijon and cracked-pepper mustard.

I smiled. I thanked people for their compliments. I wandered through the music and joy. My facial muscles grew weary under the strain of acting happy.

A guest under the influence of too much Christmas cheer brushed against the tree and knocked off an ornament. The red ball hit the floor with a crack like an egg struck against the side of a bowl. I rushed over to pick up the delicate pieces, carefully placing the jagged fragments inside the hollow interior.

A waiter moved through the crowd to assist me. He opened a napkin on his tray and allowed me to dispose of the fragile ornament. We garnered little attention, even from the man who'd sloshed·vodka and the decoration onto the floor. I relaxed my smile. I was very tired.

Too many jobs working for the beautiful people had begun to make me jaded. In the last couple of years I'd witnessed cordial smiles turn to deadly threats. A congressional candidate with a knife in his hand as he slapped your back. Marriages as brittle as the ornament I'd just picked up.

Perhaps my disenchantment with life had begun with my father's untimely death from a heart attack, and was exacerbated by the deaths of two close friends. Whatever it was, I was under a melancholy cloud that usually only hit me as a kid after the holiday season, when all the excitement, the relatives, the anticipation was gone, played out, and I was left with a bland January to face.

But it was more than melancholy. Even Keely Cohen, my writing mentor at the University of Houston, had noticed it in my work.

"I know you're struggling with a sense of purpose right now," she'd told me over coffee. "You've seen some nasty things, and lost people who were very close to you. That's how I read the darkness in your poems."

"I can't argue with that," I'd replied.

"But you can't let the darkness take over."

"I don't believe I'm being seduced to the dark side," I said sarcastically.

"Not darkness as in evil," Keely said, sipping a mocha-almond decaf. *"Darkness as in hopelessness."*

"Can't help but lose a little faith."

"I know about losing faith, Neil. When Caitlin died, a part of me died, too."

I fell silent. Keely had lost her little girl, Caitlin, to cancer a few years back.

"But you have to work through it," she added. *"And that's what scares me. I don't see you working through it. I see you dwelling in it. And soon you'll be locked inside a darkness so great no light will ever be able to seep in."*

I half smiled, swilling my coffee around in the Styrofoam cup.

"You're too sweet to let that happen to you, Neil. A poet can't lose his faith. Might turn out to be a Dadaist," she joked. Then, firmly: *"Don't dwell in it."*

Don't dwell in it, I thought as the quartet completed their program with "We Wish You a Merry Christmas."

I brought the smile back and rejoined the pretty people. I applauded as the singers wound up their program. But inside, I wasn't much better than the Christmas-tree ornament.

Hollow and broken.

Then the winds shifted. From the mountains of my childhood, a storm gathered. And at its center was the last man I expected to see.

Six Days Before Christmas

1

Perry Stevens Catering had worn me out this holiday season. Body, mind, and soul, I was plumb tuckered. Nonetheless, while Mattie Johnson's six-year-old son, J.J., was around I slapped on my game face and fed his Christmas enthusiasm. Or tried to draw from it.

For J.J., this time of year was more than the roasting of countless Christmas ducks, marinated in a rum-orange sauce and stuffed with a wild rice and pecan dressing. It was more than staying up until two o'clock in the morning to finish just one more gingerbread house. It was more than the thousands of dollars we invoiced over a few short weeks.

But I didn't feel J.J.'s Christmas spirit. Not even when he suddenly and passionately interrupted my description of one blizzard-ridden winter I'd spent in the Rockies.

"Santa!" he exclaimed, pointing out the front window with one hand, slamming the other against the stainless-steel worktable between us.

Automatically I turned to look out the window and saw an old familiar image lumbering up the driveway. I did a double take then glanced at Mattie, who'd come up behind J.J. "Oh my God," I said as much to myself as I did to Mattie. A heavy rapping hit the door. "You're not going to believe this," I added, and the door opened.

"Santa?" J.J. whispered.

"Grandpa?" I said.

I had inherited my height from my grandfather, but I was always amazed at his size, especially when I hadn't seen him in a while. At six-foot-seven, he ducked as he stepped over the threshold, leery of banging his head on the frame. With a figure so bulky it blocked the mellow December light, Grandpa was an impressive man. J.J.'s mouth was as wide open as mine.

"Hello, kid," he bellowed, and quickly closed the door. A cold spell had hit the city, and it was all of thirty-something outside, but my grandfather was sweating as if he'd just jogged a marathon. He pulled a red-and-silver San Francisco 49ers cap off his head, allowing his long gray hair to flow freely. His bushy silver beard was wilder than I'd remembered. He was wearing blue jeans, a red flannel shirt, and a red down vest that no doubt served him well at his Colorado home, but in Houston it would be as useless as a one-horse open sleigh.

"Mom didn't tell me you were coming down," I managed to say.

"Your ma and I don't speak much since your dad passed," he replied, catching his breath.

Or while he was living, I thought.

J.J. hopped down from the stool he was sitting on. "Are you the real Santa Claus?" he asked, wide-eyed.

Grandpa looked kindly at the boy, and for a split second I was jarred back to a Christmas over twenty years ago. I'd almost forgotten about the year my parents and I flew to Colorado. The excitement, the anticipation, the holiday joy all finally busted loose when our rental car coasted to a stop in his driveway, and I jumped out hollering, "Grandpa, Grandpa, Grandpa . . ." He stepped onto the deck, large as the Rockies himself, and stared down at me, a huge smile on his face.

A smile not so different from the one he now flashed J.J. "Been accused of being old Saint Nick, but my name's Stephen Marshall," he responded heartily, and offered his hand. "I'm Neil's granddaddy. Who are you?"

"I'm J.J. I'm six and a half." He gave Grandpa's hand a gentle shake. "You sure look like Santa."

"Thank you." Grandpa unbuttoned his vest and laid it

on the stainless-steel table. His wide girth became even more apparent; he was built like an old weight lifter, solid and robust, but fighting time's effect. He turned his smile on Mattie and asked, "And who is this beautiful young woman?"

"My mama," J.J. piped up.

"Mattie Johnson, meet my grandfather," I said.

"Lovely." He approached her and kissed her hand.

"Be careful, Mattie," I warned. "My dear grandpa's been married five times." My father was a product of wife number one, and as the first grandchild, I'd always received particular attention from Grandpa.

Mattie blushed. "Nice to meet you, Mr. Marshall. I can see where Neil gets his charm."

Grandpa smiled warmly, then he righted himself and ran a hand across the sweat on his forehead. "Don't suppose you have any Scotch in this place?" he asked, his expression paling. "I had a hell of a trip down."

Just then Perry Stevens, owner of the catering company bearing his name, strolled out of his office. He adjusted his reindeer-speckled bow tie. "I see we have a guest."

Next to my grandfather, my boss looked like a dapper elf. I introduced them.

"A pleasure," Perry said, stroking his red beard and craning his neck to meet Grandpa in the eye.

"Nice little restaurant you have here," Grandpa observed, "but where do the customers sit?"

"We're caterers," Perry corrected politely.

"I see." Grandpa's eyebrows furrowed as he contemplated the wire racks of canned goods, the large reach-in refrigerators, the mixers, the hanging utensils, the deep sinks, the worktables, and the knife racks. "You mean you don't even have a bar?"

"We are not a neighborhood dive."

"Shame," the old man said, and waved a thick finger toward the front window. "I got a good look at your neighborhood. A man could make a fortune with a dive."

"Please, sir—" Perry protested.

"Grandpa," I interrupted, "Perry's going to take you seriously."

The old man eyed me soberly. "Maybe I am. One thing I could always do well was make money. Buttloads of money. 'Course I blew the dough as fast as it came in. Now, what about that Scotch? Or do I have to go to that Mexican cantina down the road?"

"Well . . ." Perry started to say.

I sighed and glanced at my boss. As we were winding down this Sunday before Christmas, having just dispatched Robbie Persons and his crew to tonight's function, I didn't think it would kill Perry to serve my grandfather a warm-me-up before we left. He picked up on my vibes, albeit reluctantly, and gave in to my grandfather's request.

"By all means," Perry said slowly.

Grandpa's countenance brightened. "On the rocks with a splash of water."

Mattie jumped up. "I'll get it," she said. "Anyone else?"

Perry and I declined. I pulled a wooden stool up to the table. "Have a seat, Grandpa."

He complied. "Thank you, son. You know, this place is a bitch to find. Even with directions from that nutty landlord of yours. I think he just wanted to get me off his back porch and away from his slobbering Doberman. Nice dog, but a sorry-assed guard."

I grinned slyly. "Looks can be deceiving." I recalled how the dog had mauled a gunman who had taken a shot at me. "After all," I continued, "you have that Father Christmas appearance, but—"

"I have a generous heart, Neil," he said, cutting me off.

Perry cleared his throat. A subtle twitch at the corner of his mouth told me he was trying to make sense of what was going on and not be too quick to pass judgment. The latter was very difficult for Perry.

"Neil didn't mention his granddaddy was coming for the holidays," Perry said.

"He didn't know." The old man laughed sonorously.

Mattie set a crystal rocks glass filled with Scotch and ice in front of Grandpa.

"Thank you, my dear," he said, raising the glass. " 'Tis the season." And he drank, though he didn't appear very jolly. Of course, Grandpa's visit notwithstanding, little appeared very jolly to me at the moment, so his attitude could simply have been a reflection of my current view of the world.

J.J., still in awe, crawled into my grandfather's lap.

"You're sweaty," the little boy said.

"You get down, J.J.," Mattie said, her slender hands on her hips. "And you apologize to Mr. Marshall."

"Oh, he doesn't mean no harm," Grandpa insisted. "Besides, I'm used to the little critters crawling on me. Happens almost everywhere I go." His face beamed again with cheer, but I was beginning to notice a pattern. He was either beaming or somber, nothing in between—and he seemed mostly somber. It was a sorrow I'd never seen in him before, and the feeling was flowing from him, not me.

I shook off the rising melancholia and glanced at J.J. "That's true. Ever since I can remember, he favored Saint Nick. Perhaps your hair wasn't quite as gray, Grandpa, or beard quite as bushy, but it's been an image you've always cultivated."

"Interesting," Perry murmured.

"You don't know the half of it," I replied.

Mattie glanced at her wristwatch, then, knowingly, at Perry. "Well, we need to get going."

"Yes," he said, suddenly remembering what he'd been doing before my grandfather's arrival, and darted back to his office.

"You know what I want for Christmas?" J.J. whispered.

"J.J.!" Mattie reprimanded.

"But what if he is Santa, and I don't tell him what I want. Then I've really messed up."

Grandpa laughed. "What do you want?" he asked.

"A puppy," he whispered.

"J.J.!"

"Seems we'll have to work on your mother," Grandpa said in mock confidence, then patted the child's back. J.J. hopped down.

Mattie flashed him a *thanks a lot, that's the last thing I need* look.

Perry returned, waving Mattie's check. She accepted it, said her goodbyes, and tugged her wide-eyed son out the door.

I pulled off my apron and tossed the stained white fabric on the table. Grandpa took another gulp of Scotch, that faraway look in his eyes again. Automatically he reached into his vest pocket, drew out his pipe and tobacco, packed the bowl, and lit it up. Perry's face went pale.

"Come on, big guy," I announced. "Let's get something to eat." I slipped on my black leather jacket.

"If that's what you want, Neil," he said, and stood. Milky-blue smoke billowed from his pipe as if he were his own factory. I had to admit, though, the aroma was pleasant.

"Ah, everything's put up?" Perry asked weakly, staring at my grandfather.

"It's spotless back there, boss."

Noting Perry's gaze, Grandpa, after reclaiming his vest, shook my boss's hand with exaggerated exuberance. "Pleasure to meet you, young man," he exclaimed through a cloud of smoke. "I hope my grandson's doing a good job for you."

"A very good job," he responded, freeing himself from the huge man.

"Excellent. I wouldn't have anything less." He tossed the remainder of his drink down and fixed his cap back on his head. "Lead on," he ordered.

"Tomorrow, Perry," I said. "Have a good night."

"You, too."

I marched out, caught Grandpa hesitating, then he followed, saluting Perry with his pipe before closing the door.

"Nervous little fella, isn't he?" Grandpa asked as we hiked down the driveway.

"Maybe he caught it from you."

"What do you mean?"

"One minute you're fine, the next you're off in the ozone, or sweating, or, I don't know, just not right." The sun was almost down, a charcoal light shading the chilly evening sky. At the corner, the stop sign rattled in the gusty wind.

"Never figured it got cold in Houston," he grumbled.

"You're avoiding the subject." We stopped at my VW Bug.

"You drive this?" He was incredulous.

"It's a classic."

"Classic, hell. It's old, cramped, and has no heat."

"You think my Bug's cold and cramped, wait until you see my apartment," I shot back. "Besides, how'd you get to The Kitchen?" The renovated ranch house we worked out of had been christened The Kitchen. Perry enjoyed the sound of it—a nickname that implied both homeyness and culinary excellence.

"Walked," he replied.

"Walked? My apartment must be three miles away."

"Suspect you're right. Now, are you going to unlock this toy or are we going to stand here and freeze our balls off?"

"Hold your horses."

I slipped inside and unlocked the passenger door. He hunkered down in the seat.

"I was more comfortable riding a mule through Silver Valley when I was prospecting in the Twenties."

"Grandpa, you're seventy-two. You weren't prospecting in the Twenties."

"My soul's been here a long time, boy," he muttered.

I cranked up the Bug. "That's just fine for your soul, but why are you in Houston and not in Silver Valley?"

"I'm visiting my favorite grandson."

"Grandpa—"

"Ain't you glad to see me? You're sure acting strange. What's wrong?"

"Of course I'm glad to see you. Nothing's wrong—"

"Then why the third degree?"

"I'm not giving you the third degree," I replied, growing exasperated. "I only asked a simple question."

"Hmmph!" He grumbled something unintelligible and, in the ensuing darkness, gave no further response. There was nothing like the holidays to engender warm family feelings, I thought, and chugged around the corner toward my apartment.

"I want to change into a clean shirt," I told him, "and then we can round up some dinner."

"You look fine. Can't we just get some grub?"

"I smell of garlic and onions. And I spilled booze on me when I made the apple-brandy pâté."

"Hmmph!"

Hmmph again, I thought. Might as well be *Bah, humbug*. He was sure lifting my spirits.

"You planning on staying until Christmas?" I asked as we drove through the neighborhood streets. Live oak and pecan trees cast stark shadows beneath the street lamps.

"Don't know. What kind of chow do you like?"

"How about seafood?"

"Fried oysters?" he asked, perking up.

Like you should eat that stuff, I thought, but wisely kept the comment to myself. "I'll take you to Little Pappa's."

"Fine."

My apartment was located above the garage of my landlord, Jerry Jacoma. As I approached the area, however, I could see that something was wrong. Jerry's house was dark and his truck gone, but the front door was open, banging back and forth in the breeze. I coasted into the driveway and parked close to the street.

"That's odd," I stated absently, and turned off the Bug. "You wait here." I climbed out of the VW. So did Grandpa.

"Don't you ever do what you're told?"

"No, and that's why I'm in the—I mean, I ain't staying cooped up like a bear in a beaver bog."

I hushed him. "I'm serious. Jerry never leaves his door open."

Grandpa quickly looked in all directions.

I eased toward the porch.

"Might be wise to call the police," he whispered coarsely.

"There's a phone in the house."

"Your mother's right. You *can* act like a damned fool."

You don't talk to Mother, remember? I wanted to shout back, but again held my tongue. Quietly, I ascended the wooden steps, then paused and listened. All I detected was the banging. I caught the door on the outward swing, held it, and gently pushed it inward.

The living room was a disaster. Books scattered, tables overturned, cushions knifed, and the stuffing flung everywhere. I felt the hair on the back of my neck stiffen. I debated whether or not to call out, thought better of it, and edged back outside.

"What is it?" Grandpa said.

"Jerry's been robbed," I said. "Let's walk around back to my apartment and call the cops."

"Good to see you inherited some of my sense."

"Grandpa, I've been knocked around a time or two. I don't take too many foolish chances anymore."

"Noticed you're a bit more ragged than the last time I saw you. Your beard doesn't hide the whole scar. What caused that?"

"Not now, for Christ's sake. Come on." We scuffed up the driveway, wind cutting into us, when an image caught my attention. I froze. The back door also banged open and shut, open and shut. But down at the foot of the stairs, beneath the rear porch light, lay a dark shape.

"Oh, God," I whispered.

"They've found me," Grandpa said, voice low.

We both stared at Samson, Jerry Jacoma's Doberman, lying in a web of blood. Slowly, the dog raised his head and acknowledged our presence with a whimper.

As I knelt to examine the severity of Samson's wound, I noticed a piece of paper pinned by a knife to the porch banister. A piece of paper that, on closer inspection, was a coloring-book outline of Santa Claus.

Instead of being filled in with crayons, though, this picture was tinged with blood—and Jolly Old Saint Nick's head was skewered by the knife's lustrous blade.

2

The police officers were accompanied by a familiar figure. Tall, lean, and wearing an off-white trench coat, Lieutenant Paul Gardner appeared to slip through the shadowy street like a solitary beam of moonlight.

I wondered why Gardner was here. He was a homicide detective, not burglary.

Police lights strobed the chilly air as the three men approached. I waited, shivering by the VW, my hands jammed into the pockets of my leather jacket. Grandpa was tending to Samson, wrapping the gash above the dog's right front leg with some towels I'd fetched from my apartment.

"We haven't gone inside the house," I informed them.

Grandpa came toward us, wiping his hands on a small towel as he approached. He'd been strangely quiet as well as unwilling to explain his earlier comment: *They've found me.* What did he mean?

Gardner nodded toward the house. "Check it out," he told the two blues. The cops jogged up to the front door, hands on holstered guns, and disappeared inside.

Gardner looked at me pointedly. "I'm coming to know this driveway as well as my own." No handshake, only a piercing glare. "Where's the body?"

"The what?"

"The victim."

"The, ah, the victim?" I questioned.

"Around back," Grandpa spoke up, his tone friendly and helpful. "And he's going to need to be sewed up, real

17

quick." He'd shifted into his patient Santa voice, the one he used with children. Far different from the cantankerous old fart he'd just been with me.

Gardner stared at him. "And you are?"

"Stephen Marshall." He stretched out his hand. "Neil's grandfather."

Gardner shook his hand. "Who's been murdered? Dasher or Dancer?"

"Close," Grandpa replied, and led the way.

How was I going to explain this? I specifically told the dispatcher that the house was in a shambles and Samson had been knifed. I know I mentioned that Samson was a dog. Surely, I did. I was rattled, but not that rattled. Surely, the dispatcher misunderstood. Perhaps it was my attempt to explain the Santa picture that muddied the conversation. Still . . .

I screwed up. Damn.

I trailed them to the back porch. Grandpa pointed out the bundled dog.

"Is the Doberman dead, too?" Gardner asked.

"Hurt bad. I slowed the bleeding."

"Best get him some medical attention."

"I already called a vet friend of mine and explained the situation," I told Gardner. "He has an animal clinic on North Shepherd, and he's coming by to pick up the dog."

"I'll be damned," the lieutenant said. "Can't get doctors to make house calls, but if an animal's hurt—"

"He is a friend, of sorts. We catered the grand opening of his new hospital."

"All right, let's get down to the real business. Where's the deceased? Inside? Is it that flaky landlord of yours, Neil?"

"Uh—"

"There is no deceased, Mr. Gardner," Grandpa informed him.

"Lieutenant," he automatically corrected, then paused. "What did you say?"

"The deceased is not deceased." Grandpa again pointed. "I believe his name is Samson."

"You've got to be kidding."

"I think there was a failure to communicate when I called 911," I said meekly.

"A failure to communicate," Gardner repeated. "Sunday night and I'm fixing to go home. But no, I take this call first because, you see, I recognize the address and think to myself, *What the devil has Marshall gotten himself into now?* And it turns out to be a goddamn mutt."

"Calm yourself, Lieutenant," Grandpa spoke up, "before your blood pressure soars to the heavens and you find yourself prematurely shaking old Saint Peter's hand."

"My blood pressure tends to rise a little more each time I cross paths with your grandson."

"Have you considered meditating?" the old man offered.

"Meditating?" he repeated incredulously. "Just what I need on a cold Sunday night, a gray-haired hippie and a wounded mutt."

"Samson is hardly a mutt—and Jerry's house is a wreck," I pointed out.

He shook his head. "Not my job, unless he's in there cold as the night air."

"Aren't you going to investigate?" I asked.

"An assault on a dog? That's priceless, even coming from you."

"Someone's rifled my landlord's house, stabbed his dog, and left a cute picture of Saint Nick stuck to the porch railing like some sick message," I protested. "All this, by the way, occurs on the very day my grandfather comes to town. Who, as you've noted yourself, strongly favors the guy from the North Pole."

Gardner scratched his five-o'clock shadow, fully visible beneath the back porch light. His mouth was agape as if he were trying to decide how loudly to respond. Wisps of gray-black hair at his temples lifted in the easy breeze. He turned from Grandpa to me then back again to the old man. "You have anything to offer?" he asked at last with controlled civility.

"City folks are crazy."

"What?"

"That's why I live in the mountains and only come out a few times a year."

"How nice."

"This is serious, Grandpa," I spoke up. The tension crackling off the usually laid-back Lieutenant Gardner was enough to light the giant Christmas tree down in front of city hall.

"I've got nothing helpful to tell you, Neil," the old man said. "Reckon it's just a coincidence."

"A pretty macabre coincidence —"

The two blues came out the back door, cutting me off. I was fixing to remind Grandpa what he'd said about having been *found* while Gardner was still here. Perhaps the lieutenant could shake some information loose.

"No one's in the house," said one of the cops.

"But someone sure was," the other cop stated. "Ripped the place apart. Not like a robbery but sheer vandalism. Maybe somebody was looking for something."

"Anybody know where Jacoma is?" Gardner asked.

"No," I replied. "I've been so busy at work I haven't seen him in a few days."

"So you can't tell me if he's been around?" Gardner continued.

"Oh, he has," Grandpa shot in. "I saw the man this afternoon while I was waiting for Neil. In fact, I was playing with the dog, too. Nice animal. Strange little man, though."

"Do you know where he went today, Mr. Marshall?"

"Well, after finding out who I was, he asked me in for a beer, and he talked about some—how did he put it?— *bitchin' party* he was going to tonight. Down Galveston way, I think. I had half a mind to go with him, except he babbled like a fool, and I didn't think I could stand the ride. So I got directions from him and walked over to where Neil works."

"Invited you in for a beer?" Gardner asked. "You didn't by chance hide anything in his house, did you?"

"Like what, Lieutenant?"

"You tell me."

"If only I could think of something to hide."

Gardner drew a deep breath. "Well, if Jacoma's at some holiday party in Galveston, he's most likely spending the night. Secure the house," he ordered the cops. "And you best double-check that no one called the coroner."

"Yes, sir," responded one cop, and he left.

"And bag this knife and picture," Gardner added. "I'll send it to the lab to see if they come up with anything."

"For the dog?" The officer was taken aback. "You're investigating an assault on a dog?"

"No, I'm not investigating an assault on a dog," Gardner retorted.

"Yes, sir." The officer almost snapped to attention.

"At the moment I don't know what needs to be investigated," he added, eyeing Grandpa and me. "Take a statement from these two."

"Yes, sir."

"Neil, when Jacoma gets back, have him take inventory of anything missing and contact burglary."

"All right," I agreed. "And you'll let me know if you discover anything about the knife and picture."

Gardner's response was a thick sigh between clenched teeth. Then he turned away and strode silently down the driveway.

"Jerry's going to freak out," I said absently.

One of the cops, who appeared as happy as the lieutenant to be out in the frosty night, came up to us with a clipboard, flashlight illuminating it. Grandpa went first, repeating his story almost verbatim in the same listener-friendly style he'd used with Gardner. I was a little more tense, feeling the blood rise to my face as I relived my apparent mistake in summoning a homicide lieutenant. As he finished, a van pulled into the driveway. The cop paid little attention to Dr. Crenshaw as the vet hopped out of the vehicle and carefully approached the Doberman. With great effort, the officer mumbled a "Merry Christmas," gave Grandpa the once-over, and left.

"Someone did a nice job binding the wound," Crenshaw observed.

"Had my fair share of injured animals," Grandpa stated.

Crenshaw glanced up. His smile transformed to bewilderment, as if asking, *What kind of animals?*

"Appreciate you coming out here like this," I said.

"Chalk it up to the spirit of the season," the vet responded. In a deep, gentle voice, he soothed Samson and quickly checked the wound. "This big fella's in rough shape. He's going to need X rays and stitches, at the least. If he pulls through, he's also going to have to wear a hood so he won't reach back and tear the stitches out. It looks kind of like a lampshade that'll go around his neck."

"*If* he pulls through?" I asked, a sick feeling hitting the pit of my stomach.

"He's lost a lot of blood, his eyes are dull, and he's in shock."

"Need help?" Grandpa asked.

"Thank you, no." Crenshaw slid his hands under the dog and, for a small man, picked up the muscular animal with ease. I opened the sliding door of the van and the vet laid Samson in a large cage. A sharp whimper escaped the Doberman and the vet apologized.

"He belongs to my landlord," I told Crenshaw, "but Jerry's not around. You do what's necessary to patch up the dog. I'll see you get paid."

"I'm not worried about the money, Neil." He slammed the door shut. "I'll call you."

After Crenshaw drove off, we went upstairs to my apartment.

"Hurry and change, Neil," Grandpa announced, the coarseness reentering his voice. "I'm overdue for a big serving of oysters and a bucket of beer."

I was incredulous. "I kind of have a knot in my gut right now."

"You're right," he observed. "Your apartment *is* smaller than a miner's cabin. And you don't have any Christmas decorations up. No tree. No candles or cards. Not even a few candy canes. What's the matter with you? Where's your Christmas spirit?"

"I don't have any Christmas spirit," I snapped. "It's not on my schedule this year."

"That's preposterous!"

"I don't want to talk about me."

"Fine. But I ain't telling you a thing on an empty stomach." He rattled around the kitchen and found the tequila. "Mind?" he asked, waving the bottle.

"By all means, help yourself." As I walked into the bedroom I unbuttoned my shirt, balled it up, and tossed it toward the laundry basket. Was his mind simply wandering these days, I wondered, or was this a well-orchestrated game of dodgeball? With a little schizophrenia tossed in? Who cared if I hadn't decorated my apartment? Pick, pick, pick.

Still, I thought as I slipped on a clean flannel shirt, the mood swings were real. Something was going on. Something more than being seventy-two years old.

Grandpa smacked his lips and released a long breath as he set the empty shot glass down. "Too much will make a man loony," he said. "But a taste every once in a while ain't bad."

"What's going on, Grandpa?"

He raised a hand to me. "Not on an empty stomach," he repeated. "Now with two drinks in it," he added.

"Fine. You eat, I'll watch."

"Oh, you'll change your mind."

I put my leather jacket back on. "Doubt it."

"Look, Neil," he told me. "I'm mighty sorry about the dog. In fact, more sorry than if it'd been that idiot landlord of yours—"

"That's not really the point."

"But I don't want to stay here right now," he finished.

Someone might come back? I thought.

"Good point," I agreed. "Though the notion doesn't do much for my appetite."

He laughed, slapped me on the back. "You worry too much, son."

"Wait a minute. Aren't you the one who's worried about staying here?"

"And you take life too seriously. Knew that'd be the case when you told me you wanted to be a poet. Poet, hell. Demolitions expert of the mind."

"How do you figure?" I asked, not even trying to follow his logic. I opened the door.

"Always busting your innards out all over the place."

"I consider myself more of a miner of the soul," I shot back half-jokingly.

We stepped into the pea-sized hall, and I locked the door.

"Be careful how far you drill," he said, a sudden soberness to his tone. "Sometimes a man goes so low he takes himself to the brink of hell." With that, he stomped down the narrow wooden stairs.

3

We arrived at Little Pappa's shortly before closing. As a practitioner in the food business, I knew our late arrival didn't exactly thrill the staff. They were, however, extremely courteous, and we were seated at a table I requested near the back.

It was normally a loud place, but a dwindling crowd tonight and light music contributed to a peaceful ambience. The waiter took our drink orders and recommended the shark steaks with an olive oil, garlic, chive, and crawfish sauce. Attempting to put on my game face, and in an obvious moment of weakness, I announced to Grandpa that the dinner was my treat.

"Wonderful!" he exclaimed. "I'd like a double order of fried oysters," he told the waiter.

"Double order, sir?"

"Absolutely. Take it easy with the fries. But double the oysters. And give me . . . let's see . . ." He hesitated and guided his finger down the menu. "A cup of shrimp gumbo. Yes, that'll do fine."

"Yes, sir," the young man said, and caught my eye. "I see we have a big appetite."

I nodded. "He always has, in more ways than one."

Grandpa grinned.

"And may I say," the waiter added, "that you look an awful lot like—"

"Thank you," my grandfather interrupted gruffly. "With good service and excellent food you will undoubtedly be rewarded."

Yeah, with my tip, I thought.

I waited patiently as Grandpa received his Scotch, and I sipped on a Corona, before trying to pull any answers out of him.

Finally, I said, "Talk to me, Grandpa."

"If God had given me a choice, I'd have been a baseball player," he answered.

"That's not what I meant."

"I met all the greats," he continued. "The Babe when I was a kid. DiMaggio. Ted Williams. Fly-fished with the curmudgeon once. Drank with Mickey Mantle. Oh, he was a hell of a guy—"

"Grandpa," I said sternly. I was beginning to wonder if the man wasn't in the early stages of Alzheimer's.

"Thought you had the makings of a good ballplayer, Neil," he said. The waiter set his gumbo before him. The old man dug in. "Great stuff," he commented, wiping a drop from his beard. "Now where were we?" he asked.

"I want to know—"

"Oh, yes," Grandpa said, cutting me off. "You were a hell of a player. Great glove on the hot corner. Catlike re- actions, Neil. And a gun for an arm. If only you'd learned how to hit a curve. Had high hopes for you."

"Sorry to disappoint you." I swigged my beer.

"Oh, you've never been a disappointment. Except for maybe the poetry shit."

"Grandpa—"

"And marrying so young," he added. "Knew it wouldn't last." He waved his spoon at me. "Have some experience in that ballpark."

"I learned from the best, I suppose."

"That's the problem," he said earnestly. "You learned the wrong thing. I didn't want to see any of my blood fol- lowing my folly."

I opened a package of saltines. My relationship with my former wife, Susan, was the one thing I refused to dwell on tonight. *Or* how Grandpa had advised—no, basically told me not to marry her only days before the wedding.

His assessment of Susan's control-freak nature had been
right on the mark. "You don't see me running right off to
get hitched again, do you?" I finally asked.

"Don't get skitterish and take the relationship game to
the other extreme, either."

I didn't want to talk about the relationship game. Not
yet. Besides, Grandpa would thrash my hide if he found
out about my unresolved feelings for Keely Cohen. She
was my mentor at the university and one of the few trusted
friends I had. She was also very married.

He scraped the bottom of the cup. "Someone was
mining on my land," he said quietly.

I thumped my beer down. "What?"

"Goddamn assholes took up a claim next to me. Tun-
neled into my mineral rights."

As I leaned forward the waiter showed up with our din-
ners. I had to admit, the shark steak looked sumptuous,
and Grandpa had enough fried oysters to make Venus
squirm.

"Did you go to the police?" I asked.

My meal steamed before me. Grandpa rolled an oyster
in cocktail sauce.

"Best damn thing about Texas," he said. "The food." He
popped the oyster into his mouth, chewed slowly, and
swallowed. "De-li-cious! Plump. Tender. Peppery, with a
little cornmeal. Wonderful! And this is only the beginning.
Tomorrow, I say chicken-fried steak. Or better yet, prime
rib at The Stables. Love that old restaurant. And then
Mexican food—my mouth drools at the thought of fajitas.
What's that place you took me to last time I was down
here?"

"The Flower?"

"Have to go there."

"If we're still alive," I muttered.

"Eat, son." He ate another oyster with relish.

The image of the half-dead dog haunted me. And the
Santa picture. Reluctantly, I poked at my food. Then finished my beer and signaled for another.

"Order me a Tecate," Grandpa said. "Should've thought of that ahead of time."

I gave the waiter our requests. He caught sight of my untouched plate.

"Is everything okay?" he asked me.

"Hell if I know." I looked straight at Grandpa.

"Sir?"

People had been calling me *sir* ever since I'd received the scar on my face and subsequently grew a beard. I was too young for that shit.

"*He's* sir," I snapped back, nodding at my grandfather. "And everything's fine."

The waiter was taken aback.

"You'll be thirty this year, won't you, Neil?" Grandpa spoke up, catching the waiter's attention. "Even the coleslaw's good," he said as if in confidence, and winked.

"Everything's fine," I repeated to the waiter. "Sorry. All we need are our beers."

"Yes, sir." He reddened, rattled by my frustration, and quickly procured our drinks.

"I don't give a damn about turning thirty," I told Grandpa in a hushed voice. Did he think I was that sensitive about aging? *Just get back to the mining issue,* I scolded myself.

"Good. You'd still be in your prime if you were a ballplayer." He munched on a fry. "Maybe on the downside, but a few decent years ahead of you," he added.

"Did you go to the police?" I pushed.

"Did all sorts of things, Neil," Grandpa replied. "First these so-called investors wanted to buy me out, but I wouldn't hear of anything so ludicrous. No matter they only offered chicken feed. Could've been ten times and I still wouldn't have sold. Best I can make of it, they're fronted by a penny-ante operation, anyway. An independent company named Ledbetter Mining after Buster Ledbetter, a young upstart."

"Let me get this straight," I said. "This Buster Ledbetter's one of the investors?"

"He's the nut I talked to."

"Did the nut say who he was representing?" I studied the old man's face, trying to see beyond the matter-of-fact attitude.

" 'Course not. But Ledbetter's bush league, wanting real bad to make it to the majors. And that translates to money, so I figure Ledbetter's got to have someone or a lot of someones backing him."

"So you wouldn't sell?"

"Right."

"But he went ahead anyway?" I asked, to ensure I had a clear picture of the situation.

"Yup."

"How'd you find out he was on your land?"

"A friend of mine was on his crew. He knew they were close to my property, and he told Buster they had gone too far horizontally. Buster ordered him to shut his mouth and keep digging. Old Zach doesn't take crap like that from anybody, especially from a son of a bitch who was plain stealing, so he knuckled Buster on the nose. Damned if he didn't break it. Zach marched on over and told me what the deal was before he ducked off for Leadville to scrounge work up there. Heard they're hiring at Climax, again."

Grandpa washed down his oysters with a slug of beer. I waited, tasting the shark, determined not to allow him to ramble off track.

"He tried to use the Apex Law against me," he continued. "Citing he was a legitimate mining operation, producing results, and I wasn't using the land. But I blocked that by filing an adverse claim, then an injunction, contesting the property was mine, and private."

"What's all that mean?" I asked, not being familiar with Colorado mining laws.

"Means, for the time being, they can't mine my property."

"Why *not* sell?" I asked.

"You been talking to Walter?" His eyes narrowed.

"Walter? You mean Walter Pierce, your partner?"

"Ex-partner. Been pushing me to sell ever since our mining-equipment business hit the skids. But he don't understand that Ledbetter's a sleaze."

"You and Walter had a falling-out?" I asked. That was like Butch and Sundance going their separate ways.

"Ever since Walter went on the wagon, he's been acting like a mule with a burr up his ass."

On the wagon? Quite an accomplishment for one of the last of the hard-drinking men, I thought.

"Don't know where he is, either," Grandpa added. "Most likely sucking down Turkish cigarettes in some gambling hall. Then the fool wonders why he's busted all the time. So what does he do?" He leaned toward me as if I knew the answer, then went on. "Well, like I said, business hasn't been great—not that I'm worried. But, hell, Walter's sure we're headed for the red because our overhead's too high, so he fires our accountant, Edgar Bryant. Doesn't even consult me. Boots old Ed the day before he heads to Hawaii for a fishing trip somewhere in the little islands.

"Ed must've been plenty irked because he took off without a word to me. Can't say as I blame Bryant, as my former partner claimed the decision was a mutual one between us. I could've killed Walter. We weren't Ed's biggest clients, but we'd been together eons and had a good relationship."

"You and Walter parted ways," I repeated. "Unbelievable."

"I kicked his ass out. For all I know, Walter might've teamed up with Ledbetter. Anyway, someone's taken to dirty tricks. I found the tires on my truck slashed. Messages painted on my front door—"

"Messages? Like what?"

"Sell or die."

"Oh, to the point," I quipped, but I was stunned by the blunt statement.

"Finally, someone blasted my living-room window."

"Christ, Grandpa, didn't you go to the cops?"

"Been trying to work with them, but they claim they

need hard evidence. Guess that means my dead body." He scowled and shook his head.

"Sell-or-die messages aren't evidence?"

"Said they couldn't prove the culprit."

"Or didn't want to," I stated.

Grandpa rested his fork on his plate. "Got to admit, son, I found the gunshots disturbing. Look," he added, and pulled a small slug from beside his pocket watch.

I held the small piece of cold mineral in my palm, then handed it back.

"Dug three of them out of my wall. Gave the cops two, never heard anything back. So I called my lawyer, told him to get someone out to fix my window—"

"Your lawyer?"

"Only one I could trust." He grinned and resumed clearing the oysters from his plate. "Ironic, huh? I even just paid him his fees for my last divorce. But he's not fond of Walter, so I don't figure he'll stab me in the back. After he completed some paperwork for me, I said I was heading to Houston for a few days to visit you and clear my head."

A little bell went off in the back of my mind. "I assume the trashed house and Samson's injury are linked with this mining deal, right?" I asked.

"Safe bet."

"And the thug arrived about the same time you did?"

"Something like that."

"And the only person who knew you were visiting was your lawyer?" I continued.

"You're barking up the wrong tree, Neil," he said, finishing his beer. He shook the empty bottle at the waiter, who brought him another one. "T. R. Spence and I go back over forty years."

"Grandpa, you surprise me." In spite of my shaky appetite, I was slowly but surely nibbling the shark steak, finding it grilled to perfection and the crawfish sauce outstanding.

"Don't think me naive, Neil," Grandpa responded. "I know the man, and he has no reason to work against me."

I let it rest, though I tucked T. R. Spence's name into my memory bank. Along with Buster Ledbetter's, Edgar Bryant's, and Walter Pierce's. "You think Walter's that angry at you?"

"Don't know." Grandpa put away the last oyster then patted his belly. "Good stuff," he decreed, and raised his beer. "My compliments, people," he called over to the staff. Caught off guard, they feigned appreciative smiles. I was no longer shocked by Grandpa's antics, though I was glad the restaurant was almost empty.

"Ain't you going to eat that?" he asked me. "You're pecking at it like a bird."

I set my fork down, pushed the plate toward him. "My stomach's churning," I said.

Grandpa used his knife and fork to lift the last of the shark steak to his dish. "Love the crawfish sauce," he muttered between bites.

"Grandpa," I began.

"I don't know what to do," he anticipated. "*I'm* not thirty anymore. That's why I'm in Houston."

The penny dropped. Earth to Neil: Grandpa had come for my help. He was too proud to admit it outright. And yet he about had to. I felt dumb as a clump of dirt.

"I need to do some shopping," he said.

"Some what?"

"Let's go to that mall you like tomorrow. The one with the ice rink."

"The Galleria?" Right before Christmas it'd be easier for a hen to grow teeth than for me to get time off at work. Although I did have to meet Keely on campus in the morning to get my manuscript with her edits. Perhaps we could go there first, then somehow become detained. *Christ,* I thought. Perry—and Claudia, the kitchen manager—will kill me.

The old man finished his beer. "I'm ready," he announced.

I signaled for the check. "Now what?"

"We go to your place and sack out."

"But I thought you didn't want to stick around there."

"I was hungry and wanted you to take me out to eat. Besides, I ain't never been afraid to stay in my own house in my life. Until recently. Time to put an end to that."

The waiter brought the bill. I flashed plastic and left a generous tip, still feeling guilty at my outburst.

Grandpa stood. "You have a gun, don't you?" he asked.

I nodded.

"Good. Anyone tries to show up, we'll give him a little season's greeting."

"Wonderful," I mimicked Grandpa, the Santa with an attitude.

"Well, isn't that how you feel?"

"What do you mean?" I asked cautiously.

"You'd as soon plug someone as to wish him a merry Christmas."

"Of course not," I said a little too quickly.

"Oh." The old man rubbed his eyes. "Must be that all them oysters are making me see things."

Like what? I wondered, but didn't want to get into it. "Must be," I simply agreed, and patted his back.

Instead of walking, though, Grandpa stopped. He stared hard into my eyes a minute then began to grin. For a split second I was with him in his cabin. Twenty years ago. A child. Then he winked and, without shyness, began whistling "It's Beginning to Look a Lot Like Christmas" as we ambled out into the unusually cold Houston night.

4

On my answering machine was a message from Dr. Crenshaw informing me of Samson's precarious hold on life. The Doberman was resting but far from out of the woods, and we wouldn't know any more until tomorrow. While I listened to the message, Grandpa took the couch before I could ask him to sack out in my room.

"I don't sleep too well," he grumbled as he stripped to his underwear then crawled under a quilt.

"But I'm a night owl—" I attempted, and tossed an afghan on top of the comforter.

"And I like to be close to the bathroom," he declared. End of conversation. Okay, I'd acquiesce to the sleeping arrangements, but I wasn't finished.

"Something's bothering me," I said, and walked into the kitchen. Ice clinked into my mug as I made a nightcap.

"I detected as much, but I'm too damn tired to get into anything now. You demand a lot of energy."

I was speechless. The old man blows into town like a whirling dervish after someone's been shooting out his windows and trying to steal his gold, and immediately my landlord's house is ransacked, his dog stabbed, and a cute little picture of a bloody Santa is left for a reluctant Lieutenant Gardner to ponder. And I demand a lot of energy.

I took a deep breath. "What I meant was, whoever trashed Jerry's house was apparently searching for something."

No response at my pause.

"What do you think it was?" I prompted.

"Good question. Considering that babbling fool, it

could be anything. Drugs, a married woman's wedding ring. But I sure hope the dog pulls through. Where's your gun?"

"In the bedroom. With me."

"Hope you ain't a heavy sleeper."

"No thoughts on the break-in?" I asked, ignoring his last comment.

He propped himself on his elbows. "It occur to you the burglar figured that was your place?" he asked. "Might be you have something he wants."

"Only you would think that," I quipped. But maybe he *had* hit on something. This wouldn't be the first time someone assumed I lived in the house and not the garage apartment behind it. "Why don't we go to Lieutenant Gardner and fill him in on the rest of the story?" I suggested. "Maybe he can help."

"He's a Texas cop," Grandpa objected.

"In case you didn't notice, this afternoon's little incident took place in Texas. Besides, he has a lot of connections—"

"No." He cut me off.

"Why?"

He pulled the afghan up to his neck and fluffed his beard outside it. "Good night, Neil."

All right, I thought, biting back my frustration. The old man's not going to talk and my pushing would only drive him deeper into that mine shaft of silence. "I get up early to jog," I said. "I'll try not to disturb you."

"You do that."

"Good night, Grandpa." I closed the bedroom door behind me. Strange day, I thought. One wrecked house. One hurt dog. Cantankerous old Grandpa hiding out in my apartment. Under siege. An ex-partner who might be part of the problem. And God knew what else. I sipped my margarita, then set the mug on the nightstand.

After easing my tired bones into bed, I picked up a slim collection of poems by Keely Cohen and thumbed through it for the umpteenth time. I stopped at a piece on relationships.

A lover's grin
cut the night
like the broad curve
of a killer's knife.

Why it caught my eye, I had no idea. The lines were not typical of Keely's work. Simple and harsh, allusions to Kurt Weill's "Mack the Knife." Why the break from her usual fluency? Was this darkness as in evil? I wondered. Or darkness as in hopelessness? The lover as psychotic, or as grinning liar? Literal or figurative killing of love? Did love even exist, or was it lust in costume? A lusty grin? Was there such a thing as pure love? Or was love forever tainted by such poisons as control, manipulation, fear?

Was it Keely and Mark? It had been Susan, my ex-wife, and I.

I set the book down, decided not to prod at my unraveled nerves any further, and clicked off the light.

And at some point in the night, I dreamed.

Darkness. And in that darkness, a golden vein sparkling like Christmas garland. Then many veins like roots gripping the earth. Damp earth. Sometimes a light, sometimes not. Flashes. Hard-hat light. Grins reflect. Knife grins hacking at—a dog. Teeth fall like peeling paint scraped from a decaying wall. Legs of lead—mine—run to shake the dog's silence. *Ho-ho-ho* echoes in the cavern. A hand pulls me back, first as protection then turns to roots clutching me in a fist. I fight for air. Golden grins. Ho-ho-ho. I'm a boy. *Grandpa! Grandpa!* I call without words. *A lover's grin. A killer's knife.* Panting, panting . . .

Five Days Before
Christmas

5

I twisted awake. Beneath the thick blanket in the chilly apartment, I was sweating. I ran a hand through my long blond hair, took a couple of deep breaths. My heart pounded. Outside the window the sky was the color of ten-penny nails.

The alarm clock read seven in the morning. Time for a run.

As I dressed in a lightweight Nike sweatsuit, I noticed an enticing smell in the air. Part bacon, part coffee, and part . . . I wasn't sure. I pushed open my door.

"I underestimated you, son," Grandpa said, voice full of cheer. "I didn't figure you'd roll out of bed till nine or ten." He was in the kitchen, pulling a pan out of the oven. On the counter, bacon drained on a plate covered with a paper towel. And coffee steamed in my small Braun.

"Smells great," I responded, thinking a good night's sleep freshened him right up. "What's in the pan?"

"Finnish pancakes," he announced.

Finnish pancakes was an egg dish, rich and sweet like a custard but with the texture of Yorkshire pudding. Cut into squares and served with maple syrup, they were decadent. My mother made them each year for Christmas breakfast. She'd be humming carols at the stove while I surveyed the loot from my stocking, and Dad and Grandpa—the best years were when the old man joined us—sat quietly together in front of the tree in the living room, each smoking his pipe and drinking strong black coffee. They really were wonderful times, I thought.

How things change.

"I haven't had Finnish pancakes since I last visited Mom," I said.

"I figured as much," he said, and peered in the oven. "Appears ready." He lifted out the dish with a mitted hand.

"They look great. And I guess you weren't going to wait until nine for me."

"Nope."

"Well, don't feel like you have to wait now. I usually run before breakfast."

"Good boy!"

"So I'll be back in about half an hour."

"Wait and I'll go with you."

"What about the food?"

"It can wait," he said, and tucked the food back in the oven, turning the temperature down low. "I'd like to get some exercise."

"Uh, Grandpa—"

"Got my running duds with me," he said, rummaging through his travel bag. He pulled out a red sweatsuit. "Be right with you." And he ducked into the bathroom.

Christ, I thought. Now I'd have to worry about the man having a heart attack. There went a peaceful run and any hope of working out my anxieties.

The old man emerged appearing more Christmassy than ever in his red jogging suit with white trim. "Let's go," he announced as he slipped on his 49ers cap and led the way out the door.

After a few minutes of stretching, I started at a cautious gait. The air was brisk and dry. A hint of sunlight struggled through blankets of clouds. Cars groaned weary workers off to work, and trees waved their bare limbs like wind chimes of dangling bones. There was no sign of anyone tailing us, but I still kept a close watch, scanning for any suspicious vehicles. As conspicuous as we were, a drive-by would be easier than wringing a chicken's neck.

"You always trot this slowly?" Grandpa shouted.

"Well—"

"Anywhere around here to pump iron?" he asked.

"You're kidding, right?"

"You don't hit my age in the shape I'm in by sitting around at night drinking beer and smoking cigarettes," he proclaimed, and kicked us into high gear. I hoped he wasn't trying too hard to make a point. After a mile, though, he was still going strong, breathing steadily, and I was worrying that I wouldn't be able to keep up with him.

Grandpa wove haphazardly through the neighborhood, and I scanned the various manger scenes, brightly painted plywood figures of Santa, reindeer, and snowmen, and the multicolored Christmas lights decorating house after house. Everywhere I looked, scrolled letters reading SILENT NIGHT, HOLY NIGHT or PEACE ON EARTH or JOY TO THE WORLD jumped out at me. Some of the signs were faded or slightly soiled, brought out of storage only once a year. Words and phrases so often used I questioned whether their meaning was any longer heard. Considering how they seemed to fade each January like footprints beneath a heavy snow, I couldn't help but wonder if these sentiments ran only as deeply as the ribbons, paper, and slabs of pressed wood they were printed on. I shook my head, realizing how cynical my thoughts were. God, I was in a funk.

When Grandpa started to turn into one of the rougher neighborhoods where even plywood Santas were mugged, I took the lead.

We ended up on Heights Boulevard, the busiest street in this old section of town. We jogged past looming Victorian houses hung with holiday wreaths. Massive pecan trees and live oaks lined block after block. The trees were not, however, thick enough to hide us from passersby. Grandpa's striking red-suited figure attracted honking horns, cries of "Howdy, Santa," and supplications for desired Christmas gifts. It amazed me how many people wanted new pickup trucks, cowboy boots, diamonds, furs, and good old greenbacks.

I remembered simpler Christmases past, hiking in the forest to cut our own tree, making ornaments and gifts for each other—my mother has cherished a storybook I wrote and illustrated when I was ten. The feel of the holiday now was so foreign to what I'd grown up with I often doubted my memory. Was Christmas past really less commercial, or was I romanticizing it? Probably a combination of both.

As we cut into a quieter neighborhood I noticed a gray Taurus slowly turn with us. The hackles on the back of my neck stiffened. The car had tinted windows, so I couldn't see the driver. Grandpa appeared oblivious to this new development, his breathing hard but steady, focused on his running.

Instead of speeding up after making the turn, the Taurus eased parallel to us. I caught my toe on a crack in the street and stumbled. Grandpa glanced at me. I had to do something.

"You all right?" he asked.

"Neither of us is all right," I shouted, and lunged at Grandpa.

His eyes went wide and he gasped as I grabbed him by the waist and drove upward into his chest as if he were a tight end who'd just caught a sideline pass. A thick grunt escaped him. I pumped my legs and shoved him up onto the sidewalk and into the small front yard of a modest bungalow. We went down hard on dry pine needles and large brown magnolia leaves, coming to a stop by a cardboard Mickey-Mouse-as-Bob-Cratchit. And standing by the decoration, stretching out for his own run, was the largest African-American man I'd ever seen. He had arms the size of the Texas Panhandle and muscles as hard as the Rocky Mountains. Out of the corner of my eye, I saw the Taurus speeding down the street, too far away now for me to get a license-plate number.

"What the hell did you do that for?" Grandpa barked as he rolled to his knees.

"You mugging Santa Claus, Jack?" the man directed at me.

"A Taurus pulled up right beside us," I said.

"I didn't see any goddamn Taurus," Grandpa gasped.

"I know—"

"Want me to use these hands on this joker, Santa?"

"I ought to belt him myself." Gently, he rose to his feet, brushed off his red suit.

"Didn't you see the car?" I asked the muscular man.

He stood stiffly, and popped a fist into his open hand. "I just seen you taking down Santa in my yard."

"You okay?" I asked Grandpa sheepishly. I resisted standing, however, as it appeared the gentleman looming before me wanted nothing more than to knock me back down on my ass.

"*I'm* fine. You're the one who's not okay."

"No, you's crazy," the man cried, jabbing a finger in my direction.

"I thought we were being shadowed," I tried to explain. "It's a feeling I've learned to pay heed to."

"The only shadow you need to worry about is your own," Grandpa thundered. "Christ, you're skitterish as a snowshoe hare whose brown coat ain't turned white by the first snowfall."

"I heard the hounds."

"Stand up, sucker," the muscle man said.

Oh, shit, I thought.

"Thank you, my friend," Grandpa said, and patted the man on the back. "But don't hurt the boy. He may be loony as a june bug, but he's my grandson."

The man stared hard at me, then back at Grandpa. "You sure?"

"Don't want to spend my day at the hospital tending him."

"Thanks," I said, and finally got up.

After a couple of stretches and a little jogging in place, Grandpa headed down the street. "You keep a couple of lengths back," he told me, then called to the man, "A Merry Christmas, friend!"

Grandpa's newest fan grinned and waved.

Damn, I thought, maybe I did overreact. I wiped pine needles off my legs, dodged the piercing gaze of the large man, and slowly began to follow Grandpa.

The Taurus had been there, I reasoned. The car had hovered next to us. I knew it. So why did I feel so foolish?

We wound back home, coasting to a stop in the driveway. As we paced to walk the jog off I offered, "Reckon we ran a good four miles."

"Four miles and one crack-back block. Thought seriously of letting Mean Joe Green back there eat you alive."

"Damn it, Grandpa, I'm sorry." I glanced around for our unwelcome company. Nothing.

He grumbled, paced, and spat. Finally, softening his tone, he said, "Don't apologize for doing something you thought was right."

"So you believe there might've been a threat?"

"No."

I took a deep breath and steadily blew it out.

"But you did," he added. "And you didn't break my bones. 'Sides, something occurred to me the last half mile. This is your territory. You're going to pick up the danger signs before me. Next time, though, give a little warning."

"Sure," I responded, flexing my right knee. I was glad the old man wasn't hurt, but I realized my knee felt smartly banged.

"But if there was someone following us, why didn't he take a potshot or rush us or something?"

"You saw the size of your protector back there," I replied. "Reckon he influenced the situation."

Grandpa nodded, accepting what I said. "What time you figure that fella will show?" he then asked, and pointed to Jerry's house.

"If what you said was true, he'll be too polluted to travel much before noon."

"Oh, what a man will do to himself in the name of fun." He stretched back, hands on hips.

I laughed. "You've not exactly led a preacher's life yourself, Grandpa."

"Compared to some of the preachers I've known, I've been saintlier," he fired back.

"Sorry I brought it up."

"Why, I remember this one man of the cloth," he began as we made for the apartment door. "He had eyes for Louise, my third wife. Chased that poor woman till I thought I was going to have to break a commandment before he did."

"What happened?" I asked. I closed the lower door behind us and made sure the knob was locked. The wooden stairs echoed hollowly as we climbed up the steps.

"She ran off with the son of a bitch, Neil," he said with sudden sadness. "Hadn't been married a year and she skipped town with that scrawny Bible-thumper."

"Sorry," I said weakly, caught off guard.

"Don't be. Heard they got busted fleecing God's flock, as they say. Dipped their hands in the till once too often. Around San Antonio. Made me glad I let them go to their just reward."

I unlocked the door. "Instead of breaking a commandment," I added. We entered the living room, the fine scent of breakfast in the air.

"Exactly."

As a child I received only bits and pieces of Grandpa's escapades. Not until I was in my early twenties did I receive honest answers from my parents to questions I had. Sort of. "Grandpa, is that story true?"

"Rumor is I took up with that miner's wife," he commented, and pulled off his cap. He Frisbeed the hat onto the couch. "Well, I fancied the woman, sure enough. But I was quick to realize I was in a spot where her crazy husband might stick a shotgun in my face. So I backed out of that situation right quick." He paused, wiped sweat from his forehead with the sleeve of his sweatsuit. "What I told you just now is as true as I'm standing here, and as Louise and the preacher man had to spend every cent they had to stay out of jail."

Still, I wondered how he figured his checkered past made him more saintly than the men he put down. And he read my thoughts.

"I ain't never claimed to be more or less than I am,

Neil," he said. "Done some things I ain't proud of, and many I am. I've always been front and center, though. Never hid behind anything. Not God, not money, not some crazy cause, and not someone else's ideas of morals."

"That's why I've always been proud of you, Grandpa."

"Don't mock me, boy."

Mock, hell, I thought. I was going to write a poem about the man.

"Let's eat," he said.

And we did, sticking to small talk. The rise of the Houston Rockets and a small debate over their drafting Olajuwon—which overjoyed me—over Jordan years and years ago. Each had more than one championship ring. Then we turned to the fate of the Oilers, Nashville bound. Grandpa favored the Denver Broncos as well as the 49ers, though he agreed with me the beginning of the end for the Oilers was the firing of Bum Phillips nearly a generation ago. After thirds on Finnish pancakes, and polishing off a pound of bacon between us, Grandpa was ready to act.

"Let's go shopping," he announced.

"What?"

"I told you yesterday—"

"I have things I need to do, first," I objected. "But don't you reckon we ought to talk to Lieutenant Gardner before doing much else? We can't ignore the threats against you. For Christ's sake, gun blasts and slashed tires are serious. And last night wasn't a case of kids tossing toilet paper in the trees or soaping a car."

"I have a commitment, Neil, and there's nothing that's going to keep me from it. Your lieutenant can wait. Besides, I'm not so sure I want to parley with him."

"Grandpa—"

"You do the dishes. I'll shower."

"So you get all the hot water."

"I'm the guest."

I threw up my arms. "Go."

"You are a magnanimous host." He grabbed his overnight kit and went into the bathroom.

Right, I thought. My landlord's coming home to a trashed house and a damaged dog. Grandpa's being followed and threatened, but won't trust the police. In an hour I'm supposed to meet Keely Cohen at the university and talk about my manuscript, which was time off from Perry Stevens Catering I'd had to scratch and claw for. And now the old guy really wants to go Christmas shopping? No doubt about it, Grandpa's clutch was slipping.

Or mine was, for allowing myself to be taken on this holiday roller coaster.

And, damn, my knee hurt.

6

When we reached the sleepy English building I asked Grandpa if he'd like to come in and meet Associate Professor Keely Cohen. The sprawling, wooded campus had that between-semesters tranquillity, and Grandpa, pipe out, was ready to sit on a bench beneath a loblolly pine, smoke, and wait for me. At the invitation, however, he changed his mind, tucked the pipe back into his pocket, and followed me inside.

Keely was in her office as promised. From the looks of the sweater she wore, a sweater you could get away with only down here in the South—red, white, and green with a Christmas bear pattern and bows and bells tied on—she was in one of her lighthearted moods. Every once in a while Keely would act a little silly as a reminder not to take herself too seriously. In the often stale atmosphere of academia, her attitude was fresh as clear mountain air.

Through the partially open door, I saw that she was hanging a framed print advertising the Gauguin show that took place in Washington, D.C., a number of years ago. Her slim figure stretched high and her dark hair bobbed back as she attempted to place the print exactly right. I tapped on the door.

"Hey, Keely, let me help you," I said, and limped into the small office.

She jumped. "My God, don't sneak up on a girl like that."

I saw the hook she was trying to catch the print on, took the Gauguin notice, and easily hung it.

"Thanks. I like to change pictures around every once in a while so I'm not staring at the same old ones all year.

Though I'm not sure I should bother, with that job offer—"
Then she caught sight of my grandfather, cap in hands,
and came to a dead stop.

"Is there a faculty Christmas party I don't know about?"
she asked.

"This is my granddaddy," I told her. "Stephen Marshall."

"Santa's come to town," she commented.

"Nice to meet you," he replied, a broad smile on his face
and a twinkle in his eyes. Then again, Keely brought that
look from many men.

"You going to tell him what you want for Christmas,
too?" I asked, and related our jogging experience without
my all-pro, open-field tackle. Thankfully, Grandpa didn't
bring the hit up, either.

"How charming," she said, and leaned against the
corner of her tidy desk, arms crossed. "But did you pull a
muscle, Neil? I noticed your hobble."

"I strained my knee."

"It was a valiant run, though," said Grandpa. For which
I was grateful.

"Oh," Keely said, slightly confused.

"He loves that kind of attention," I threw in.

"And I bet he gets it all the time. How long are you in
town, Mr. Marshall?"

"Please, it's Stephen. And I'm not sure."

"Well, I hope you have a wonderful time. In Neil's company that's a given. You have a delightfully talented
grandson," she added, and shot me a wink. The gesture
didn't go unnoticed by Grandpa.

"Thanks—guess you liked the manuscript," I responded.

"Loved it."

"But what did you mean by *that offer*?" I asked, coming
back to what she'd said earlier.

Before Keely could answer, though, Grandpa asked,
"You're the poet, aren't you?"

"Yes, I write poetry," she replied, surprised at the re-
mark, and obviously pleased. Her light brown eyes glistened like root-beer candy.

"I have one of your collections," he continued. "Let's see, *Kissing the Sunset,* right?"

"Why, yes."

"Very sensuous, young lady."

Keely actually blushed.

"And very good," he added. "If I were a young man, I'd snatch you up in a New York minute."

"Thank you."

"I have to admit Neil recommended the book to me a couple of years ago. He holds you in high esteem."

The old man didn't know the half of it, I thought. But at the moment my fondness for Keely was quivering from a fearful chill. I cleared my throat. "That job offer?" I asked Keely.

"Oh—um, I've been invited to teach at another university," she said hesitantly. She unfolded her arms, walked around the desk, and sat down.

Suddenly my heart ached like a disappointed child on Christmas morning. "Another university?" I repeated. I sank into one of the chairs in front of the desk. Grandpa, scrutinizing the scene, took the other.

"Tenure-track position," she added. "In California."

California? I thought. "Wow," I managed. "Congratulations. When?"

"Next fall."

"You accept it?"

"Not yet. Mark's being . . . resistant."

"Who's Mark?" Grandpa asked.

"My husband. He's not crazy about moving to the West Coast."

"Your husband," Grandpa said. "I see. Well, husbands can be like that." He stood. "It was very nice to meet you, young lady. Think I'll step outside for a smoke and leave you two to your business." He pulled the pipe from his pocket.

Keely also stood. "Great to meet you, too, Mr.— Stephen. Hope to see you again before you leave."

He nodded, tipped the pipe at her, and slipped out of the office.

"I like your grandfather," Keely said.

"So do I." I had wanted to tell her about the trouble the old guy was in, but now I didn't feel like it. All I could think about was her leaving. If I'd had a hollow feeling before, now my insides were cratered.

But why should I care? After all, she was married. And parting was bound to happen. I would eventually gain my master's or doctorate. She would leave. It was part of academic life. But why did it have to happen so soon?

Keely set my manuscript before me. "As I said, I love it," she began. "Strong images, great metaphors, but perhaps, most importantly, you've found your voice. The pieces that don't work—and most of them, as we've discussed, are your recent endeavors—are too caustic, bordering on bitter. They don't have the same sharp wit to them as the others do, and they're—"

"Too dark," I suggested.

She shook her head. "Without purpose, except perhaps as a catharsis for you. Put that batch away for the time being. Let them rest. In a few months I think you'll view them differently."

With you gone, I'm not so sure, I thought. But I simply nodded.

Keely continued in a professional manner to cite certain poems, their strengths and weaknesses, and made suggestions on how to improve them. All of the pages were marked with comments. It was an excellent, well-thought-out critique.

"So, here you go, my friend," she said, forcing a smile.

"You should take the job, regardless of Mark," I found myself saying.

There was a hitch in her breath. "It's not that simple, Neil," she replied. "Of all people, you should know that."

"I do," I said, resigned and thinking of my divorce from Susan. "But—"

"And I've built a life here," she pointed out.

"You've wanted a position like that since I first met you," I argued.

"I'm well aware of that, Neil," she said sharply.

"Sorry." I picked up my poems.

She reached out and touched my hand. "So am I," she told me. "Mark won't move."

"What are you going to do?"

"I don't know," she replied, pulling her hand back. "Mark's territory is Texas. He doesn't want to leave it."

"None of us want *you* to leave. Sondra won't want you to leave. John Carlyle won't want you to leave," I said, naming two members of our writing class. "And I don't."

Keely ran a hand through her hair and twisted back in her chair. "I know, Neil," she said, then turned forward. "And it's sweet of you to put those feelings aside and tell me to go. It means a lot."

I nodded, shifting my weight from foot to foot. Her leaving wouldn't be easy, but I didn't want to think about it now. As a heavy silence began to slip between us like a glass door sliding closed, I quickly shifted conversational gears. "Grandpa wants to head over to the Galleria now. It's going to put Perry in an ornery mood when I don't show up on time."

"No doubt, as this is your busiest season."

I could only nod again, feeling like one of those damn plastic birds that bobbed into puddles of water. "I best be going," I finally said.

"Give me a call and we'll get together for some coffee and poetry over the holidays," Keely offered.

"How civilized." I returned her smile then trudged down the hall and out of the long, cavernous building.

Smoke from Grandpa's pipe whispered upward like shadowy fingers struggling to clutch the air. I sat next to him on the bench beneath the loblolly pine. He calmly eyed me.

"How can you run so well and still smoke?" I asked.

"Gave up cigarettes."

"So did I. Damn if I wouldn't like one now, though. It's always a battle, isn't it?"

"That's why I puff on the pipe once or twice a day," he replied. "Represses the urge. That and my last memory of smoking cigs. One morning, I coughed and hacked my way out of bed to the deck, ready to light up, when I noticed, as if for the first time, all the white cigarette butts scattered on the ground. Quite a sight. They were like the teeth of a great beast that'd been chewing my lungs. I knew then I could never live with the beast, and so I threw in the towel and bowed out of that ring. 'Course, you're right, that's when the real battle began."

"Nice story," I said, "but I still hanker for one of those damn cancer sticks."

He changed the subject. "Your professor's a right handsome woman."

I rubbed my sweaty palms on my pant legs and stood. "She's been a good friend."

Grandpa rapped the ashes from his pipe then ground them with the toe of his boot. "And her husband? He ever stuck a shotgun in your face?"

"Never gave him a reason to."

He rose, still holding the pipe to allow the bowl to cool. "You're a better man than I am, Neil."

Or an idiot, I thought.

"Let's go shopping," he announced.

"On one condition. I'm taking a risk by skipping out on work," I told him. "When I get back to The Kitchen, they'll be ready to boil me in my own pudding."

"What do you want?"

"Talk to the cops."

He pointed the stem of his pipe at me. "I'll consider your request."

"Grandpa?"

"It'll be on my mind the whole time I shop, I swear."

My patience was playing out. But I decided I owed him some slack after having blindsided him on our run. Perhaps I was jumpy. After all, I recalled the feeling of being followed and didn't cotton to it one bit. A touch of paranoia could've slipped in. So I decided to drop the subject of going to the cops. Sooner or later the old man would have to open up.

7

The Galleria was part of Uptown Houston. On one side rose the Transco Tower with its Romanesque waterfall and horse-and-carriage rides. Snuggling the north side of the complex was traffic-congested Westheimer. There were now three sections to the Galleria full of swank shops and power business offices. Area hotels hosted thousands of international travelers yearly. During this festive season, red Christmas bows, garlands, and white lights abounded.

Grandpa and I were fortunate to find a parking place in the garage beneath Galleria III. Attendants reluctantly waved my poor Bug down into a tight spot near a thick concrete beam. With some maneuvering between door and rock, Grandpa wedged himself out.

"If you drove a respectable car—"

"Don't even go there." I cut him off and closed my door.

He laughed. "You're so much like your father. He stood up to me from the day he was born. Never hesitated to express his feelings."

A wash of emotion suddenly covered me, catching finally in the corners of my eyes. "We did our share of butting heads, too," I said softly.

"I miss him, too," he told me, and slammed his door shut.

I changed the subject. "Where to first?" My voice and our footsteps echoed in the underground cavern. "Macy's? The Sharper Image? Or maybe a stretch of the legs to Tiffany's or Neiman Marcus over in Galleria I?"

We climbed a short flight of stairs and were soon in the

mall. The dull throb in my knee was growing stronger, informing me that I best not spend all day hiking around on it.

"Find me a toy store," he ordered.

"A toy store? Why?"

"So I can buy toys."

"No kidding," I said. "For who?" I searched my mind and couldn't think of any cousins still at the toy stage, or any who had given Grandpa great-grandchildren.

"Boy, you have an irritating habit of asking a lot of questions."

"Pardon me."

He pushed his hair back over his ears and adjusted his cap. "I want to see the ice rink, too," he told me.

"Yes, sir." Toy stores? Ice rinks? What in hell was the old man doing? Or was he just that, an old man who needed a reality check every few miles? He had that somber, distant look in his eyes again, failing even to notice the small children pointing at him or the curious stares from many of the mall's patrons.

We wound over to the Galleria Tower, where many of the offices were, and then into the original section of the complex. As the area schools hadn't yet released for the Christmas holiday, the skating rink wasn't nearly as crowded as it would be during vacation. A few people of various ages were broken into groups taking lessons from a team of instructors.

Grandpa leaned over the railing and gazed down. The music of Mannheim Steamroller was a flurry of tiny crystal snowflakes in the arena. Across the rink a frosted sports-shop window displayed mannequins of Mr. and Mrs. Claus decked out in matching sweatsuits and the new Air Jordans.

"When's the last time you went skating, Neil?"

"Probably the last time it snowed in Houston. Six or seven years ago, I bet."

"Been longer than that for me. I've got a hankering to take a spin or two around the rink."

"Grandpa—"

"Sometime before I leave. But not today, so don't get your dander up. My side's achy due to the overzealous actions of my self-appointed bodyguard."

"Knew you wouldn't let me off the hook that easy. You'll ride me on that the rest of your life."

He grinned. "At least the rest of my trip." He pushed himself from the rail, and we turned together.

"There's a toy store—" I began, but failed to complete the sentence when I stepped square into a short, stocky man. Slightly embarrassed, I muttered, "Excuse me." And then I felt the unmistakable pressure of a gun barrel pressed into my gut.

"I said excuse me," I repeated.

"Don't be a smart-ass," he responded curtly.

I glanced at Grandpa. Another man had drawn up on his left side, poking a handgun in his ribs.

"Where is it, Pops?" Grandpa's assailant asked. If not for the power of the automatic weapon, Grandpa could've backhanded the scrawny man as easily as a grizzly swiping away a pesky mutt.

"Gentlemen, this is not the place to discuss business," Grandpa replied.

"It's the perfect place," Mr. Stocky told him. "Ain't no security guards around, and we open fire you think any of these housewives is gonna help you? They gonna grab their babies and run."

"Easy," Grandpa said. "I don't want anyone to get hurt, especially not a kid."

"I don't whack kids, old man. Leastways, I don't whack 'em on purpose. That ain't my style."

I registered the *on purpose*, knowing he'd do whatever it took to do his job. We had to move very slowly so no one got hurt.

"But say you don't want to talk business here," Mr. Stocky continued, "then we just take you back to Denver for the reward. Either way we win."

"Reward?" I asked, and stared at Grandpa. The bewilderment in his eyes told me he was as lost as I was.

"Yeah, so where is it, Pops," Mr. Scrawny repeated. They were both dressed in blue business suits, but the scrawny man appeared as out of place in the clothing as a Christmas tree on the Fourth of July. His long hair was greased back, and the beard on his thin face was patchy, giving him a sleazy rat look.

"What the devil are you talking about?" Grandpa demanded.

"Come on," Mr. Stocky said. "If that's the way it's going to be, then we gonna walk." Except for his diction, my aggressor seemed more at home in his suit. Clean-shaven, short black hair, a briefcase in his hand would've been as natural as the gun. It was also obvious he was in charge.

He jammed the barrel of the gun into me. "I said walk. And you try anything, I'll plug you and anyone around you."

"I believe the man, Grandpa," I stated calmly, though the blood was whipping around my system so fast my ears were pulsing.

"Whatever you say, Neil."

"Whatever *I* say," Mr. Stocky corrected. He eased the gun away from me and hid his hand behind his suit coat. His partner did the same.

"Me and you go first," he instructed. "Side by side. They follow, same way. We go down the stairs, not the escalator. And you fuck with me—"

"I know," I interrupted, wiping the sweat from my palms onto my sleeves. "You play terminator."

"You got it. Let's go." He bumped his shoulder against me to show the way.

Slowly, with my tender knee, I walked, eyes darting in a desperate search for help. Nothing. I was feeling terribly claustrophobic. It reminded me of the time I was trapped in the old refrigerator in Grandpa's barn. I was a kid, alone, playing vampire, and I decided to use the refrigerator as my coffin. And when the appliance locked me in darkness, it almost was. At that time refrigerator doors had handles that locked in place rather than simple suction grips. I was trapped in the airtight appliance. Sweat poured off me then, too. I screamed, banged, and kicked on the door until my voice was hoarse, my arms were one great bruise, and my feet hurt. Finally, the old man found me. I was short of breath and wild with tears. He was full of fearful anger as he clutched me to his chest and lashed out at me with his tongue. The next day he hauled the refrigerator off.

We reached the stairs. "Nothing funny," Mr. Stocky reminded me.

I nodded, breathing deeply, knowing I was as trapped now as I was that scary childhood day. Trouble was, Grandpa was in the coffin with me, not outside ready to open it. There had to be something I could do. It was time to pay the old man back. But Grandpa spoke first.

"Never did tell me how you got that scar, Neil. Was it when you killed that guy?"

"No, after," I replied.

"Shut up," Mr. Stocky said.

"He never killed nobody," Mr. Scrawny spoke up.

"Drilled him through the heart with a 30-30," Grandpa told him. There was some truth in that. I had been charged with justifiable homicide, and cleared of any wrongdoing. But I'd shouldered the false charge in order to protect someone else.

"You lie," Mr. Scrawny said.

"It's true," I spoke up.

"Yeah, well, fine," Mr. Stocky piped in. "But you ain't got no 30-30 now, so shut up."

We inched down the stairs, and with each step it felt as though I were crawling deeper and deeper back into that refrigerator. Except for an occasional glance at Grandpa, people passed us without much fanfare, and I still didn't spot any security guards. I heard Grandpa grumble and looked back.

"Don't try nothing," Mr. Stocky said.

"You're still limping, Neil," Grandpa observed, "from, you know."

"An old sports injury," I explained to my unwelcome partner. I caught Grandpa's drift, though, and was trying to figure how to make another fierce block work. It would all be in the timing.

As we reached the bottom of the stairs my anxiety rose as I noticed a large group of kids. Kindergarten age, I guessed. A woman leading them was saying, "Now, hold your partner's hand. We'll be at the ice rink in just a minute." A few mothers with the group kept them corralled like sheepdogs moving a flock.

A field trip to the Galleria. Kindergarten was life. *But get them out of here,* I thought desperately.

When Grandpa hit the ground floor behind us, though, all hell broke loose.

"Santa Claus!" one of the kids exclaimed, and a wave of shrieks crackled through the class. Suddenly my worst nightmare played out as the group converged on us.

Sweat streaked my glasses. "Stay cool," I told Mr. Stocky as his hand beneath his jacket twitched. "They're just kids." Not that he had ever been a kid, or cared one way or another.

"Get the brats away," he growled to Grandpa.

I stepped to the side as the tots jumped around Grandpa's feet like puppies anticipating food from their master.

"Ho, ho, ho," Grandpa played up, "you caught me."

One little girl leaped into his arms. Mr. Scrawny's head jerked back and forth. He was panicking.

"Tell him to be calm," I said to Mr. Stocky.

"What are you doing here?" the little girl asked.

"Checking out the toy stores," he replied, setting the girl down.

"But don't you make your own?" she asked.

"He sells toys to the stores, dummy," a small boy interjected.

"Yeah, that's how he can buy reindeer food," another boy said.

"Tell your buddy to be calm," I repeated to Mr. Stocky. Mr. Scrawny's eyes were crazed, mirroring an unbalanced mind.

"Relax, all of you," Mr. Stocky snapped.

"You're all quite right," Grandpa informed the kids. "But I've got to go now. I have a lot of work to do before the big night."

"Come on, children," the mothers called, rounding them up.

"I'm sorry," the teacher apologized to us.

Mr. Stocky forced a smile and jerked a short nod. Given the depth of his irritation, it was remarkable he didn't draw out his gun and pop the woman on the spot. Sensing his antagonism, the teacher ushered the stragglers toward the main group.

"I love you, Santa," the little girl called, and waved as they meandered away.

So do I, I thought. Grandpa smiled and waved. Stocky and Scrawny muttered to each other, eyes on the kids. Then slowly, too slowly, still distracted, they turned to close in on us again. And I, with the children out of harm's way, spotted my opening. "Hey, Santa, are you ready for some football?"

With all the force I could muster, I drove my elbow into my distracted escort's chest, forcing him backward. Grandpa, with linebacker quickness, grabbed hold of Mr. Scrawny's shoulder and flung him into his partner. Their heads collided like a couple of coconuts banging together, and they went down. Miraculously, they each held on to their guns. A woman nearby yelped. "What the hell?" her male companion said.

We ran.

Or, rather, I tried. The stiffness that had settled in my knee forced me to skip awkwardly every few steps on my good leg.

"I ain't about to carry you, son," Grandpa barked.

"I can hold my own."

"Yes, I reckon you can."

Instinctively, I headed for the security office. Grandpa, however, turned down a corridor that led outside. He was a good five yards ahead of me, and as I didn't want to lose him, I had no choice but to hobble along and follow.

"You're taking us to the parking lot," I called.

"I've had enough shopping for one day."

"We need to find help."

"I'm not sticking around. I won't be the cause of a gun battle and get some little kid killed."

If Grandpa had attracted attention before, his racing through the mall brought even more stares from Christmas shoppers. When he reached the door, he paused and waited for me.

"We left them a little loopy," Grandpa said. "They're not behind us."

"Now do you believe me about the Taurus?"

"It was smart of you busting your knee and slowing us down."

"For crying out loud, Grandpa. Oh, let's find a cop and take care of those thugs the right way."

"There must be one outside," Grandpa said, and he pushed through the door.

In the parking lot cars were packed tight as needles on a spruce bough. Valet parkers assisted the well-to-do and attendants directed the rest. In a surprise move, Grandpa hailed a cab.

"What are you doing?" I asked.

"Get in."

We both jumped in the back.

"Where to?" the cabbie asked.

"The parking garage beneath the third Galleria," Grandpa instructed.

"You're joking."

"Very serious," Grandpa told the driver.

He shrugged. "It's your dime."

The cabbie maneuvered through the thick traffic like a

water moccasin through a brush-infested bayou. In the distance I spotted the two thugs as they emerged from the mall. I poked Grandpa and pointed a thumb toward the men. He hunkered down in the seat, but I doubted we'd been seen.

The VW was right where I left it and intact. The driver's mouth, though, fell to his lap.

"I figured you for crazy money people, taking a cab from one end of the Galleria to the other. But looking at that car, I think you're just crazy."

Grandpa tossed him a five.

"Sure that's not your life savings, old man?"

"And a merry Christmas to you, too, sir," Grandpa replied.

"I want to put some distance between us and those idiots," I said, and unlocked the door to the VW. "I imagine they'll be after you again for whatever it is you won't tell me that they want."

"Reckon it's the deed to the mine, or my will. And I don't figure it's just me they want."

"Your will?" We were both in. I started up the Bug. "And what do you mean it's not just you they want?"

"Walter Pierce isn't the executor of my estate anymore," Grandpa informed me. "You are."

8

"They'll find us again," I announced and shifted the Bug into fourth as we climbed onto Loop 610. The ache in my knee intensified each time I moved my foot from the gas to the brake.

"They think you live in the house, not the apartment." Grandpa edged down in the seat, raising his knees toward the dash in an effort to reach a comfort zone.

"Those muscle heads don't know whether to scratch their watches or wind their asses—"

"Them's my words," Grandpa broke in.

"I'm speaking in terms you'd understand," I countered, then completed my thought. "But it doesn't take a brain surgeon to make the connection."

He didn't argue.

"What inspired you to name me executor of your estate?" I asked.

"I trust you."

"Why not your lawyer? You said you trust him."

"Not that much. Besides, T.R.'s almost as old as I am. Leave it to him to croak before he completes my business and send everything into the mess I want to avoid." He looked straight at me. "You afraid of the responsibility?"

"I've done it before."

"Maybe I'm putting too much of a burden on you."

A touch of sarcasm rose to my lips. Burden, of course not. Thugs pulling guns on me is old hat. But something hit me. I realized with all the loss I'd suffered, compounded by the fact that Keely would probably leave, I was in danger of facing yet one more key blow. Something could easily happen to Grandpa. And he knew it. Problem was, I didn't know if I had the foresight, faith, confidence—whatever you wanted to call it—to assure him that everything would be all right. I was beginning to expect the worst.

"Let's have no talk of burdens," I said forcefully. Who was I trying to convince? "Now, did I understand you right? You have the will and the deed to the mine with you?"

"In a safe place." He unbuttoned the front of his down vest.

"You didn't stash them in Jerry's house, did you?"

"There you go again with all the questions."

"It's the only way I can help you," I replied calmly, and continued digging. "Doesn't your lawyer have a copy of the will?"

"Not yet. I was in the process of making some alterations when I decided to leave town."

"You're cutting Walter out," I stated.

"Damn right."

Now we were getting somewhere. "Does Walter know?"

"I informed him."

"Don't imagine he took it too well."

"He didn't."

"Was he angry enough to send someone after you?"

"Reckon he was, but I never thought he'd stoop so low," Grandpa replied, the sharpness in his voice dropping to silence like a hammer's final blow against the head of a nail.

The VW sputtered along in a futile attempt to keep up with the flow of traffic. So many pickup trucks and Cadillacs roared past us, shaking my car to its soul, I began to worry we'd be blown away like an old piece of wrapping paper at the mercy of an ill wind. Grandpa cracked open the window.

"Gotten warm," he muttered.

"Don't know if it's the weather affecting you."

"Coming from subzero temperatures in the mountains, forty, forty-five degrees feels pretty damn good," he responded plainly.

"We pay for our mild winters with blistering summers," I said to keep the dialogue open. Actually, I was trying to figure out what to do. Where to hide Grandpa? Who to call about the two thugs? Private investigator C. J. McDaniels or Lieutenant Gardner? Grandpa would probably talk to C.J. before Gardner. Finally, before I lost my job, I had to get to The Kitchen and begin planning and prepping for the Gilcrest Christmas Eve dinner. And then there was the condition of Samson. How was the Doberman doing?

"Yeah, I was in Houston in the summer," Grandpa stated. "Once. That's when you need to pay me a visit."

"Just might take you up on that. Tell me why you have the deed with you. Why isn't it locked in T. R. Spence's safe?"

"I've always taken care of my own paperwork."

"Simple as that?"

"Simple as that."

We passed a billboard of the Budweiser Clydesdales pulling a sleigh through a snowy forest at night, with red, yellow, green, and blue lights twinkling in a distant window. Sentimental, I thought. Pastoral. And anything but Houston. Every few years there'd be a dusting of snow. Rarely did it stick, and even less often did the white stuff last for more than a day. No, nothing for Santa to touch his sleigh down on here. I glanced at Grandpa. And the last thing I wanted was for the jolly old guy to crash-land.

I chugged over the Katy Freeway, the overcast Houston skyline in the distance, and around to 45 North. I felt obligated to run by the apartment to see if Jerry was back, and to explain the situation to him. Also, I could run in and quickly phone C.J. and solicit his help.

"Where are we going?" Grandpa asked.

"My place."

"I'm beginning to question your judgment."

"We won't be long."

"Good. I'm hungry."

I exited at Airline, cruised by the Farmers' Market, a den of fresh produce that was humming as usual, and drove directly to my apartment. Sure enough, parked in the driveway was Jerry Jacoma's truck.

"The nut's back," Grandpa commented.

"Be nice," I told him as we disentangled ourselves from the Bug. "This incident's going to be quite a shock to his fragile system."

Jerry burst out the front door. "Oh, man! My God! My house, my poor house. We didn't even leave the party pad in Galveston as trashed as my poor house." He was talking to himself until he caught sight of us. In one swift motion, he jumped off the porch, avoiding the stairs.

"Neil, man, my house looks like someone locked a damn Brahman bull inside. You didn't have no party, did you?" Jerry was breathing heavily. His round face glistened with sweat and dampened his Fu Manchu mustache.

"I didn't have a party in your house," I replied, unable to mask the irritation in my voice.

"Someone broke in," Grandpa informed him. "The police have already been out."

"Lieutenant Gardner wants you to take inventory and let them know if anything's missing," I added.

"Of course things are missing. I've been robbed."

"The police believe whoever broke in was looking for something specific," Grandpa explained. "You still have your stereo, VCR, television, and such."

His face went pale. Grandpa and I looked at each other.

"What are you worried about, Jerry?" I asked.

"Nothing, man. I mean, I buy my drugs honestly. I don't cheat anyone."

Grandpa rolled his eyes.

No, I thought, after the bloodied Santa picture and then the Galleria fiasco, I was convinced the intruder had no idea who Jerry Jacoma was or that he had a weakness for weed. The criminal had broken into Jerry's house for an unknown reason that most probably pertained to Grandpa.

The old man cleared his throat. "Neil, you best tell him about Samson."

"What about Samson?" Jerry asked.

"He was hurt during the break-in," I said. "Dr. Crenshaw is tending him. Samson's in a bad way."

Jerry opened his mouth, but it took a couple of attempts for the words to escape. "Crenshaw? Where?"

I swallowed hard at his swell of emotion. "Shepherd."

"The new hospital?"

I nodded. "He'll be okay," I tried to comfort him.

Without another word, Jerry jogged to his truck, hopped in, and took off.

"He's annoying," Grandpa said, "but he didn't deserve this."

I set a hand on the old man's shoulder. "Let's run upstairs. There's a phone call I need to make."

Once we were inside, the clouds opened up and a steady rain began to drum against the windows. C.J. wasn't at his office, so I left a message with his answering service. Grandpa peeked out the window at the driveway below. "Sure wish the dog was down there," he said. "Fierce barking's a great alarm." He let the blinds go.

"I called a private-investigator friend of mine," I told Grandpa. "But I'm sure he's going to advise you to talk to the police."

Grandpa's response was to spy back out the window.

"I'm just warning you," I said, picked up the phone again, and tried to decide whether it was better to grovel for Perry's forgiveness over the cordless or in person. I set the receiver down. In person.

"A cab pulled into the driveway," he stated.

"Those morons wouldn't take a cab here."

"Someone's gone around to the front door."

I stepped beside Grandpa and peered out.

A figure wearing a beige London Fog and a soft matching hat wandered around to the back. The Yellow Cab, lights on, windshield wipers swiping the rain, waited.

"It's a woman," I said, noting her high heels and narrow waist brought out by the belted coat.

"Not just any woman," Grandpa added. "That's Christine Cooper, wife of mining magnate and all-around son of a bitch, Albright Cooper. Now, what in the name of dickens is she doing here?"

9

Upon seeing Grandpa and me emerge from the apartment, Christine Cooper waved the taxi off. The Yellow Cab shone like a cat's eye before pouncing into the misty afternoon.

"Christine?"

"Hello, Stephen."

My boots scraped the pavement, catching the woman's attention. She looked as if she belonged in a Bogart movie—Lauren Bacall paying a visit.

"My grandson, Neil."

"Can we get out of the rain, Neil?"

"Yes, ma'am."

I led them up to my apartment. Grandpa took the umbrella and guided the woman behind me.

"How quaint," she commented on my modest flat. Undoubtedly, her bedroom closet compared in size.

"He needs some Christmas decorations," Grandpa grumbled. "Best time of the year and he's passing it off like the plague."

"Because this time of year works me to death," I retorted.

Something about this meeting made me nervous. I'd never heard of the woman, didn't know the woman, and the small talk and guarded presence that Grandpa exuded set me on edge.

"Coffee?" I suggested.

"That would be wonderful." A smile flickered and then faded from her face like a dying lightbulb. It was obvious that Christine had once been a very beautiful woman.

Now, though, even a heavy dose of makeup couldn't mask the wrinkles that had invaded her high cheekbones and surrounded eyes that were both dark and sad.

Grandpa directed her to an easy chair. He took the couch, and I slipped into the kitchen. A glance outside showed nothing but the rain darkening the driveway and glistening against the rounded form of my VW. Beneath the sound of the rain was the murmur of the stereo I'd left on all day. Garth Brooks's version of "Santa Looked a Lot Like Daddy" rocked soft and low.

While I dumped out this morning's coffee grounds and proceeded to make another pot, they spoke.

"What are you doing here?" Grandpa asked.

"If Albright knew, he'd kill me."

"Oh, he'll find out. He always does. But you aren't afraid of that, or you wouldn't be here."

"Not true," she hedged.

I poured water into the Braun and then drifted back into the living room.

"Did Walter put you up to this?" the old man asked.

"No," she said, eyes darting. "Not exactly."

"Don't even try to snow me, Christine. I know you and Walt are an item."

"Stephen, please—"

"Walt send you to patch things up?"

The thick aroma of coffee stretched to all corners of the apartment, countering the chilly rawness that had overtaken the afternoon. It also underscored my growing hunger, which reminded me how late it was getting and heightened my anxiety about work. I was beginning to wonder if having guns pulled on us at the Galleria was a good-enough excuse. I could hear Perry say, *You shouldn't have even been at the Galleria. . . .*

I caught myself and focused on Christine's response.

"I'm here because of Walter," she said with great effort, "but I'm afraid it's not what you think."

Grandpa leaned forward. "Christine?"

"Walter's dead, Stephen."

The old man's face turned ashen. Only a twitch below his right eye betrayed any further emotion. He stood, faced the window.

Before he said anything, though, Christine continued. "Apparently he died of gunshot wounds." She took a deep breath.

"By who?"

"I don't know. But the police think they do."

I set a cup of coffee before her, along with sugar and milk. The full weight of what she'd said hadn't sunk in yet. In spite of their recent argument, I had always liked Walter. When I was a kid, he encouraged me to call him Uncle Walt, would slip me candy or money—one Christmas he gave me a pouch that contained five silver dollars, and I thought I was rich. Then there was the time he encouraged me to take a slug from his whiskey bottle. *Go ahead, kid, it'll put hair on your chest.* And I almost took a swig. Grandpa was ready to knock Walt silly. Still, to me, he and Grandpa were simply a couple of grumpy old men.

"Neil, do you have anything to give the coffee a little body?" she asked, voice trembling.

"Bourbon?"

"A touch, please, to calm my nerves." Her hands trembled as she handed the cup and saucer back to me.

I returned to the kitchen and splashed in half a shot of the liquor.

"What do the cops think?" Grandpa asked, still facing the window.

"Thank you," Christine said as I set the cup and saucer before her. After a couple of strong sips and a heavy breath, she told us, "Walter's body was discovered on your property, Stephen."

He whipped around. "What?"

"In a cavern in the mine. Apparently there'd been some sort of fire, too, but I don't know much about that."

"Jesus, Joseph, and Mary."

"Buster Ledbetter found him," she added.

"That bastard's supposed to keep clear of my land."

"Don't worry about that, now. You have bigger problems."

A dreadful feeling syphoned the strength from my legs and threatened to tear my heart from my chest. "When did Walt die?" I asked.

"I'm not quite sure, but some days ago."

"When Grandpa was still in Colorado," I murmured. "So the cops think he murdered Walter, then ran."

"Stephen's the police's number one suspect," she confirmed. "Ledbetter's screaming he now understands why your grandfather wouldn't sell or work with him. In turn, the authorities have issued an arrest warrant with extradition orders back to Denver. Your lawyer claims he doesn't know where you are," she told the old man. "I didn't believe him, but he stuck to his story. Then it dawned on me where you'd go. The way you brag about your grandson, it was obvious. And if I figured it out, the police soon will, too."

"How do you know all this?" I asked.

"In part from the news, much from overhearing my husband talk. Albright knows everyone and everything that has anything to do with the mining industry."

"He know Ledbetter?"

"I'm sure he knows of him, but I don't believe they're friends or anything like that."

Grandpa was visibly at a loss as to what to do. For a moment he stood there gazing from Christine to me then blankly into space. Finally he managed to work his way back to the couch.

Well, I knew what to do. First thing was to make like a reindeer and dash away from this place.

"We're leaving," I told Christine. "Can I drop you anywhere?"

"Yes, Stephen, leaving is a good idea. Perhaps even out of the country for a while."

Whoa, I thought. Out of the country? C. J. McDaniels's office was more to my liking.

"Why are you here?" Grandpa suddenly asked, a no-nonsense tone in his voice.

She took a drink of the spiked coffee, then set the cup down and knelt before him. "I don't want to see you in jail, Stephen. I came all the way to Houston because I care about you."

"The same way you cared about Walter?" he shot back.

"Contrary to what you may believe, Walter and I were friends. I care about you."

"Damn it, woman, you're married."

"That's my problem. Your immediate problem is to get out of the country. Come to Buenos Aires with me."

Color was returning to Grandpa's face. Slowly, he shook his head. "No, Christine. It was no before, and it's still no."

Christine pursed her lips, dug her nails into the couch, then pushed herself up. "You'll change your mind," she said, "when you get it into your thick head you could spend the rest of your life in jail. Or be given the chair."

"Do they still use the chair in Colorado?" I asked. "Texas is up to lethal injection."

The glower she directed toward me was meant to rip me to shreds. "There's nothing amusing about this situation."

"Absolutely not. So we're leaving. And I'll be glad to drop you somewhere." I went into the kitchen and turned off the coffeemaker.

"I'll call a cab," she announced.

"That really isn't necessary," I countered.

"Is the Volkswagen down there yours?"

"Yes, ma'am."

"I'm not going to stuff myself into that capsule." She picked up the phone and muttered, "And they say everything's big in Texas. Ha!"

"Need a phone book?"

"I recall the number." And she did.

Grandpa was eerily silent. "Grab your bag," I told him.

He rose. "You really do need some Christmas cheer in this place," he said. "A little tree. A wreath. Maybe ribbons. You know, dressing a place up for Christmas is something your mother can sure do. First time I walked into your folks' house I thought I'd entered an enchanted cottage in Candy Land."

"I know, I know." I touched the old man below the elbow, but he pulled away.

"Don't insult me, Neil," he said, voice low. "I'm not a doddering old fool."

"I'm not trying to insult you, and I certainly don't consider you a doddering old fool."

"Okay, well, don't insult me."

I sighed, let it go.

As the rain was falling hard, I traded my black leather jacket for a brown duster. I also grabbed my battered and grungy straw cowboy hat.

"You figuring on joining the Texas Rangers?" Grandpa asked.

"Might need them before we're through."

Christine hung up the phone. And we all returned to the damp afternoon. After cinching her belt, Christine opened her umbrella. I tossed Grandpa's duffel bag into the trunk and unlocked the doors. Before the lean woman got away, however, I asked her a couple more things.

"Mrs. Cooper," I called. "Did you come to Houston alone?"

"Of course."

"Then do you know of anyone else, besides yourself and the police, of course, who'd also like to locate my grandfather?"

"Really, Neil," she said, her composure back, "how would I know? As far as I'm concerned, your grandfather's a sweet, lovable old man."

"That's why I won't go anywhere with you, Christine," Grandpa barked, hand on the passenger door. "You're so full of shit."

"Such gratitude, Stephen."

"There's something you're not telling me."

"You moron! You absolute moron! I'm standing in the pouring rain talking to a lunatic miner who's spent too much time underground." She paused, held the umbrella with both hands, and calmed herself. "You're shooting the messenger, darling. The messenger who sounded the warning call."

"You want something," the old man said, his beard soaked with rain.

"You're right—*you!* But, dear Stephen, you said no. So I lost, didn't I?"

"Sounds to me like Walter's the biggest loser in this story."

"For the time being," she declared, and faced me. "Young Neil Marshall, you'd better know one other thing."

"And that is, ma'am?"

"He won't take my advice, so you'd better know what the hell you're doing or they'll bring him down." With that, she swung herself around and over to the front porch to await her cab.

"Who's *they?*" I called.

"I ain't scared," Grandpa hollered, "and I ain't running away!" He jerked open the door and got in.

For a second I stood, more than a little stunned. Rain peppered my brown duster and ran down the rim of my straw hat. My fishing hat, in fact. I took it off and tossed it onto the backseat before settling in. Fishing, I thought. Never really fished at Christmastime before. But I suspected I was about to begin. Only trouble was, I needed to find a top guide. One who could navigate the waters of breaking and entering, attempted kidnapping, and murder.

It was time to visit C. J. McDaniels.

10

C. J. McDaniels's office was located above a new-and-used record store off Westheimer in the Montrose area. I parked next to his red Mustang, which glowed brighter than a neon sign in the dull afternoon. Quickly, we hustled—or rather, Grandpa hustled and I hobbled on my bruised knee—out of the rain and up to his office. The door was unlocked, and he was inside, all right. Feet propped up on the front desk, thick arms folded over his massive chest and ample belly, he leaned back in the wooden chair, his bald head dipped forward and his eyes closed. He appeared to be very much asleep.

"Good thing I'm not a desperado," I said loudly, "or you'd be one ventilated detective."

" 'Bout time you got here," C.J. replied. He tilted his head back and slowly opened his eyes. "Got your message, tried ringing you back. Had a strong feeling when no one picked up you were on your way."

"Cocky bastard," Grandpa commented.

"That's what makes him so good."

"You're limping," C.J. observed.

"It's a long story." I hung my hat on the antique hat tree, then drew a tissue from the box on the desk and wiped off my rain-speckled glasses.

"Sit down," C.J. invited, waving a hand at the chairs in front of his desk, "and tell me who's in trouble—you or the big elf."

After introducing C.J. to Grandpa—who grumbled to the detective he was hardly an elf—we sat, and I related to him the break-in at Jerry's house, the dog, Ledbetter mining on Grandpa's land, the threats, the gunmen at the Galleria, and finally Christine Cooper's visit with news of Walter's death and the warrant out for Grandpa's arrest. During my briefing, C.J. swung his feet down, leaned forward, and lit a cigarette. Only the teeth of Grandpa's beast image kept me from bumming one.

"Let me get this straight," C.J. said. "The Cooper woman flew down from Colorado—"

"I don't know that she flew," I interrupted.

"If she's taking cabs, she doesn't have her car, so she flew. Now, don't cut me off." He blew out a cloud of smoke, then crushed out the butt in a Texas-shaped ashtray.

Aye, aye, Captain, I thought.

"She flew down," he repeated, "to warn you about what's going on in the Rockies." He pointed at Grandpa. "Why?"

"Christine has a thing for me," Grandpa replied. "Been chasing me for years. In fact, I think she took up with Walter to make me jealous."

"Been chasing you for years?" the detective echoed.

"Getting tired of running, too," the old man said matter-of-factly.

"Where is her husband in all this? Indifferent or stupid?"

"Albright Cooper is a neurotic, narcissistic twerp, which doesn't make him indifferent. Blinded, maybe. He is not, however, stupid."

"He the type to pull a gun on you if he didn't like what you were doing?" C.J. asked.

Grandpa hesitated. "Albright has a king's treasure chest. For him, money is the meaning of life. He'd rather see a man reduced to panhandling, spirit broken, than six feet under."

"So the answer's no?"

The old man shrugged. "Mostly. Any man can commit the darkest act under the right circumstances."

"I agree, but where does that leave us?"

"With a big mess," Grandpa answered.

Rain beaded on the window that overlooked Westheimer, and an overhead fan lazily swept at the smoke from C.J.'s latest cigarette. "Why did you and your partner part ways?"

"He called me a selfish old fool for not selling the mineral rights of my mine to Buster Ledbetter. I told Walter to go to hell, he hadn't been pulling his weight for years, then gambled most of what he had away. He threatened to sue me. I asked for what? He said for his share of the business, including the mine. Finally, I swore to him if he tried jumping my claim, I'd kill him."

His words set off ripples of horrible feelings in me— fear that the police actually had a case, anxiety that there was more going on than I was aware of, worry that such information might dig us into an even deeper hole.

"That's the holiday spirit. Where did you have this conversation?" C.J. said dryly.

"At a bar called Glittering Gold."

"Anyone hear your argument and ensuing threat?"

"Sixty, seventy people. We ended up in a shouting match."

C.J. ground out another cigarette and leaned heavily back against the chair. "Santa," he said, "you're in deep reindeer shit."

"What do we do?" I asked.

"I guess going to the cops is not an option."

Grandpa's expression had a *you have a better chance of canceling Christmas* look.

"You guessed correctly," I affirmed.

"Then we need to find someplace for you to hole up for a while," he told the old man, then turned to me. "A motel's the best option. Paul Gardner and Vic Hernandez know all my sources. If we tried to stash him at Linda's or Mama's, they'd be on your grandfather like cold on ice."

I agreed. Linda was C.J.'s daughter, and Mama was an old family friend who'd helped raise McDaniels. Lieutenant Gardner and Sergeant Hernandez knew them both well.

"I'd like to talk to Christine Cooper," C.J. stated. "Where's she staying?"

Grandpa and I looked at each other in embarrassment.

"Don't tell me," the detective said. "You didn't ask."

"No," I said, a near whisper, "we didn't." I felt my cheeks redden.

He sighed. "Well, I can probably trace her through the cab company. You do know the cab company." He fumbled with a pencil and drummed the eraser end against a large desk calendar.

"Yellow," I replied.

"Well, that's a start. Neil, keep an eye for those gorillas that jumped you at the Galleria. Sounds like they're serious. You need to spot them before they corner you. And let me know. I want to see if they can shed some light on the situation."

It would take punching their lights out to get any information, I thought. But then C.J. wasn't above such tactics.

"The solution to your predicament, Santa, is actually simple," C.J. continued. "All we have to find out is who murdered your partner."

"Your encouragement is overwhelming," I said.

"He's right, Neil," Grandpa said.

"I might need to run to Colorado," C.J. added.

"I have money," Grandpa told him.

"Well, it's refreshing to meet a Marshall who can pay for services rendered."

"Next time you get shot, don't ask me to drive you to the hospital," I shot back. That was the precarious way in which we met—he was the victim of a drive-by shooting, and I happened to jog up in time to witness it.

"So you're the man my grandson saved," Grandpa chimed in.

"And I've been paying for it ever since."

A short chuckle escaped the old man.

I rose. "If I care to keep my job, I have to get to The Kitchen."

"I'd like some chow," Grandpa announced.

"You go on, Neil," C.J. directed. "I'll take Saint Nick out for a burger then set him up with a room. The bozos following y'all won't be looking for me."

"True."

"So, like I said, keep your eyes open."

"Count on it."

"You still haven't explained the limp."

"One of the best blindside knocks anyone ever laid into me," Grandpa interjected.

C.J. immediately caught on. "He hit you?"

"Once a hero always a hero," the old man said.

"I'm going to be glad to be out of here," I muttered.

"Just pass the fugitive around," Grandpa said, taking out his pipe.

"I'll be in touch later." I retrieved my hat from the rack, gave it a shake, and put it back on.

"I'll call you at work," C.J. said as he lit another cigarette.

As I eased my knee down the stairs I heard Grandpa say, "Chicken-fried steak sounds good."

"I was thinking of McDonald's."

"Never touch the stuff."

"A quick bite is best," C.J. reasoned.

"Not a quick McFat heart attack."

"Chicken-fried steak's any better?"

"If I'm going to keel over, it's going to be on tasty food."

"Are all Marshalls this difficult?"

"Who's being difficult?"

I closed the outside door believing they deserved each other.

Twenty minutes after leaving C.J.'s and five hours late, I drifted to a stop by the curb in front of The Kitchen. Perry's Lexus was absent. But the old silver Cadillac belonging to kitchen manager and self-appointed field marshal Claudia Perry was standing guard. With the deftness of a cat burglar, I slipped into my place of employment. Robbie Persons, beverage manager and close friend, was busy with some paperwork in the office.

"The prodigal employee returns," he said, and swiveled around in the chair to face me.

"Perry angry?" I asked.

"Irritated you didn't make this morning's staff meeting, but I jarred his memory that he'd given you permission to meet your professor at U of H. He left right after the meeting, so he's unaware you haven't been here all day."

"Claudia will be sure to draw it to Perry's attention." I unbuttoned my duster. I'd left the hat in the car.

"She will unless you smooth her feathers."

"I spend half my life doing that."

" 'Cause you spend the other half of your life ruffling them. I had to help Claudia and Mattie finish Mrs. Gilcrest's desserts for this afternoon's tea. If we'd blown that little function, she'd surely have hired someone else for her Christmas Eve dinner, even at this late date."

"I didn't see Trisha's Honda out front," I observed about one of our newest employees. "Did she feel it necessary to drive herself to Mrs. Gilcrest's tea?"

"Oh, no, she didn't decide that."

"What do you mean? Mattie's not working the job alone, is she?"

"Not at all, and the function is under control."

"Okay, then what's *not* under control?"

Robbie looked at me with a deadpan face. "Trisha didn't come in today, either," he explained. "The spirit didn't move her."

"What?"

"The bad weather was a message she shouldn't venture out."

Trisha was a New Age student, and a brilliant pastry chef—especially with the orders for gingerbread houses we'd received. But every ounce of talent was balanced by a very unique approach toward life. For instance, Trisha didn't own an alarm clock because she believed she should awaken in the morning when the spirit guided. Today, however, was the first time the spirit indicated she shouldn't show altogether.

"How did Claudia respond to that?"

Robbie stood. He was almost as tall as I was and lean as the line of hardworking ranchers he came from. "You think my mama raised a fool? I told Claudia that Trisha was sick."

"Might not be too far off."

"Neil—"

I hung my coat in the closet. "So what'd y'all discuss at the weekly meeting?"

"That Christmas can't come too soon."

"Amen." Neither one of us had enjoyed an entire day off since Thanksgiving. "I used to love Christmas, Robbie. Since my grandfather arrived, I've been thinking about how much fun it was when I was a kid. Now it's just excess work and stress."

"God, you're in a funk," Robbie observed. "I'm tired, too, but I still love Christmas. Maybe you should come over to my place this year. I'm planning a big party. There will be people you know. My sister's driving in from Amarillo. Bring Grandpa," he suggested, and laughed. "You might even have some fun."

"Thanks, Robbie, but I think we're going to Candace's. I need to talk to Grandpa," I said. "And pray he can make it," I added under my breath.

"You best pray, seeing you just arriving," a voice behind me scolded. In spite of her recent weight loss from battling cancer, Claudia was still imposing, especially in the small office.

"I know. I'm sorry. I'm not even going to try to explain."

"You got yourself in some kind of trouble again, didn't you?"

"Not me," I evaded. "My grandfather's down from Colorado and demanding a certain amount of attention."

Her eyes narrowed as she tugged at the black scarf wrapped around her head. Fingerprints of flour left impressions on the dark material. Not even a hint of a smile tugged at her cracked lips. Her drawn face, weathered from a hard life and recent chemotherapy, looked like the worn leather binding of an overused Bible.

I cleared my throat. "What's on my agenda?" I asked.

"Only time you's late is when you knee-deep in problems," Claudia muttered. "Someone else's problems," she added, stepping out of the room.

"She's tired," Robbie spoke up.

"I know. And she won't slow down."

"You coming?" Claudia screeched from the front room.

"It's the way she hangs on." Robbie stretched and playfully punched my shoulder.

"She doesn't need to hang on to anything. The good Lord's going to see Claudia receives all the treatment she needs in order to keep her down here as long as possible."

"To torment you, no doubt."

"No doubt."

"Neil Marshall!"

"Yes, ma'am." I pasted on my best smile and followed her irresistible request to join her in the other room.

"This just a social visit or are you fixing to do some work?" She'd slipped on her bifocals and peered at me over them, a fistful of papers in her grasp. I was reminded of crabby old Mrs. Baggly, my third-grade teacher, who ruled with a stiff yardstick and a tongue so acerbic she could reduce the toughest of us to bawling fools.

"I intend to do my job," I said, calmly countering the Mrs. Baggly image.

Claudia grunted, shuffled the work orders. "We got a lunch tomorrow. The chutney-glazed game hens will wait till morning. But you can make the wild-rice-and-hazelnut stuffing. And prep the asparagus. Bake the cheese rolls—"

It took a few seconds, but I noticed the pause.

"You listening to me?" she asked.

I snapped to attention, half expecting the slap of a yardstick across my knuckles. My mind had drifted off to C.J. and Grandpa. Where would the detective stash the old man? Considering how well they'd hit it off, I hoped they'd bonded just a little so C.J. wouldn't abandon Grandpa under some bridge.

"Yes, yes. You have my undivided attention."

"Good. You can throw a couple of apple strudels together."

"Apple strudels? You going to be here to help me stretch the dough?" The dessert was a popular item of ours, served warm and with a rum sauce, but the dough needed to be worked and stretched until it thinly covered the length and width of a butcher-block table. The process made for a great demonstration, as we'd done several times at Macy's and Neiman Marcus. Problem was, it took two people to pull it off.

But it wouldn't be Claudia who helped. "No, honey, I'm going home."

"As you should," I agreed.

"We're goin' to need a few strudels for the Gilcrest Christmas Eve dinner, too."

"I know."

"Might as well do them at the same time, but set those in the freezer and we'll cook 'em later."

I'll be here until ten, I thought dejectedly.

"The Gilcrests is also having rack of lamb with Texas pesto."

"I know."

"The lamb's gonna need to be trimmed and the chops separated."

Too early for that yet, I thought, but grinned and nodded.

"And the Texas pesto gots to be fixed."

Not too difficult as we used a basic pesto recipe, added pecans instead of pine nuts, cilantro instead of basil, and a touch of jalapeño, but these projects were beginning to add up to an all-nighter. And I had Grandpa to think about. Shit, Grandpa.

"Neil!" Claudia snapped. "Texas pesto, too. Where is your mind?"

"Enough already." I tugged at my collar. Claudia *is* the reincarnation of Mrs. Baggly. I wanted to run out of The Kitchen screaming, *No, I don't know my multiplication table, and you can't make me cook everything tonight!* I took a deep breath. "I get the picture. We have *beaucoup* to do. I'll be sure to hit the priority stuff first."

Claudia set the work orders down. "You do that." She untied her apron and tossed it in the laundry bag. "I'll see you in the morning. Early."

Robbie came up with his denim jacket and a baseball cap on. "I need to run by the warehouse, and then I'm going to work out," he stated. "So I'm gone, too."

"Later." Suddenly it struck me how quiet The Kitchen was about to get. "Where's Conrad?"

"Our trusty dishwasher is meeting with his parole officer," Robbie informed me. "Don't expect him."

I sighed, feeling as if I were being punished for taking time off while they worked.

"I'll enjoy the quiet," I rallied. And washing my own dishes. Right.

Claudia straightened her coat, grabbed her purse, and dug out a wad of keys big enough to be used as brass knuckles. "I'm fighting death, myself," she suddenly told me, her head cocked back. "I can smell his bitter odor wherever it is. You *is* in trouble."

Robbie stopped short of the front door.

"No, ma'am," I managed to reply.

"Your mouth say no, Neil," she said solemnly, "but your eyes say yes." She rattled her keys, and I heard the echo of Mrs. Baggly's yardstick. My stomach churned the same as it had in the third grade, the day I ran into the street without first looking for cars. A station wagon had screeched to a stop inches away from me—and Mrs. Baggly had seen it from her classroom window. Once I was inside, she'd stood there, tapping the yardstick against the palm of her hand, talking to me about danger, about dying, about never doing anything foolish like that again.

Yes, ma'am. Tears welling in my eyes.

You foolish, foolish little boy.

Yes, ma'am. Barely audible.

"Yes, sir," Claudia muttered, and brushed past Robbie. "Danger. I can smell it."

Damn her intuition.

11

I lost myself in preparing the wild-rice-and-hazelnut stuffing, carefully roasting the hazelnuts so they didn't scorch, then adding healthy amounts of fresh tarragon, sage, chives, and garlic. It wasn't until I began the apple strudel dough that C.J. called to say he'd set Grandpa up in a cheap motel off South Main near the Astrodome.

"Nice neighborhood."

"That's what the old man said. Sure glad I'm appreciated."

"You are," I replied. "And actually I feared that after spending time with Grandpa, you'd leave him under the Pierce Elevated near the bus station. So I'm much obliged. Now what are you going to do?"

"Must say you don't take the long way around the barn anymore," he grumbled. His raspy voice had the pitch of a bass sax.

"Didn't intend to be presumptuous. Just getting to the meat of the matter."

A short chuckle. "Fair enough. I have to wrap an insurance investigation. Linda's onto the initial digging to confirm Christine Cooper's story. In the morning I'll follow up and be in touch."

"Sounds like you've done this before."

"Once or twice, and some clients like your granddaddy even paid." With that jab, he hung up. Always had to get the last word in. Oh, well, he'd eased some of the anxiety that Claudia had raised. And at least we weren't sitting around like victims, waiting for events to catch up to us. We were moving, causing our own waves—little as they were, but better than nothing. And who knew what the surf would wash up? Pray God, a solution.

I was kneading the last of a half-dozen apple-strudel doughs, listening to *All Things Considered* on the radio, when keys jangled in the front door and in popped Mattie.

"Good timing," I declared. "I need a pair of capable hands to help me stretch these doughs."

"Neil, I'm exhausted," Mattie responded, and set a white container full of knives, utensils, and condiments on the stainless-steel workbench.

"It won't take long."

"I'll help," a familiar voice announced from the doorway.

I glanced over. "Candace Littlefield, what are you doing here?" Candace was like a baby sister to me. She was a spunky barrel racer who aspired to be a large-animal veterinarian. We'd become close when a mutual friend of ours, Jason Keys, had died.

"Working, silly." She thumped a tub of silver serving pieces next to Mattie's.

"Stupid question," I agreed.

"Trisha was supposed to help Mattie, and when she couldn't, Robbie called me." The smile on her eighteen-year-old freckled face was a sight for sore eyes.

"Mattie, darling, you're off the hook," I announced.

"Thank you, Candace," Mattie said with relief.

"My pleasure," the girl said. "You go on and pick up J.J. and I'll unload this stuff before I help Neil."

"Bless your heart." Mattie collected her purse and, after a Merry Christmas from Candace, was out the door and into the rainy evening.

"I've been meaning to call you," I told Candace when we were alone. I spread a film of flour across the cotton tablecloth that covered the butcher-block table.

"Heard that before." She winked. "And if you had, you'd know that I aced all my finals."

"I'm proud of you."

"Thanks. First semester of college and I think I'll pull straight A's."

"Look out world, genius at work." I patted the first dough out on the table, floured the springy mass, and began to roll it out. The elasticity in the mixture caused it to recede back with each push like a turtle's head ducking into its shell. "My grandfather's in town," I told Candace.

"Cool." Then a hesitation. "Or is it?"

"No, very cool. He and I are close. There's just a minor problem." I flipped the dough over, dusted it with flour, and rolled a little more.

"Oh?" Eyebrows raised.

"We have to move quickly while this is still warm," I explained. Using the backs of our floured hands, we carefully but deftly stretched the dough until it was as transparent as a lace curtain. As we worked I explained Grandpa's situation to Candace.

"Neil," she said slowly, "now, don't get me wrong, but do you believe your granddaddy didn't, you know, waste his partner. I mean—"

"I know Grandpa didn't kill Walter." I choked back a flare of anger. After all, Candace hadn't suspected her grandfather was a man who'd commit such a heinous crime. Neither had I, until one night he'd confronted me with a shotgun in my face, crumbling the walls of deceit that he'd built around my friend's murder. A murder that sprang from his ignorant attempt to protect Candace. And then there'd been the truth. *Truth,* I thought. C.J. would get to the truth. Not a dishonest truth as a lawyer's biased argument or a politician's twisted view, but a bittersweet truth where the taste would last forever.

We hooked the ends of the dough over the corners of the table, and I brushed on the butter while Candace followed, sprinkling the cake crumbs. We then drained the apple, raisin, and pecan filling, and spread it on one end. Cinnamon and dark rum spiced the air.

"Did I make you mad?" she finally asked.

"No, honey." Using the tablecloth, we tightly rolled the

strudel until it resembled a large, pale cigar. "I know where you're coming from," I added. "It's okay."

"You sure? I mean, you don't seem much like your old self. You seem kind of, well, angry."

"Sorry, kid. I'm fine."

"Well, whatever you say. I tell you, though, you're going to like what I got you for Christmas."

"Candace, you don't have to—"

"Oh, shut up, Neil."

I smiled in spite of myself. "Reckon I'll have to break down and pick something up for you, too."

"Don't hurt yourself." Candace shook her floury hands at my face, setting off a slight flurry that landed on my beard and hair.

"I'll keep that in mind," I replied, and puffed at the powder in my mustache and on my lips. We lifted the strudel with the cloth and rolled it diagonally onto a greased baking sheet. Then we set up the table for the next round.

Two hours, six strudels, and a clean kitchen later, Candace and I were ready to call it quits. I had to get to Grandpa for fear he was going cabin crazy in flat country and would do something foolish. Like decide he couldn't live anymore without food and go hiking out for all the world—or rather underworld—to see.

"Where's your truck?" I asked Candace.

"Around the side by Nick's Produce."

"That's why I didn't notice it when I drove up. Since you have your ride, I'm heading off to see Grandpa."

"Can I come?"

"I don't know if this is the best time." I paused, tried to qualify what I was saying. "I mean, some mean-ass vermin—"

"Don't go there, Neil. I'm not afraid—"

"Candace—"

"Besides, I've got a 'thirty-eight with me."

"What!"

"Oh, it's crazy that I'm too young to be licensed to carry

a concealed handgun. I'm responsible. And I figure it's for the best while I work in this neighborhood and live at the trailer."

"Responsible?" Nothing could've hidden my shock. "Carrying a gun is anything but responsible."

The girl straightened her auburn ponytail then pulled on her blue jean coat. "I shouldn't have told you. I knew you wouldn't approve."

"Approve? Jesus, Candace, you're inviting trouble."

"Well, ain't that the pot calling the kettle—"

"No," I interrupted, "that's not the issue."

" 'Course that's the issue. It's all right for you to have a gun—"

"I don't tote them like I'm Wyatt Earp." My voice rose in volume.

"Maybe you should," she shouted back, hands planted on hips and chin defiantly stretched forward. Her emerald eyes smoldered.

"Like a gun would've helped me at the Galleria today," I answered sarcastically. "Either the thugs would've grabbed the piece or some kid would've gotten shot." Not that I was antigun, but there was a place for such an instrument of danger, and it wasn't in the purse or truck of an eighteen-year-old.

"You just don't like it when I do things on my own."

"That's ridiculous," I said.

"Ridiculous! Now I'm ridiculous."

"Don't bend my words."

"Don't treat me like a kid."

"My intentions are not to treat you like a kid. I am, however, questioning your horse sense."

"I'm leaving."

"Candace, you're acting irresponsibly."

"I'm not going to end up a statistic floating naked and facedown in the bayou because some nut jumped me and I couldn't defend myself. Christ, Neil, look what happened to that judge. If he hadn't had a gun, that lunatic would've beaten him to death."

She referred to a Houston judge who'd chased down a mentally impaired man who'd stolen a lawyer's briefcase, only to have the man turn violent on him. And Candace was right—if the judge hadn't had the gun, he probably would've been seriously hurt. Instead, the judge shot and killed the man. But the judge was licensed to carry the piece.

"I'm not going to get into a debate over the concealed-handgun law. My point is that in your situation what you're doing is illegal and—"

"And I'll take my chances," she snapped, and unlocked the front door. Her final statement was the reverberation of wood on frame rattling throughout The Kitchen.

"Well, Neil," I told myself aloud, "you handled that like a pro. A pro bonehead." I sighed. Maybe I worried too much about other people and situations I couldn't control. Candace was entitled to make her own decisions. And being one who'd illegally carried a handgun more than once myself, who was I to preach? A concerned big brother, that was who.

On the radio, the London Symphony Orchestra sprang into its version of "Hallelujah" from Handel's *Messiah*. I clicked the music off, then hit the lights and locked up.

"Hallelujah"? I thought. *More like "Blue Christmas."*

And I cared for that Elvis tune about as much as I did the raw, wet weather I trudged into.

12

Rain blistered my windshield. The colors of Christmas glistened with moisture like tears gathering around sad, red eyes. The stretch of road I approached had long ago seen its heyday. Gone was Christie's Seafood. Gone was Kaphan's, one of *the* places to dine in the Fifties, and for thirty years afterwards. Gone was the Shamrock Hotel, a buttress between the Medical Center and South Main—I recalled having a drink in the lobby bar one summer evening and spying the Los Angeles Dodgers, led by Steve Garvey, checking in. The wonderful old Shamrock, built by oilman Glenn McCarthy—famously portrayed by James Dean in the movie *Giant*—was now a parking lot. Soon even the Astrodome would be history, as a bond had passed to build a downtown stadium. I shook my head to release the growing melancholia. It was starting to overwhelm me, distract me from what was important. I couldn't help but notice that in the charcoal night even the giant star atop the dome seemed to have lost its luster.

As I cruised into the rocky parking lot of a dingy little motel, my mind was on how I could've handled Candace better. No matter how mature she often seemed, I needed to remember she was still a teenager. And in our argument I allowed myself to be brought down to a teenager's level. Once that happened, I lost. Perhaps Grandpa would have a few words of wisdom.

A train whistle and the ensuing thunder of steel that echoed in the night called to mind the lonely songs of Luke the Drifter. Within that memory, the place also

91

brought forth the picture of a dive I'd once spent the night at in Raton, New Mexico. Not too far from railroad tracks, those rooms, I learned, went by the month to laborers, by the night to wayward travelers such as myself, or by the hour, for obvious reasons.

A sparse string of lights that surrounded the words *Jesus Lives* blinked at the main office. After a token glance to assure myself all was well, I crunched across the gravel and located Grandpa's room, ground level. I rapped on the door.

"It's me—Neil," I announced.

Hesitation, then the clinking of chains, and the door opened.

" 'Bout time you got here," the old man said. "A body could starve to death."

"That all you think about?" I entered the room, shutting the door behind me.

"At my age I consider it a blessing I still have food to think about. And I don't want to waste any time not taking advantage."

I looked around the room. Small TV secured to a stand, watercolors of bluebonnets screwed to the wall, and a double bed and two chairs that appeared more like a hospital setup than a hospitality pad. "Everything okay?"

"Jim-dandy, if you consider sitting in this whore's nest watching *Sally Jessy Raphael* your idea of a swell time."

"An old bear's not as grouchy as you."

"Hunger and fear have that effect on me."

I kicked myself for not rounding us up a bite to eat at The Kitchen. Of course, at Candace's departure, eating was not the foremost thought on my mind.

Arguing with Grandpa about the dangers of going out would do no good, so I didn't even try. I figured we'd head southwest down South Main toward the Stafford, Missouri City, and Sugar Land area and see what we could find. Far from my usual stomping grounds, no one would look for me there.

"I suppose it wouldn't hurt to grab a quick meal," I told Grandpa. "Maybe pick you up some reading material, too, so you won't be stuck with only talk shows to entertain you."

"They've got a dirty-movie channel, but it costs extra."

"Good thing or you might want a little dessert tonight."

"Neil Marshall," the old man boomed, "I ain't been with a hooker since I was in the marines, and even then it was because I got snookered and my buddies thought it'd be a great joke. That was in Cuba. Most expensive night of sleep I ever had." He grabbed his down vest, pulled on the 49ers cap, and we were off.

Twenty yards into the stony parking lot, though, we walked straight into the thugs from the Galleria.

"You're beginning to irritate me," Mr. Stocky declared in a voice so cold it could've sucked the energy from a strand of Christmas-tree lights.

I darted to my left, but Mr. Scrawny was there, holding the flank. The guns in their hands—9mm from the looks—were as conspicuous as Rudolph the Reindeer's nose.

"We're going back to Colorado, old man." Scrawny laughed. "What about the kid?" he asked his partner.

"Tie him up and leave him in the room."

Scrawny appeared disappointed, but I reckoned he'd still get his jollies in—a few licks to jaw, stomach, and kidneys. My heart was off at the races. How could I have been so stupid to have missed them following me? That's the only way they could've found this place. Too damn self-absorbed.

All right, I told myself. *But now it's time to focus.*

"Who has the key?" Stocky asked.

"I do," Grandpa said calmly. Without hesitation, he took it from his vest pocket, and tossed the shiny metal deep into the night. From the sound of the clink, the key careened against one of the cars parked beneath a blackened streetlight.

"A wiseguy," Stocky said.

Scrawny came up from behind and struck Grandpa between the shoulder blades with the butt of his gun. The old man staggered forward, but didn't fall. Anger flaring, I instinctively rushed forward, but Scrawny backhanded me with the flat side of his piece. A flash of white, my head buzzed, and the next thing I knew I was on my back, staring straight into the rain, my glasses skewed and beading with water.

And then the image of Scrawny straddling above my legs, the barrel of his gun aimed right between my eyes.

"Leave him be," Grandpa barked.

I heard cars swishing water on South Main. In the dull light, steam escaped from Scrawny's clenched mouth. But I wasn't scared as my senses rallied to get on track. My head throbbed, but logic dictated if they killed me, they'd also have to kill Grandpa. And I didn't believe they wanted to do that. I straightened my glasses.

"Shoot him," Stocky ordered.

Of course, logic had never been my strongest suit.

Before I could react, however, I heard a shout.

"Police! Raise your hands above your heads. Now!"

And then the firing commenced.

But not at me. Stocky let off a round toward the voice as he crouched and ducked into the shadows by the main office. With Scrawny still above me, I whipped my legs around after he'd turned his back, caught his shin, and sent him tumbling forward, facedown. The shot exploding from his gun nearly took his partner's head off.

"Goddamn!" Stocky exclaimed, and clutched his ear.

Grandpa grabbed my shoulders and yanked me up before Scrawny realized what hit him. We hustled into the cover of the motel.

"You ain't very good at not being followed," Grandpa grumbled. "Either I get smacked around by the goons or arrested by the cops."

I felt foolish, having led everyone but the FBI to Grandpa, so I didn't even try to defend myself. Not that there was time.

Bullets sizzled through the rain. Scrawny even took one potshot in our direction for good measure. After it skimmed off the brick facade, we scurried north and then east around the complex until we hit South Main. There, to my surprise, a pickup truck screamed to a stop next to us. The passenger door whipped open.

"Get in!" Candace yelled.

Grandpa recoiled.

"Trust me," I shouted, and gingerly climbed in. The old man followed and slammed the door. Candace pumped the accelerator.

In the confusion, no one caught us, but the rearview mirror displayed a hell of a lot of blues bringing Christmas cheer to the small motel.

"You followed me, too?" I asked.

"Something told me you were about to get into a great big pickle," she replied, and ran a red light. "And I spotted a car pick you up from the feeder street near The Kitchen. I'd waited in my truck until you left."

"Easy, baby sister," I said. "I don't think anyone's on our tail."

"How would you know?"

"But there will be, if you don't slow down."

Candace huffed but let up on the gas. Her hand trembled as she brushed a strand of auburn hair from her eyes.

"Young lady," Grandpa spoke up, "I surely appreciate the lift. I'm Stephen Marshall, Neil's grandfather."

"I figured as much, Mr. Marshall. Candace Littlefield." She nodded.

"Please, call me Stephen."

"I wasn't raised to call my elders by their first names. Besides, if I did, I'd call you Nick, as in Saint Nicholas."

"That's fine, too."

"Perhaps I'll stick to Mr. Marshall for the time being."

"Whatever makes you comfortable, child. I'm obliged to you."

I cleaned my glasses with my shirttail, my heart finally downshifting. "I'm obliged, too," I said. "I'm glad you picked us up instead of participating in the firearms melee."

"Some thanks."

"Is there something I should know?" Grandpa asked.

"Candace likes her guns."

"Good. A girl needs to be careful in a crazy city like this."

She shot me a smirk that read *checkmate*.

"Never mind, we won't go there."

"Young people," Grandpa said, exasperated. "Do we have a plan?"

Candace glanced at me. "I'm just the chauffeur."

For a moment the only sound was the rhythmic windshield wiper and the low country music on the radio. The singer was crooning about what Christmas was like in Dixie.

"Another motel in the area probably wouldn't be a great idea," I thought aloud. "Not my place, for sure. Or the stables, Candace."

"Crossed my mind."

"Cops will be checking it."

"So what, then? Conroe? Beaumont?"

Something clicked. "Pull into that Texaco station," I said, waving ahead to the left.

"That'll point us back the way we came," Candace stated.

"You're right. It's the only thing I can think of."

The girl obeyed and crossed over to the gas station. I dug out a quarter. Beneath the cold beam of the streetlight, the rain seemed to float like long strands of silver ribbon. The first phone was out of order—someone had pried at the change lock and managed to separate the whole unit from its base. Fortunately, the second, though putting forth a scratchy dial tone, was usable. I hesitated, questioning my judgment, then dropped the coin in, anyway. She's a big girl, I told myself as I punched in the number. If she has reservations about helping, she'll say so.

"Keely, it's Neil," I said, after she picked up on the second ring. "I need help."

"Speak up, it's hard to hear you. What's wrong?"

"Grandpa and I have been jumped and shot at by the bad

guys and almost cornered by the good guys. Now we're on the run."

"Run? Run from what?"

"It's too long a story to tell you over a pay phone."

"Are you all right?"

"For the time being. Is anyone staying at that rental house you and Mark own?" She had offered the bungalow to me, but I'd declined, not wanting the responsibility of upkeep or roommates to help pay rent.

"As a matter of fact, we leased it last week."

"Damn," I muttered.

"What? This connection is horrible."

"Nothing."

"Neil, if you need a place to collect yourselves, you can come here. Mark's out of town. Even if he wasn't, he'd welcome you, too," she quickly added.

Sure, I thought, but said, "Keely, I don't feel right about that. I'm not certain where we stand legally, and showing our faces at your house might land you in a spot of trouble."

"How? Aiding and abetting a fugitive?"

"Exactly."

"Oh."

A pause. The crackling of the phone line. Rain dampened my hair and ran down my collar. Nearby Candace's truck rumbled. I noticed in the air the scent of grilled meat from a local restaurant.

"Thanks, Keely," I finally said. "I've got to—"

"Neil, just come on. What is anyone going to say about me having my prize student and his grandfather over for dinner?"

"Candace is with me, too."

"Oh, Neil, get out of the rain."

"All right. But if you have a change of heart, or unexpected visitors, turn off your front light and we won't stop."

"How cloak-and-dagger."

"I kid you not, my friend." And I hung up. In my mind I

could see the momentary amusement in Keely's light brown eyes quiver to a wince.

I shivered and pulled up my collar. Even Houston grew cold on occasion. And tonight the weather was wet and bone-chilling. Stepping quickly to the truck, I glanced at Grandpa. The old man was in the midst of a spirited talk. His gestures and Candace's grins were out of sync with the situation, like they were on a hayride instead of on the lam. I didn't get it. For me this was one of the coldest Christmases on record. And who knew what the new year would bring?

Or who would be around to ring it in?

13

The white light illuminated Keely's front door like the crisp sheen of a Christmas candle. Candace parked a couple of houses away in between streetlights. The rain had lightened, but the rawness in the air continued to feed the chill along my spine. Grandpa had been entertaining Candace with stories about me. She laughed particularly hard at the time when I was two or three and escaped through the screen door at Grandpa's cabin. Seemed I took off after a skunk that had wandered up from the creek. "He'd have gotten close enough to get sprayed, too, if his dad hadn't cut him off. Boy, your father was fit to be tied with me. I was supposed to be baby-sitting while he did a little fishing. Instead, I was napping."

I didn't remember the incident, though I'd heard about it throughout my childhood. A smile crept to my face. He could tell stories all night, and I could listen to all of them. Later.

When we left the confines of the truck, however, it was like a curtain fell on Grandpa's performance. No one spoke. Candace and the old man followed my lead.

Keely met us at the door, alone. There was no dark figure emerging from the shadow of a nearby mimosa tree or lurking behind the neighbor's willow. I didn't see a police car, or a Taurus, or even C.J.'s red Mustang—and it was a sure bet he'd received word of the fracas by now—cruising down the street. There was only the wind rustling through the trees and twisting the garlands of lights like a young girl fidgeting with her bracelets. Quickly, we were ushered inside.

"You three look grim," Keely started to say in a light tone. She locked the door. "What's the matter, the Grinch steal—" Then she noticed the side of my head. "Oh, Neil."

Automatically, I touched the welt, remembering its throbbing presence. "I'm all right. Only a little more Christmas cheer."

"God, I'm going to start calling you Ebenezer." To Candace and Grandpa she said, "Have a seat, y'all, while I get Neil some ice."

We flopped down on the plush white furniture. Candace and Grandpa took chairs. I opted for the couch. The ceiling fan hanging from the cathedral ceiling was still, and a small gas fire flickered in the white brick fireplace. To the left of the fireplace near the front window was a tall ponderosa pine adorned with white lights and fine ornaments. Topping the tree, though, was a simple cutout of an angel crudely colored with crayon. I glanced at the charcoal sketch of a little girl framed and carefully preserved over the mantel and knew the value of the angel.

"Festive house," Grandpa commented, and broke the silence. "Unlike some I know."

I chose to ignore the old man's chiding.

"What are we going to do, son?" In contrast to the tone of his storytelling, a weariness now slipped from his voice.

"I don't know," I replied.

Keely burst through the saloon-type doors that led to the kitchen. "Here," she said, handing me a washcloth wrapped around cubes of ice. A small piece fell to the wooden floor. I started to reach for it.

"Don't worry about that," she said, and swiped at the ice with her foot. It skidded across the planks and into the kitchen. "I'm brewing coffee," she added.

I leaned back, gently placing the ice to my head.

"Someone want to fill me in?" Keely suggested.

"The less you know, the better off you'll be," I replied.

"Shut up, Neil, and tell me what's going on."

I grinned at the contradiction.

Keely slapped my shoulder. "You know what I mean."

"I'm wanted for a murder I didn't commit," Grandpa stated.

"His ex-partner," Candace added.

"A little bird flew down from Denver to pass on the information," I jumped in.

"That's what's kept us a step ahead of the law," Grandpa explained.

"And the bone-crushers, too," I said. "Don't forget our two lovely friends."

"This has something to do with a guy—what's his name?" Candace asked.

"Buster Ledbetter," we answered in unison.

"Right. Old Buster's trying to steal Mr. Marshall's gold."

"The gold Walt wanted me to sell."

"Someone tried to convince Grandpa with a shot through his cabin window," I said.

"And a thug shot at us tonight, too," the old man continued.

"Our bone-crusher friends, after whacking me on the head."

"And I saved them," Candace announced. "These two," she added, pointing at us in response to Keely's quizzical expression. "After Neil was followed to a sleazy motel."

"McDaniels left me there."

"They have a dirty-movie channel," I threw in.

"I didn't watch it!" Grandpa proclaimed.

"Oh, men!" Candace spat.

"Don't forget what happened to your landlord's house." Grandpa changed the subject.

"Trashed," I told Keely.

"And the dog," Grandpa reminded me.

"Knifed. Don't know yet if he'll pull through."

"Wait till I get my hands on the bastard that did that," Candace shot in.

"And I should mention that Christine Cooper, our little bird, is married but was having a fling with Walter," I said.

"To make me jealous," the old man concluded.

Keely's forehead was furrowed. She rubbed her temple.

"I'm sure, Grandpa," I said.

"He's probably right," Candace defended.

"Wait a minute!" Keely exclaimed, waving her arms like an umpire calling a runner safe. "I have no idea what y'all are talking about."

"Seems clear to me," I told her.

"What don't you understand?" Candace asked.

"I'm just in a shitload of trouble," Grandpa finished.

Keely eyed me incredulously. "How much of what y'all said is true?"

"All of it." Slowly, I unraveled the events sequentially, and more seriously. I didn't regret the lighthearted volley we'd just undergone; it seemed to have loosened the three of us up. Which was certainly what I needed. Perhaps a plan would now unfold from my feeble mind.

When Keely had the whole ball of wax, she quietly paced the room.

"Told you it wasn't pretty," I said, and took the ice off my head.

"Sooner or later Lieutenant Gardner will seek me out, too," she said.

"I wondered about that. Guess I was betting it'd be later, though that's hardly fair to you."

"I don't want you to leave. All I'm saying is that time is running out."

"Which is why I have C.J. working with us."

"And I figure those thugs are guests of the city," Grandpa piped in. "Cops don't like being shot at."

"I'll get the coffee," Keely said. "Sounds like we need a bull session."

"I'd like mine with a touch of—"

"Whiskey, Mr. Marshall?" Keely addressed the old man. "I can do that. Anyone else?"

"Black for me," I told her. "And for Candace."

The young girl rose. "I want cream and sugar, but no booze. I don't drink hard stuff," she said indignantly. "I won't put a thief in my mouth to steal my brain."

"That's what the girl tells John Wayne in *True Grit*," I explained to Keely.

"Admirable," Grandpa stated. "But I—"

"No problem, Mr. Marshall," said Keely.

"Stephen."

"Okay, Stephen."

"I'll help," Candace announced, and went with Keely through the swinging doors into the kitchen.

Grandpa bent toward me. "I'm proud of you."

"Why?"

"You've been very tense."

"It's a tense situation."

"The girl touches a part of you, and you're responding."

"I like being around Candace—"

"Not Candace, you idiot, though I adore that child. I mean the married one."

"The married one, as you put it, is a good friend. Leave it at that."

Grandpa dug his pipe and tobacco out of his down vest before he pulled it off and dropped it on the floor.

"I don't think Keely likes smoking in her house," I said. To deaf ears. He packed the bowl and lit up.

"You come alive when that professor's in the room," he continued on his own track. "You wouldn't have bantered earlier if she hadn't been here. I was glad to see it. Frankly, I've been worried about you—"

"You've been worried about me?"

"Definitely. Whatever becomes of me, well, I'm old. You have a life in front of you, son, as I did once. And I had a woman who put the spark of life in me." A large, billowing puff, and he pointed the pipe at me. "Your grandmother. Your real grandmother, I mean—your father's mother. She was the pistol I compared every other woman to. Which, I'm certain, was why I was married so many times after her. I unfairly compared them to her."

"A car accident took her, Dad said."

"So it did. Many years ago."

Keely and Candace returned with mugs of steaming coffee, the rich aroma blending well with Grandpa's pipe smoke.

"I detect a hint of black cherry," Keely said, and handed him his coffee.

"If you find it offensive—"

"Not at all," she replied. "My father used to smoke a pipe. I find the smell very comforting."

Grandpa nodded, puffed, and sipped his coffee. Appearing quite content for someone wanted for murder, he asked calmly, "What are our options?"

"Go to the police," Keely said.

"I say we call C.J. first," I offered, and tasted the coffee Candace gave me.

"Why?" the old man asked. "I don't see how you can have faith in a pigheaded Neanderthal who thinks the special sauce on a Big Mac is a culinary masterpiece."

"So you got stuck with fast food after all."

"Yes," he grumbled.

"Well," I explained, "short of going to the cops, it's the only course of action I can think of. Unless you want to leave the country with Christine," I added dryly.

"That's beginning to look like a viable option."

"The longer you run from the police, the guiltier you're going to appear," Keely added.

"But I haven't been served an arrest warrant."

"The police are aware you're avoiding them," I pointed out.

Candace asked bluntly, "Who do you think murdered your partner?"

"Good question," I said, and picked up Keely's cordless phone. "Why don't you give us your thoughts on Walter?"

C.J. wasn't home, so I left Keely's number on his answering machine.

"When the doctor told Walt to quit drinking or he'd die," the old man began, "something snapped. You'd think a man would mellow out in that circumstance, but for him it was like a great void that needed to be filled. He took to gambling heavily in Cripple Creek most every day. Tried hitting me up for money, got rather persnickety when I wouldn't cooperate."

"Christine know about his gambling?" I asked.

"Can't imagine she didn't. Reckon she even staked him a time or two."

"So she approved?"

"It'd be the kind of excitement Christine would like."

Maybe we were getting somewhere, I thought. "You suspect Walter racked up a huge debt?"

"Possible. He was sure interested in the mine once he discovered it was worth something. I told him the mine was my baby."

"Are you talking about the ghost mine?" I asked, jolted by the sudden recognition. "When I was a little kid," I told Keely and Candace, "Grandpa used to tell me the mine was haunted by the ghosts of miners who'd died there. In reality, he just didn't want me exploring and getting lost."

Grandpa nodded. "The one and only. I'd been working that hole for years. First as a hobby, then as a quest—I knew in my bones there was gold on that land. Eventually I came across a streak of small veins that melded into a large one. Gold's down there, all right. And that's my legacy to my heirs.

"Made the mistake of asking Walter's opinion. That was when he'd first quit drinking and I didn't know about the gambling. When I told him, I saw the greed on his face. The beginning of the end." He took a sip of his coffee.

"I've sweated, hoped, and prayed too hard to sell that piece of land," Grandpa added. "Especially to some crass hack."

The phone rang and Keely answered. She handed the cordless receiver to me.

"What the hell did you and the big elf do tonight?" C.J. bellowed. "Gardner's livid."

"We got caught between a rock and a hard place."

"Sloppy work, Neil."

"I'm not a cop."

"I expect more from you."

"Okay, I screwed up. What do you know about the thugs?"

"Serious trouble," C.J. said. "Both convicted felons—extortion, assault, the usual mess. Floyd 'Fats' Corbett wounded a cop. Arthur 'Rat Face' Kern took off a piece of his partner's ear."

"That was my fault. I leg-whipped Rat Face when the police jumped us, and his gun went off. The cops did nail them, right?"

"They're in custody. Not talking, of course."

"So you don't know who they're working for?"

"Positively, no. But Sergeant Hernandez let it slip to Linda that Fats's phone call was to the Lancaster Hotel."

I caught Grandpa's eye. A cold wash doused me. "The Lancaster Hotel?" I repeated.

"Left a message for a Catherine Flanners."

"Who?"

"You tell me."

"Hold on." I recaptured Grandpa's attention. "You know anyone named Catherine Flanners?"

The old man paled, and nodded slowly. "Where'd you hear that name?"

I briefly explained C.J.'s findings.

"This has got to be a bizarre mistake," Grandpa said. "Catherine Flanners died a couple of years ago. She was Christine Cooper's mother." As he completed his thought I noticed the shock melt to understanding.

"Christine Cooper's late mother," I repeated into the phone.

"A rather obvious pseudonym," C.J. commented.

"Christine would do something like that," Grandpa told me. "For instance, use her mother's driver's license, thinking she was being clever."

"All those years with Albright didn't sharpen her intellect any," I told them both.

"Even if she did step into her mother's identity, that still doesn't explain why Rats and Fats called her from the slammer," the detective pondered. "I thought she was on your side."

"In her neurotic way, so did I, C.J. So did I."

Four Days Before Christmas

14

In the morning I felt a great need to do something. Keely graciously agreed to harbor Grandpa for the day. I asked Candace to run me by The Kitchen, where I kept a change of clothes, and where I had a lot of work to do.

Keely's mouth hung open. "You're going to work?" she asked. We were sitting around her glass breakfast table, sipping coffee and poking at a Canadian-bacon-and-cheese frittata Keely had made.

I shrugged. "I can't afford to lose my job. Besides, consider me a decoy. The police will make an appearance sooner or later, and it's best that they find me there rather than plod and plot and eventually end up at your doorstep."

Keely raised her eyebrows.

"I'm going to call C.J., too, and have him swing by and help me get my car. Also see what he discovers at the Lancaster Hotel."

"Hope your VW's not impounded," Grandpa said.

"Aren't you afraid the police will lock you up?" Candace asked.

"For what?"

"Obstruction of justice, not to mention aiding a fugitive," Grandpa replied.

"You're a beacon of optimism this morning," I stated morosely.

"Don't want you losing sight of reality with all this fool talk of decoys and thinking the cops won't throw your butt in jail."

"As long as they're focusing on me, they're not focusing on you," I replied.

"I question your reasoning," Grandpa said, "and setting too much stock in McDaniels."

"You came to me for help. I'm giving it to you the only way I know. So you just stay put."

Grandpa huffed. I reckoned he had a crappy night's sleep on the couch.

"And you tend to the horses at the stables," I instructed Candace. "Follow your usual routine, and if the police talk to you, you haven't seen us."

"Well, I do have a passel of chores," the girl admitted.

"I'll be in touch."

"Reach me at Sondra's," Candace said.

"Okay." Sondra Anderson was a fellow writer and good friend. She and her husband had welcomed Candace into their home after the girl's grandfather had died, and it had only been a few months ago since she'd moved to the stables. The fact that she wanted to stay with them indicated how nervous she was about the situation. I thought it was a good idea.

"So it's just you and me today, Stephen," said Keely.

"At least I'll have pleasant company." He glanced at me.

"Too bad you can't say the same for Keely," I shot back, finished my coffee, and Candace and I hit the road.

The storm clouds had cleared and the sun god, Apollo, stretched his golden muscles across the early-morning sky. He was limbering up for what appeared to be an easy jaunt. A brisk wind played in the trees and tousled our hair. Up in New England this would be a spectacular fall day. Octoberish. For Houston, such weather was a treat, rarely occurring in autumn but, as in this case, on the first day of winter.

"It's going to get cold tonight," Candace observed as she dropped me off at The Kitchen. "Wind's from the north and there's no cloud cover to blanket the warmth in."

"I'd say you're right."

"Take care of yourself."

"Always do."

"I mean it. I'm worried you're slipping past the point of caring. That's when people do foolish things."

"You in league with Grandpa?"

"If that's what it takes to keep you in one piece."

"I'll be fine," I assured her, winked, and closed the door. Candace hovered until I had hiked up the driveway, unlocked the security gate, and ducked inside The Kitchen. As I keyed off the alarm system I heard her truck speed away.

I flicked on the lights, opened the blinds on the front windows, then locked and secured the door.

After changing into the fresh clothes I kept stashed in the closet, which included a pair of blue jeans and a red-and-black Perry Stevens Catering jersey, I left a message for C.J. telling him where I was. I also asked if he could run by to help me get my car. This would give me time to talk to the detective and hopefully get some questions answered.

I punched on the stereo, scanned the work orders, donned a Houston Astros baseball cap, and tied on an apron. The Gilcrest feast was foremost on my mind. I covered the menu item by item:

Hors d'oeuvres
Mushroom Strudel.
Mini Crab-Artichoke Cakes with Fiesta Salsa.
Basil-Chicken Salad on Sourdough Toast Rounds.

Starter
Stilton and Jicama Salad: crumbled Stilton and julienne strips of jicama served on a bed of mixed greens, garnished with leaves of Belgian endive and lightly toasted pecan pieces, and topped with a honey-mustard dressing.

Entrée
Roasted Rack of Lamb with Texas Pesto.
Jalapeño-Corn Pudding.

Steamed Asparagus with Bay Butter.
Brown and Wild Rice with Shiitake Mushrooms.
Cracked-Wheat Rolls.

Sorbet
Cran-Raspberry Sorbet to cleanse the palate.

Soup
Crawfish Bisque Garnished with Chives and a Twist
of Lemon.

Dessert
Apple Strudel with a Creamy Rum Sauce and
Assorted Cookies.

This was a menu Grandpa would go wild over. A
Christmas Eve sit-down dinner that would take a good
three hours just to serve. I hoped to be around to partake of
the festivities, not choking down city food while sharing a
cold cell with a gorilla named Butch.

I checked off items that were completed, or as completed as they could be before the job: the apple and mushroom strudels, the sorbet, and the Texas pesto. Mattie, I
figured, could fix the cracked-wheat rolls, the sourdough
toast rounds, and the cookies. I opted to start at the beginning and prepare the basil-chicken salad and the crab-
artichoke cakes.

Half an hour into the basil-chicken there was a rattling
at the front door and Mattie appeared. "You trying to earn
brownie points?" she asked.

I scraped a cup of finely chopped walnuts into the
chicken mixture. "Figured I'd better make hay while the
sun was shining," I replied, and ran a few stalks of celery,
four cloves of garlic, and half a bunch of green onions
through the food processor.

Mattie smiled and hung up her coat. "What do you want
me to do, boss?"

"As I'm not the boss, I really can't say, but I'll give you my advice." I did.

"Aw, Claudia only *thinks* she runs this place. Same with Perry. Really, it's you and Robbie that hold The Kitchen together."

I added the onions, garlic, and celery and gave the salad a good stir. The sweet aroma of the basil tickled the air. "If that's true, where are the big bucks?"

Mattie, a wisp of a woman, had to wrap the strings of her apron around her waist a few times before tying them. "In your Christmas bonus, I'm sure."

"I'm sure."

There was another jingling at the door, and then a knock. My blood pressure shot up, thinking Gardner and company were finally here. When Mattie opened the door, however, it was only Trisha. An elfish smile covered her cherubic face. She bounced in with nary a care in the world. Her energy and youthful appearance reminded me of Mary Lou Retton—though Trisha was much heavier than the former gymnast.

"So the spirit directed you to work today," I observed.

"So she did."

"And you're even on time."

"Funny how cosmic energy works, isn't it?" She walked right over to me, smiled sincerely, and stared me straight in the eye.

"Hysterical."

"You should try trusting in the universe. Answers are always there. All you have to do is let go, lighten your load of worry, and tune in."

"You do infomercials, too?"

"Oh, you!" Trisha swatted my shoulder and turned. "Good morning, Mattie."

" 'Morning, Trish."

In a matter of seconds, Trisha was in her pastry coat and setting up to work on the front stainless-steel table. She was out to polish off the orders of gingerbread houses.

Soon she was plugged into her Walkman, listening to Kenny G or Yanni, oblivious to the rest of us.

I squeezed some lemon into the basil-chicken salad, added a touch more mayonnaise, and ground in coarse black pepper. The chicken itself was all white meat, skinned, grilled, then cut finely so it would set on the toast round. I tasted the sweet and creamy mixture, very tender, then adjusted the seasoning with salt and pepper, and was finished.

Again the front door opened and in ambled Conrad, the dishwasher and general maintenance man. His first duty of the day was to sweep the driveway, which he did in his quiet manner.

With all the activity that now buzzed, it was difficult to focus on my own thoughts. As neither the police nor C.J. had shown up, my anxiety level was rising despite attempts to distract myself. A heavy sigh passed between my lips while I began dicing artichoke hearts for the crab cakes.

Not five minutes later Robbie arrived, and with him was C. J. McDaniels.

"Someone to see you," my coworker said.

I set the chef's knife down and wiped my hands on a kitchen towel.

C.J. nodded toward the outside. I followed.

"I realized," McDaniels began, "that I don't have a clue what Christine Cooper looks like. No picture, no description."

"You been to the Lancaster yet?"

"Nope. Think you should come with me. Then I'll run you by to get your car."

I untied my apron. "Sounds like a plan."

"Where's the big elf?"

"With Keely."

"Smart. Gardner won't go there—until he follows you."

"Funny."

"I guess our natty lieutenant's not caught up to you, yet."

"No. Why?"

"You're still here."

"Comforting." I stuck my head back into The Kitchen, tossed my apron onto the butcher-block table, and called to Robbie that I was going out for a few minutes, but I'd be back later.

"Claudia's not going to be happy," he singsonged back.

"She told me to be at work early. I was here early."

"I think she meant for you to stay."

"A detail she neglected to mention." And I closed the door.

C.J. deftly lit a cigarette in spite of the wind.

"You need to quit smoking," I blurted out.

"What!"

"You always have a cigarette hanging out of your mouth."

"Linda call you and put you up to this?" he asked, referring to his daughter.

"Good for Linda," I approved as we approached his Mustang. "About time someone got on your butt for that nasty habit."

"I ought to belt you one. You having withdrawal, again?"

"I don't know," I said, though I felt my nerves jingling and jangling.

"Well, don't take it out on me. Linda's enough to deal with. I don't need the happy warrior coming after me, too."

"Happy warrior?" I got in the car.

"Seems to fit you," he replied, and blew smoke at me. "Or it did, until you started acting like a shit."

"I'm not acting like a shit."

"You weren't a curmudgeon when you were helping me."

"You're not my grandfather," I fired back, then realized I was shaking. "C.J.," I explained, softening my tone, "I lost my dad. I can't lose him, too."

"Then shut up and let's go to the Lancaster."

"Yes, sir."

And as we pulled onto the feeder to the freeway, I caught out of the sideview mirror the image of a baby-blue police cruiser coasting to a stop at the base of The Kitchen's driveway.

15

The Lancaster was all class. A small hotel located across from Jones Hall—home of the Houston Symphony—and near the Alley Theatre and Wortham Center, the Lancaster had the Victorian feel of the Old South. Plush carpet and curtains patterned mostly in red, polished wood, crystal lighting, and a wonderful dining area that catered to patrons of the arts before and after performances as well as hotel guests—often visiting musicians and actors. I knew Marsha Boyd, the food-and-beverage manager, because Perry Stevens Catering had once provided desserts for the hotel. Although Perry and Marsha had a falling-out, I remained friends with her. I passed this information on to C.J. and asked him if the connection would be of any use.

"At the least she might prevent us from getting thrown out of the lobby." He knifed through traffic down Louisiana Street, paying little heed to the business people who tried to anticipate the light change and get a jump on the crowd.

"You're going to kill someone," I warned.

"If someone's stupid enough to get in front of me, then he's no asset to the business he's in."

"Sounds like you'd expect a letter of thanks."

"On the CEO's stationery."

We zipped around until he found a place to park half a block from the Lancaster. "You find anything out from the cab company?" I asked.

"Christine Cooper was dropped off at the Galleria after

she left your place. There's no further record of her calling that company."

"That's odd." I jumped out of the car and put a couple of quarters in the parking meter. "You'd think she'd stick to the same service."

"I agree. But you know how many cabbies hang out over there. Could be as simple as her flagging one down at random. Or it could be a deliberate act, a switch because something, or someone, spooked her."

"If Catherine Flanners is Christine Cooper, then I vote deliberate," I said. "But why? What does she know?"

"Ain't that what we want to find out?"

"She plain offered herself to Grandpa."

"Safe to say her marriage isn't quite perfect?" C.J. gave me a sideways glance.

"Safe to say."

"I have Linda poking into who Albright Cooper is, too," he added. "I want to know what kind of man would let his wife run to another city to warn a potential rival of trouble."

"She never told us he let her. In fact—"

"If your granddaddy's picture of Cooper is accurate, men as powerful and controlling as that don't allow their wives to do anything they don't approve of or expect to gain from."

We hiked down the breezy street to the Lancaster. I pulled up on the collar of my duster. Candace was right. There was the feel of a good cold snap in the air.

Inside the building it was warm with a slight musty smell. Gold and silver garlands outlined the lobby, and a tall blue spruce covered with white lights and gold and red ornaments stood in one corner. C.J. unzipped his leather jacket and approached the desk. A large wreath covered the front of the dark wood. "I need to leave a message for Catherine Flanners," he said.

"I'm afraid Ms. Flanners has checked out," the man responded.

"When?"

"Late last night."

"You know where she went?"

"No, sir."

"She take a cab?"

"I don't know. I wasn't on duty. All I know is that she checked out and her room is now vacant."

"Who was on duty?" C.J. continued.

"Really, sir, are you a police officer?"

"A detective."

"I understood from Louis, the night clerk, the police already asked these questions. Have you any identification?"

Just then I heard a call from across the room, "Neil Marshall, what brings you here?" A very poised woman strode over to me. Her blonde hair was pulled back in a bun, accentuating her angular face. She had to be six feet in flats, and with heels on came close to looking me in the eye.

"You're as lovely as ever, Marsha." I took her hand in mine and noticed how snappy she appeared in her black pants suit. "This is a detective friend of mine," I said, and introduced her to C.J. "Actually, we're here trying to track someone down."

"Really? Who?"

"She has a Lauren Bacall look to her," I explained. "In her late fifties or early sixties, dark eyes, brownish hair, lean, has an air of money about her."

"I know who you're talking about. She wears a matching hat to go with her London Fog. Exudes style."

"You recall her name?" I asked.

Marsha shook her head.

C.J. looked at the desk clerk.

"Yes," he said reluctantly, "that sounds like Ms. Flanners."

I nodded at the burly investigator.

"She place any calls while she was here?" C.J. asked.

"I can't release that information, sir."

"I can get a court order," he bluffed.

"Find out for them, George," Marsha intervened.

"But, madam—"

"George, you're already on rocky ground for being rude to Mrs. Twombly."

"I won't take responsibility."

"Of course not, I will," she said curtly.

George picked up the phone, turned from us, and muttered into the receiver. He then jotted something on a notepad.

Marsha rolled her eyes and whispered behind her hand, "Old Mrs. Twombly's been staying at the Lancaster for a hundred years, going to the theatre numerous times a season, and this twit insults her by denying her the room she's had forever because the maids hadn't cleaned it yet. Outright refused. I could've wrung his neck."

"One call," George told us after setting the phone down.

We smiled pleasantly at him.

"To this exchange." He tore the piece of paper off the pad and handed it to C.J.

"Much obliged," the detective responded.

"Of course."

"Yes, thank you, George," Marsha said, overly polite, and walked with us away from the desk.

"What about the cab?" I asked C.J.

"There's only a couple of prominent companies that work out of this area," he responded. "I'll check them. If I come up empty-handed, then I'll talk to the night clerk later."

"Won't you stay for a croissant and a cup of coffee?" Marsha asked. "On the house."

"Thank you," I replied, "that's quite tempting, but I've got too much to do today."

"Perry Stevens working you ragged again?"

"Among other things."

"You need to slow down, Neil, and enjoy the finer aspects of life."

"Perhaps after we get out of this wretched Christmas season," I said.

"Oh, bah humbug," she responded, and gave me a peck

on the cheek. "Do come back," she added as we left the confines of the hotel.

"Absolutely," I returned. And we were outside.

"You should've stayed for the roll," C.J. told me.

"I have before. Marsha's a little too aggressive for me."

"You're a fool, Neil Marshall. A young fool."

Probably, I thought, and shrugged. But my interests lay elsewhere.

Before heading to the car, though, C.J. suddenly walked over to a cabbie parked near the entrance and signaled for him to roll down his window. "I'm a private investigator," he told the old man, and handed him a card. "I'm looking for a woman who left this hotel late last night. Could you call your dispatcher and ask if anyone from your company gave her a ride?"

"The lady in trouble?" he asked.

"Don't know. Might be in danger."

"Danger? What kind of danger?"

"A couple of men—the type who shoot at cops—called her from jail," C.J. said. "Now she's gone. I'm worried."

The man thought a moment, looked from C.J. to the card and back. "She seemed skittish."

"You drove her?"

"This is my beat. Been pulling double shifts since my wife done broke her hip and can't work. Yes, sir, I drove her."

"Mind telling me where?"

"Mind telling me why?"

C.J. hesitated. I found the difference in the way the private investigator dealt with the cabdriver as opposed to the desk clerk vastly interesting. There was much more respect for the cabbie, as indicated by C.J.'s direct approach. The desk clerk he'd bluffed and outright lied to. Curious behavior for a man who'd been raised by wealthy parents in River Oaks.

"Like I said, she might be in danger," C.J. repeated.

"Not enough."

"Those men who contacted the lady have also been

threatening clients of mine. I need to know why she checked out of the hotel in such haste and appeared, as you put it, skittish."

The old cabbie rubbed the white stubble on his face and thought a minute. "Dropped her off at the Radisson Hotel over off I-10 and Beltway 8," he said. "Carried her bag. She gave me a twenty-dollar tip, so after that I called it a night."

"She seem scared?"

"Yeah, and nervous."

"Thanks," C.J. said, and tapped the roof of the cab, "you've been a great help."

"Just make sure nothing happens to that lady," he called. "It's Christmas. Nothing bad ought to happen to a person at Christmas."

"Nothing bad ought to happen anytime of the year," I muttered. "What's Christmas, its own world outside the calendar?"

"You'd think there could be at least one day of truce a year," C.J. replied to my musings. "Why not Christmas?"

"For someone grounded so strongly in the reality of the streets, that's a strange comment." We cut over to his Mustang. "Just a few minutes ago you were all set to plow over pedestrians."

"Reckon I'm not making much sense to you, son, but I've had some odd things happen to me at this time of year. Things that can't be explained away."

I hesitated, waiting for him to unlock the doors. "If you tell me you've seen an angel, I'm not getting in this car."

"I won't even go into it since your attitude's in the toilet." The locks clicked up and we climbed in. He revved the engine and burst into the traffic.

"My attitude's not in the toilet," I mumbled.

"I knew that old man in the cab had driven Christine Cooper," he continued, ignoring my last comment. "Just a gut feeling, but as soon as I was outside, I felt pulled to the cab."

"That's good instincts."

"Call it what you may. Times like that, like stumbling right upon the very cab a missing woman took, don't happen. They just don't happen," he explained.

"But it did."

"Exactly," C.J. replied.

"Because it's the Christmas season."

"Uh-huh," he grunted.

"You need a vacation, C.J."

"No, son, you do."

Was I the only one anchored in reality? I wondered. C.J. pumped the Mustang out of downtown and onto the Southwest Freeway.

"We going to the Radisson?" I asked.

"Figured we should."

"Your little angel whispering Christine's there?"

"Nope."

"No whispering angel, or the woman's gone?"

"The woman's gone."

And she was.

16

My VW was right where I'd left it. And in one piece. No bullets had careened off the rounded chassis or perforated the windows. The tires were intact. Even the hubcaps were still on.

C.J. cruised to a stop beside the Bug. In daylight the parking lot looked much smaller than it had felt in last night's darkness. And, if possible, much less inviting.

"In and out of the hotel in just a matter of hours," C.J. mused. "Sounds to me like she's more than skittish."

"You mean like scared to death."

"Takes another cab to the Galleria."

"Then switches cabs?" I asked. "Or meets someone? Maybe she's heading home. After all, she placed a long-distance call."

C.J. dug out the number. "Let's see what we have here." He punched his mobile on, tapped in the exchange, then turned to speaker-phone so I could hear. The Mustang idled quietly.

The connection was clear. "Silver Creek Mining Corporation, Albright Cooper's office."

"Albright Cooper," C.J. said.

"May I ask who's calling?"

"Floyd Corbett."

I stared wide-eyed at the detective as he was put on hold.

"What the hell!" a gruff voice barked. "I told you never to call here."

"Had to," C.J. muttered.

"Why? And how'd you get out of jail? I haven't been able to arrange bail yet."

"Your wife."

"My wife?" A sudden pause. "What does she have to do with anything?" he asked, a shade of suspicion entering his voice. "Christine's in Dallas visiting her sister."

"I don't think so."

"This isn't Corbett. Who is it?"

"I'm someone who knows that Corbett and Kern are in a Houston jail, and that your wife called this number last night."

"Who are you? What do you want?"

"I want to know why you sent two thugs after an old man?"

"What the blazes are you talking about?"

"Let me ask the questions, Cooper. You answer them."

"I have nothing to say. You don't even have the guts to tell me who you are."

"C. J. McDaniels, a friend of Stephen Marshall."

I touched my forehead and wondered why he'd given his name. What was the point of bravado right now?

"That murderous adulterer," Cooper scoffed. "The police will have his ass."

"Then why send a couple of goons after him?" C.J. asked.

"I didn't send anyone after *him*!"

"After who, then? Christine?"

"This conversation is over."

"Christine's—" *Click.*

"Missing," I finished for him. C.J. pressed the mobile's power off. "Did we get anything out of that?" I asked. "He did, he got your name."

"Cooper would know of me eventually. Might as well stir the stew and see what's served. As for what we learned, not much. Cooper does know Corbett and is connected to them. He hates your grandfather. He talks arrogantly, like he's used to giving orders and getting his way. And he's a liar." C.J. lit a cigarette, cracked his window.

"That's an understatement. I don't know what to believe."

"He obviously sent the thugs after the big elf."

"Why? He claimed he didn't go after *him*."

"Like I said, he's a liar. Cooper wants the old man before the police do. As for the reason, we need to pump old Grandpa."

"Then what's the deal with Christine?"

"Maybe they were supposed to get her at the same time."

"But she apparently left word Fats and Rats were in the slammer and needed help."

"Then fled the scene," C.J. said. "She doesn't want to be found. And when she realized we knew where she was, she panicked. But not before passing along the message to her husband, which tells me she was afraid not to do as Corbett instructed. After all, she didn't call Albright at home. She chose to call his office, where, late as it was, there was little danger of catching him."

"Rather telling on Christine," I commented. "Seems to be running away, but she doesn't want to make them too mad in case they catch up to her."

"You mean *when* they catch up. Her pseudonym trick didn't work for crap."

"So how does all of this tie in to the death of Walter Pierce?" I asked.

"I have no idea. Somewhere in your grandfather's old mind, I suspect he holds the key."

"Wonderful. I might bleed it out of him by Easter."

"Can't figure where Ledbetter fits in," C.J. wondered. "I thought he'd been the aggressor."

"Find the tie from Ledbetter to Cooper and we get our answer," I ventured.

"Still leaves Walter's murder in the dark."

"Ledbetter?"

"Kills Walter, plants him, then finds him?" C.J. asked. "Not many murderers purposely place themselves in the middle of an investigation."

"Fats and Rats?"

C.J. rolled his window halfway and tossed his cigarette to the gravel. "Implicates Albright Cooper."

"And the problem with that?"

"Like the old man said, I have the impression Cooper gets his kicks driving men to the ground, not underground."

"Still my bet. Or Christine?"

"She's running from her husband, not from a murder charge," C.J. said. "I mean, if you'd aced someone, would you warn the person who's accused of the crime and draw the attention from him to you?"

After a moment I said, "Christine was having an affair with Uncle Walt. She's not guilt-free."

"Affair sparks jealous rage, which points the finger of guilt for the murder more toward Cooper than her."

"So the culprit has to be Cooper," I deduced.

"Doesn't add up." He shifted his bulk in the seat and popped out another cigarette. I choked back a comment on secondhand smoke.

"Why not?" I asked. "His wife's having an affair with the man. He hates Grandpa. Do away with Walt and make it look like Grandpa murdered him. And then the mineral rights on the old guy's land would be easy pickin's."

C.J. exhaled slowly. "Tight scenario, but something about it bothers me."

"The little angel speaking to you again?"

"Go to hell."

"Been there, done that—"

"Get to your car. I have work to do."

"So do I. I'll be at The Kitchen."

"Until Gardner arrives. Then you'll be sitting at the police station trying to explain what's going on, and where your grandfather is. Better you than me."

I swung out of the Mustang. "You're all heart."

"Thanks." He sped off after I closed the door.

No more angel jokes, I thought.

I began to unlock the Bug when I remembered Grandpa had his stuff in the motel room. And that he'd tossed the key into last night's darkness. Now, where were we when he threw it?

His room had been on the ground floor facing the parking lot, and when I located it, I began retracing our steps. I was close to the point where I'd figured we'd been jumped when an old man with a scraggly white beard hobbled from the office to meet me. Attached to his arm, on a strong chain, was a pit bull.

I hated pit bulls.

"You looking for something, sonny?"

"Lost my room key," I said casually. My mind spun as to what to do. And then: How would C.J. act?

"I don't recollect you checking in."

"A woman gave me the room," I shot back, hoping he wasn't the only person who ran this trailer park without wheels.

"Oh, Maude," he said more to himself than me. "She's sleeping it off right now."

"That's my car right there." I pointed. The attack dog's silence was unnerving. And the old man didn't appear strong enough to hold him should the pit bull lunge.

"Saw you in a Mustang, too."

"What with all the excitement last night, I didn't much feel like coming back till morning. Was leaving with a friend when it happened. Done dropped my key in the process. You know what went on here?" I asked, hoping to gain his confidence.

"Police don't tell us nothing. Just use the office and drink our coffee. All I know is some fool shot a cop and then the yard lit up like the Fourth of July. That's what I heard, anyway. Maude told me after I got back with our Christmas tree for the office. 'Course, she was in her cups by then.

"I know what you're thinking," he continued when I didn't respond. "Kind of late for a tree, ain't it? Well, I'll be damned if I'll spend a fortune on foolhardiness—why, some of the prices they get you'd think the needles spun gold. So I wait for the clearance. Great deals. Got me a Scotch pine for ten bucks, not too brown, either. Now, I'd as soon use the fake tree, but Maude won't hear of it. See what I have to put up with?"

The negative energy flowing from the pit bull made me think I heard growling. "You strong enough to hold him?"

"You mean Nixon? He's a pussycat 'less someone's scared." He gave the dog a swift kick, spinning the pit bull over and back onto his feet. "Now, you behave, Nixon. This young man's just searching for his key."

The mean dog felt only meaner for that act. I was about to give up when I spied a glint in a patch of weeds.

"There it is," I said triumphantly.

"So it seems. Guess you was telling the truth."

"You doubted me?" I flashed a broad smile.

"Come on, Nixon," the old man said, and yanked on the chain containing the compact poundage of hate. " 'Bout time we woke Maude."

Have a good day was on the tip of my tongue but wouldn't slip out. "Be seeing you," I managed.

The old man shuffled to the office. A gust of wind kicked a cloud of dust up from the gravel lot. I glanced around then walked to the motel room and let myself in.

The air crackled with silence, an overwhelming stillness like the feel of a funeral parlor. The ghosts of a thousand previous occupants filled the room, but none so powerfully as the one who'd rifled through Grandpa's belongings.

Clothes were strewn across the bed and floor. The duffel bag had been cut, partially turned inside out, and pockets torn. A book lay like roadkill in a corner, pages stripped, binding resting helplessly on top. Nothing had been spared. Overnight kit spilled onto the bed. The lining of his robe ripped out. Even the inside soles of his boots yanked up.

I rubbed the robe between my forefinger and thumb. My heart hurt taking the sight in. It was highly unlikely the police had done the damage. But who, then? Fats and Rats were detained. Who else knew the old man was here?

As if to answer my questions, I heard a pop behind me like someone had cracked a knuckle. I stiffened and turned just in time to glimpse a heavy object slam into my already tender head.

Lights flickered. I dropped to my knees.

A foggy image and the sound of the door.

Then I was out, the soft feel of the robe still between my fingers.

16

I heard moaning and then realized it was me. In the haze I heard Grandpa encouraging me to fight my way out. Then a glimpse of Walter, his drawn, grizzled face appearing behind Grandpa, smiling, and raising a pickax. Slowly I pushed myself to my hands and knees to help Grandpa—he didn't see the danger. The pickax. Walter. I opened my eyes. Not two feet away, peering at me like I was a Christmas turkey, was the pit bull. It growled. I squeezed my eyes shut and said a quick prayer. Grandpa and Walter faded. But the dog was still there when I looked again.

"Back off, Nixon," I heard the old man say. "Give the boy some breathing room."

I gingerly touched the welt on top of the welt on the side of my head.

"That's the trouble with you big guys," he continued. "When you get whacked, it's extra hard on account of your size. Bet you got one hummer of a headache, ain't ya?"

"One hummer," I repeated, and lifted myself so I was sitting on the bed.

"You want me to call the cops?" he asked hesitantly. "I hate to do it seeing they was here last night—not good for business having them around all the time—but I will."

"No, don't." I brushed the hair out of my face. "You see who did it?" I asked.

"No, I was in the back room fetching Maude some coffee. But Nixon seen it. He was barking so hard I thought he was going to chew through the wall."

Great, I thought. My only witness is a mean-assed dog with a Neanderthal's mentality. I stood, straightened Grandpa's bag as best I could, and randomly tossed clothes inside it.

"You get robbed?" the old man asked. "We get street people in here all the time causing trouble."

Automatically I touched my back pocket. My wallet was still there. "I guess I interrupted him."

"So he was inside here already? Huh, wonder how he got in?"

Like this place's Fort Knox, I thought, but said nothing and finished gathering Grandpa's stuff. I was on my way out the door when I heard, "Merry Christmas to you, boy."

There was a blue hammer pounding in my head. "You, too," I heard myself reply.

"And I hope the new year's better than the old," he added, but I didn't respond. I drew in a couple of deep, sharp breaths on my way to the car. An old woman in a flowery housedress drank coffee and stared at me from the office. She was only fairly more attractive than Nixon, the pit bull. Hi, Maude. I shot her a quick smile. Tie one on for me, dear. Looks like we both need it.

It was unfair a day so beautiful should turn on a guy like that. From losing Christine Cooper to getting whacked on the head, again, to driving up to The Kitchen and discovering Lieutenant Paul Gardner and his entourage patiently awaiting my return—things were just getting worse. Crunch time.

"A little trouble, Mr. Marshall?" Gardner asked, examining my bump.

I brushed it and realized there was dried blood in my hair. "Banged my head getting into the car."

"On your left side? Were you getting in backward?"

"It was a fluke." Two blues filed in behind the tall lieutenant. "What can I do for you?"

"Cut to the chase, Neil. You and your grandfather were

in an altercation last night. But luckily, we happened to be there, too, and saved you from a couple of undesirables."

"True we were jumped, and thank HPD for being on the scene, because we were in a bad way. But I thought we were just victims of street crime. A random act of violence. They were out to rob us."

Gardner smiled thinly, his eyes cold. "You're lying."

I feigned shock. "No, sir."

"What were you doing at that motel?"

"My grandfather and I'd had a disagreement and he took off. That's where he ended up. He doesn't know Houston too well."

"Where is he now?"

"On his way home, as far as I know."

"Neil . . . Neil . . . Neil." He shook his head. "You're as aware as I am that the old man's wanted for suspicion of murder."

Again shock. "Murder! You've got to be kidding. Who?"

"The body's not been positively identified—"

"What?" This time genuine surprise.

"I said the body's not been identified." He watched me carefully, reached into his coat, and pulled out a small notebook. "But it's believed to be the remains of Walter Pierce."

"Grandpa's partner," I said slowly. "Who's saying the body is Walter's if it's not been identified?"

"Don't know." Now he was lying. "Would you?"

"Not a clue. But why is the corpse presumed Uncle Walt's?"

"Uncle Walt?"

"We were close when I was a kid. I don't get what's going on here."

"Neither do I. From what I understand there's remains of a ring, glasses, and a—" He stopped. "And where's your grandfather, Neil?"

"And a what?"

"Answer my questions, Neil. Where is he?"

"Told you, Grandpa's headed home, as far as I know. Did you ever get anything from the picture and knife?"

"Nothing but dog's blood and a ruined coloring-book page. However, I must again remind you to let me ask the questions."

"Yes, sir."

"So your grandfather's not staying for Christmas?"

"We argued."

"Over what."

"Family matters."

"What family matters?"

"He doesn't like my mother. You didn't get *anything* from the knife and coloring-book page?"

Gardner sighed, closed the notebook. "Neil, let's go over to the station for a while."

"Am I being charged with anything?"

"Not if you come willingly."

"And if I don't?"

"Harboring a fugitive, obstructing justice. I'll think of something."

At this point the charges wouldn't stick. I knew Alice Tarkenton, my crotchety old lawyer, would blow them out of the water. But was it worth the hassle and the time I'd be locked up?

I pointed to The Kitchen. "Can I inform the crew I have to go with you? Might lose my job, anyway, but I surely will if Claudia and Perry believe I left this morning and didn't come back."

He nodded. I jogged up the driveway and opened the door to the smells of onions, garlic, sage from the back, and hints of ginger and cinnamon candy from Trisha's houses. It triggered my appetite. I announced I was having lunch with Lieutenant Gardner at the police station—hopefully not dinner and breakfast, too—and I'd return as soon as possible. Mattie looked forlornly, already over-whelmed. Claudia huffed and walked off. Robbie's concern was evident, and Trisha grinned, bopping to the sound of her music. I closed the door.

I spent the remainder of the morning and most of the afternoon in one of the interrogation rooms. The black, clothlike walls made the space feel small, and Gardner's looming presence while he paced came close to fulfilling his intentions—intimidation and wearing down.

"Tell me what you know, Neil," Gardner had begun. He ran the side of his hand across his immaculate hair.

"I only know what you've told me."

"How does your landlord's break-in tie in with the murder charges?"

"I don't know. I was hoping you'd come up with something from the knife and—"

He cut me off. "How were your grandfather and his partner getting along?"

"Best buddies."

"I heard the old man was last seen threatening Walter Pierce."

"They always fought, like an old married couple. But they stuck together through thick and thin."

"They always fought? Ever come to blows?"

I was determined not to say anything he could twist. "Argued, yes. Punched, no."

"Where is your grandfather?"

"On his way home, as far as I know."

"Why do you keep saying *as far as I know*?"

"Because he has a mind of his own and often changes it."

"So he could still be in town?"

"I doubt it."

"But he could?"

"Yes."

"Where?"

"I don't know."

And around we went until Gardner was as tired as I was. I expected the cavalry in the form of C. J. McDaniels to arrive, but he never did. So I drew my wagons in a tight circle to wait the lieutenant out.

Finally, Gardner said, "Mr. Marshall, I *will* catch you in

a slipup. Perhaps not today, but perhaps tomorrow—or the next day—I will catch you."

"Only when there's something to slip up on. Can I leave?" I decided the potential significance of the knife and Santa picture would come up later, if there was one, and that to push him on it one more time would mean only more time chatting with the lieutenant.

"Yes," he replied, a quiver of frustration in his tone, "you can leave."

"Has anyone ever mentioned you bear a strong resemblance to T. S. Eliot?" I asked at the door.

"I swear you compare me to a different poet every time we meet."

"And one of these days I'll get it right."

"Yes, cracking the nut. I understand perfectly."

The winter afternoon was losing its luster. I decided not to go back to The Kitchen and pull another long night. Whatever needed to be done could be tackled tomorrow. Question was, would there be a tail on me?

I drove straight home, wished for a stress-relieving run in the waning evening, but, still in limp mode, opted for a long, hot shower instead. After carefully rinsing the flakes of blood out of my hair, I dressed in gray sweats with a Houston Astros logo. It hit me then that I hadn't eaten all day. I resolved to wait until I caught up to Grandpa and Keely. With my luck today, they'd be dining elegantly after I'd choked down a tuna sub.

Feeling a touch paranoid, I didn't call Keely's before heading over to her house for fear my phone was being tapped. It was probably only a television mystery scenario rolling through my mind, but I wasn't willing to take a chance. In fact, I took a circuitous route to Keely's place, running a couple of red lights, backtracking, until I was comfortable no one was on my tail.

I parked between the same streetlights Candace had the night before. The thudding in my head had dulled until I almost forgot it was there. I grabbed Grandpa's bag from the backseat before I locked the car and jumped to the sidewalk. With a quick tug I pulled the zipper up on my black leather jacket and jammed my fist into a pocket. Suddenly a voice spoke from the shadows while I was cloaked in streetlight.

"If I hadn't known where you were going, I'd have lost you."

A streak of panic, then I relaxed. I smelled the cigarette smoke.

"You checking up on me?"

C.J. emerged from the darkness. "Caught you pulling out as I was driving up. What happened to your head? Looks worse than it did this morning."

"I was rounding up Grandpa's goods," I said, shaking the bag, "when someone blindsided me."

"Any idea who?"

"None. I went into a funky dream of Grandpa and Walter. Shook that off then went twelve rounds with Gardner after I reached The Kitchen. He hauled me to the station."

"Figured he would."

"Was hoping you'd pop by."

"Was kind of busy."

"Learned something interesting," I told him. "The body on Grandpa's land hasn't been officially identified as Walter's."

C.J. puffed a billow of smoke. "I was going to tell *you* that. Linda called me. She used a connection through Vic Hernandez to Denver PD." Sergeant Hernandez was Linda's on-again, off-again boyfriend.

"What do you think?"

"Someone either wants the body to be Walter's and sent the investigation in that direction, or someone *knows* it's Walter's. And whoever knows it might not be able to prove it without implicating himself."

"Linda say why it's been so hard to identify the remains? Walter's not exactly been missing for months."

"There was a fire in the shaft after some kind of explosion. Linda wasn't clear. One of the miners died, and that was how they found the body, retrieving the miner and cleaning up."

"Christine vaguely mentioned a fire. Dental records?"

"I don't know. The cops must be having trouble finding records to match."

"Including Walter's?"

"That'd be my guess." C.J. toed out his cigarette. He walked with me toward the house.

"So is there a warrant out for Grandpa?"

"Oh, yes."

"How? They can't even identify the victim."

"Someone can, or thinks so, and has convinced the DA."

"It doesn't make sense," I said.

"No, it doesn't. There has to be a trump card waiting to be played."

"Question is," I asked, "who holds it?"

18

There was a pause before Keely unchained the lock then let us inside. Immediately I noticed a brightness in her light brown eyes that was in stark contrast to my weariness.

"You're chipper," I commented.

"I've had a delightful day. Hi, C.J."

"Ma'am."

She slipped the chain in place then twisted the lock on the doorknob. "Your head looks worse," Keely added. "I'd think it'd start looking better by now."

"Probably would if I hadn't been slugged again."

"Slugged? How dreadful. By who?"

"Never saw what hit me." We entered the living room.

"I guess I can't comment now on why you're limping."

"You just did," I told Keely, "and he told you."

"I was going to say it appears you had cause to injure yourself, and your grandfather made it sound amusing in an affectionate way. Now it doesn't seem so amusing."

Grandpa emerged from the kitchen carrying a glass of red wine. Smoke curled from his pipe.

"Hello, Neil," he said cheerfully, then added almost under his breath, "McDaniels."

A short smile broke across C.J.'s face. I believed the private investigator enjoyed irritating the old man.

"I've had a day to forget," I said.

"That's a shame," Grandpa told me. "I finally got some shopping done."

"Shopping?" I wanted to check my ears for wax.

"There's a number of wonderful stores around town."

"You left the house? To go . . . *shopping*?" The last word slid from my tongue as if I were unsheathing a knife.

Grandpa simply set his wine goblet on the glass end table and settled into a big plush chair. "With this lovely young lady's assistance I accomplished all I wanted to in one day. Amazing."

I glanced at C.J. His indifference was indicated with a short shrug. *It's his neck*, I could almost hear the burly detective say.

Keely smiled meekly. "The stores we patronized were out of the way," she attempted to explain. "I saw no harm. Besides," she said when I started to speak, "it was for a good cause. And *I* was certainly not going to stand in his way. You'll understand later, Neil."

Here I was being beaten, grilled by the cops, and jeopardizing my job—all on account of Grandpa—and the old man was Christmas shopping. My blood pressure rose, until reason stepped in. *Oh, don't whine, Neil,* reason said in a voice that was strangely similar to my father's. *Let it go. The old man's always done things his way and always will. You just have to accept that.*

So I swallowed hard, and did.

"Have y'all chowed down?" I asked.

"We were waiting," Grandpa replied. " 'Bout ready to give up on you, though."

"I picked up a beef tenderloin," Keely added. "We cut filets and wrapped them in bacon. Not very healthy, but your grandfather made my mouth water when he described the wild-mushroom-and-red-wine sauce he prepared to go with the meat."

My mouth was watering, too, not to mention my stomach grumbling.

"There's plenty, C.J., if you'd like to join us," Keely invited.

"Providing you don't mind real food," Grandpa shot out.

"Much obliged, Mrs. Cohen, but I've got to be leaving soon," C.J. responded, ignoring the old man. The PI was strangely formal to Keely. Perhaps it was because he disapproved of my attraction to her—the fact he addressed her as Mrs. Cohen didn't escape me—over his daughter, Linda, whom I'd had a brief interlude with.

"Would you like a drink?" Keely persisted.

"No, thank you."

"I'll take a beer," I spoke up. "I've earned it."

Keely strode off to grab me a beer. I dropped Grandpa's bag beside his chair and sat opposite him. C.J. remained standing.

"Someone broke into your motel room and searched your stuff," I told Grandpa.

"That where you were jumped?"

"I didn't know anyone was in the room with me. What was the intruder looking for?"

"Beats me."

I might, I thought.

He placed his pipe in a large ceramic ashtray. "Told you before," he said, "probably my will or the mine deed. But they weren't in my overnight bag."

"The identity of the body found on your land is in question," C.J. announced.

Grandpa leaned forward. "Then why are they saying I killed Walter if they're not even sure he's dead?"

"The evidence they have include remains of a ring, glasses, clothing fibers, and though the body's in bad shape, a witness. Who'd try to railroad you?"

"Buster Ledbetter," he answered. "Albright Cooper."

"That's obvious," C.J. said. "Anyone else?"

Silence, then, "Not that I can recall. At least not recently."

Keely handed me a Newcastle Brown Ale.

C.J. sighed. "I'm heading out. I'd strongly suggest you move the big elf tomorrow," he told me. "Sooner or later Gardner and his men will swing by here. We surely don't want the old man in custody if there's funny business going on."

Disappointment marked Keely's face.

C.J. started out of the room then hesitated. "If it wasn't Walter in the mine, any idea who it could've been?"

"None," Grandpa said.

"Figures."

"It didn't seem prudent to ask Gardner," I said, "but do you know if Fats and Rats are still incarcerated?"

"Relax. Corbett shot a cop. Bail was denied. Then again, as for Rats, I don't know."

"That ought to rattle Cooper's cage some."

"Hope so." Then Keely, after peering through the peep-hole like a member of the French underground fiercely guarding our secrecy, allowed C.J. back into the crisp night.

"Let's fix dinner," Grandpa said. "I'm ravenous."

"The potatoes au gratin is warming in the oven," Keely informed me. "All we need to do is steam the asparagus and grill the fillets. The wild-mushroom sauce, prepared by your grandfather, smells heavenly."

"Neil's not the only chef in the family. In fact, his daddy was a good cook, too."

I leaned forward in the chair. "I remember the time y'all let me make the gravy," I said. "Christmas Eve dinner, and I couldn't have been much more than eight or ten. It was so much fun. Then, either you or Dad informed me that chefs made decent money, and it wasn't a bad idea to learn a trade along with all the college smarts I'd get. Well, that really sunk in. But y'all were wrong about the money. God, I miss my dad."

"As do I, son." Grandpa fumbled with his pipe, then scraped the ashes out of the bowl and into the ashtray with a pocketknife. "Left my tobacco in the kitchen," he said absently, and ambled into the other room to get his pouch.

Keely came up behind me and stroked my back.

"It's a treat now to have people cook for me." I forced a smile, but my mind was preoccupied about what to do with Grandpa in the morning. Keely picked up my vibes.

"Let's enjoy tonight." She massaged my shoulders. "You're so tense."

The soothing effect rippled to my toes. I set my beer on the table and closed my eyes.

"We'll have a celebration of the season," she continued. "Let the world turn without us for a while. Tomorrow we'll make a plan." Her deep voice had a sultry edge. I felt lost in it, drifting. "Mark will be home soon, anyway, so it's just as well that Stephen leaves. I couldn't have him as a guest without explaining the situation. And I'm not quite sure how Mark would react." She paused a moment then resumed the massage. Her thumbs rubbed in circles on the upper portion of my back, near my spine, while her fingers went across my shoulders and up the base of my neck. I moaned.

Keely whispered, "Relax, just relax," and kept talking, but I lost track of her words. Instead, I sank deep within myself, pulling the sound of her voice with me. Rich as a fine Cabernet. The tingling from her touch. *A fine figure of a woman,* Grandpa had said, and he was right. My chin touched my chest. I floated on her tone as if I were riding a snowflake. My breathing fell into a deep rhythm.

And then I awakened myself with a snore.

"Don't relax that much," Keely said, slapped my biceps, and wandered around the front of the chair.

"Pure delight."

"You're welcome."

"You could make money as a masseuse."

"I'll keep that in mind if my writing ever dries up."

I rolled my neck. "God, I could kiss you."

Keely's face flushed.

"Ah, ah," I stammered, "what I mean is, ah, thank you."

"Of course, I know that." Her face flushed more.

Hit a little too close to home. I rubbed my temples.

From across the room, Grandpa cleared his throat. "Why don't we nibble on the Roquefort cheese and French bread we bought," he jumped in. "Then we'll have dinner. You might want to switch to red wine, Neil, in order to fully savor the taste. Keely bought that Texas Cabernet you like, Sainte Genevieve."

"Good idea." I polished off the last gulp of beer and

Keely fetched the cheese and bread while Grandpa poured me a glass of wine.

The tangy cheese cut by the full-bodied wine was a wonderful combination. We stuck to mostly literary conversation, though when I questioned Keely on the job offer, she was noncommittal and changed the subject to politics. I had intended to go back to my apartment for the night on the off chance Christine might return, and to display my car in its usual spot in case someone was checking up on me. However, the back rub, wine, and pleasant company mellowed me for the first time in a dog's year, and I lost myself in the evening until I had no desire to venture out.

Three Days Before Christmas

19

Morning rose gray and ragged like a whore straggling home after a rough Saturday night. My head felt like it'd been stomped on by a mule, and the silence of the house only emphasized the pounding. Surprisingly, Grandpa, the early riser, was still asleep in the guest bedroom. I swung my feet off the couch, slipped on my sneakers, then stiffly limped on my gimpy knee to the kitchen and made a pot of coffee. Keely hadn't awakened by the time I poured myself a cup, so I left a note saying I'd be back in a while, grabbed my leather jacket, and went out to face the day.

I drove to my apartment, showered, and dressed in a khaki L.L. Bean shirt and blue jeans. As C.J. had advised, Grandpa needed to be moved. The only thing I could think of was another hotel, though I wasn't really keen on the idea. I'd rather have him someplace where someone could keep an eye on him. Of course, I'd thought Keely was a good candidate to corral the old man, and they'd ended up Christmas shopping. Christ, his neck was on the line and he was too busy buying into the commercialism of the season to care. I shook my head. Christmas shopping. Bah, humbug!

The light flashed three messages on my machine. First Candace asked how we were faring, then said she'd see me at work this afternoon. The next two were hang-ups. I hated hang-ups. Imagine receiving a blank letter in the mail.

Three days before Christmas—and less before the Gilcrests' feast—the smart decision would be to run by

The Kitchen and put in a few hours of work. Lately, however, smart decisions came to me about as often as blizzards hit Houston. Instead of The Kitchen, I decided to head to C.J.'s office.

Again the sky threatened rain. I hesitated at the VW wondering if I should switch out of my leather jacket, when the back door of Jerry's house opened and my landlord appeared on the back porch.

"Time for a mug of coffee?" Jerry's hair was disheveled, his feet were bare, and the tail of his shirt stuck out of his pants.

"Afraid not. How's Samson?"

"Hanging in there." There was a hitch in his voice. "Might know more by the end of today."

"For what it's worth, the idiots who I think busted up your place and hurt Samson are in jail." I pulled the collar up on my jacket and zipped it a few inches.

"I'll kill them if my dog dies."

I knew that was emotion speaking, so I didn't respond.

"Why did they do that?" he asked.

"I don't know," I said, not wanting to delve into the whole scenario. Though I added, "They have no conscience." I unzipped my coat.

An angry sigh escaped him. After a moment he said, "Oh, some woman was by here looking for you and your granddaddy."

"What?" My interest was piqued.

"God, she was pounding and kicking so hard on your downstairs door I thought she was going to knock it down."

"Who was she?"

"Didn't leave a name. And I flew out onto the back porch so fast I think I scared her. That, my snappy attire, and the shotgun I waved in the air." A short smile touched his face.

I described Christine Cooper and asked if it had been her.

"Yeah, sounds like the broad."

I bristled at the word *broad* and normally would've

given him hell over it. Now, though, wasn't the time. "She happen to say where she's staying?"

"No. But I gave her The Kitchen's address and said y'all might be there."

What in the world is she up to? I wondered, and swung open the car door. "Thanks, Jerry." I fumbled with the zipper again then decided to leave the jacket open.

"She acted nervous," he told me. "You know, like you do when you're in trouble."

"I don't act nervous."

"Then stop playing with your damn coat."

I smoothed my hands down the sides of the leather. "Keep me updated on Samson's condition."

"Will do. You want me to give this woman any message if she comes back?"

"No, what you told her was fine."

"Be careful."

"Always." I climbed in and closed the door.

"From the looks of your head, I don't believe you," he called.

I simply waved, started up the engine—a smart twinge knifing my knee each time I clutched—and rumbled off.

Now what? I asked myself. The Kitchen? If there was a chance Christine would come to us, I supposed I had to be in the position to field her company. But why would she seek us out? Another warning? Maybe the thugs spooked her and Christine felt she needed to tip us off on their presence. Little did she know. Why not call? Or had she—the hang-ups?

Or was she scared and wanted our help?

Again I was the first to arrive at The Kitchen. After I opened up the place, I called and left a message for C.J. Then I phoned Keely to let them in on the latest development.

"You snuck out early," she said.

"Couldn't sleep. When does Mark get back?"

"This evening."

"Okay if Grandpa sticks around a few more hours?"

"Absolutely." A pause. "What are you up to?"

I told her about my conversation with Jerry. "So if I hang at The Kitchen, I might be able to help Grandpa and at the same time keep my job."

"Hang at The Kitchen like a sacrificial lamb, you mean. Surrounded by so many wolves. And between the police, whoever conked you on the head, and the Cooper woman, I don't know which beast is worse."

"Neither do I," I replied, and got off the line.

To imagine that the dead man found on Grandpa's land wasn't Walter felt like wishful thinking. Not that I desired any poor soul untimely vanquished from this world. I opened the meat cooler and retrieved the airtight packages of lamb racks.

But if it wasn't Walter, Grandpa acted like he had no clue as to who it could be.

After tying on an apron, putting on my Astros cap, and setting up a cutting board, I slit the plastic, pulled the lamb out, and discarded the covering. I drew a boning knife from the magnetic rack and briskly sharpened the blade against a kitchen steel. And if the deceased was Walter, and meant to set up Grandpa, then why was identifying the body so difficult? It sounded like someone claimed he or she could. Why was identification still in doubt? Had the corpse been burned that badly?

Trimming the lamb was a painstakingly slow process. The top of the bone had to appear flawlessly smooth for presentation purposes, and while I wasn't going to separate the individual chops until after I grilled the rack, all signs of fat or gristle had to be cut away. Each guest would receive two chops, but Mrs. Gilcrest wanted seconds passed, which meant I had to figure an average of three per person. The bottom line was I had a small flock to tend to.

Each rack I completed I set in a large, deep container and covered with a marinade of olive oil, red wine, minced garlic, coarse black pepper, and chopped cilantro. I worked steadily and didn't realize the depth of my concentration until I heard a thud at the front door that nearly caused me to jump out of my socks.

Mattie smiled wearily, then spotted me checking my finger.

"You cut yourself?"

"Almost." I'd just missed my knuckles. More importantly, however, I inspected the lamb and found no gouges or slices where there weren't supposed to be.

"Claudia will be in this afternoon," she informed me.

"All right." I wiped off my hands and fetched a mug of coffee. "I might be here."

Mattie raised an eyebrow but said nothing. Next Robbie and Conrad arrived, and finally the spirit whisked in Trisha, who went right to her job.

"How long are you going to be here, today?" Robbie asked.

"As long as the forces that be allow."

Trisha gave me the thumbs-up sign. "That's it, Neil, don't be a prisoner to stress."

Robbie rolled his eyes.

"There's plenty of jobs out there, Robbie Persons," Trisha called as he disappeared into the office.

"Remember that," he replied.

"You bet I will, and so will Neil."

"Trisha—"

"Well, you're a damn good chef, and you need to be someplace where you feel appreciated."

"I feel appreciated."

"Do you?"

"Yes."

The door swung open and Perry entered.

"Do you appreciate this man?" Trisha asked my boss, hands on her hips.

Perry pulled his head back, his eyes widened, and a cautious tone waxed his voice. "Of course."

"Trisha—"

"Hear that, Robbie?"

"What's going on?" Perry asked.

"Nothing," I said quickly.

"Neil's got the spirit," Robbie called.

Perry's countenance turned more quizzical.

"You can't be a slave to stress," Trisha spoke up. "It brings on more health problems than any disease."

"Then you should be the healthiest person in the city," Perry told her.

"Thank you."

"Have you finished the Steins' gingerbread house yet?"

"Give me an hour and it'll be ready to move into," Trisha answered, plugged into her earphones, and bounced along her way.

Perry's eyes narrowed, and he waved a thumb at our diminutive New Ager. "You're not—"

"Don't worry." I cut him off.

"Okay." And he eased around the worktable to join Robbie in the office.

I sipped my coffee. The lamb beckoned. And then old faithful appeared in the guise of Lieutenant Gardner. I caught sight of him gliding up the driveway, followed by a uniformed cop, and went outside to meet them.

" 'Morning, Lieutenant, Officer. Care for some coffee?"

"No, thank you," Gardner answered for them both. "I'd care to locate your grandfather."

"So would I."

"He's not inside, is he?"

"No, sir. You're welcome to look."

"I will."

I drank more coffee.

He scratched his head and thumbed through his notepad. "What do you know about a man named Albright Cooper?"

I thought a minute, then decided what the hell, I'd spill some information and see what I received in return. "He's a big-shot miner."

"Your grandfather do business with him?"

"I don't know for sure."

"What do you think?"

"I doubt it," I said. "They aren't very friendly toward one another."

"Why is that?"

"I'm only guessing—"

"So guess."

"From my understanding, Cooper's wife had taken a shine to Walter."

"What's that got to do with your grandfather?"

"Maybe Cooper saw Grandpa as covering for them. I don't know."

"Sounds like you're fabricating a case to draw attention from the old man."

I tossed the remainder of my coffee into a hibiscus bush. "Told you I was guessing. Why are you asking me about Albright Cooper, anyway?"

"Just a name that came up."

"Last I heard he was trying to bail the thugs out of jail."

"And how'd you hear that?"

"Through C.J."

"Well, one of them's out. The skinny one, Kern. Since Corbett shot a cop, he's being held without bail."

I nodded, feeling an icy tingle on the back of my neck.

"You hear anything else through McDaniels?"

"Nothing." I continued to keep Christine Cooper's visit and subsequent follow-up to myself.

"You still don't know why Jacoma's house was torn apart?"

"No."

"Could it have been for the ledgers?"

"Ledgers?"

"Do we have to go back to the station, Neil?" He shifted his weight from foot to foot and adjusted his gray hat. The blue stood stoically behind him.

"I honestly don't know what you're talking about."

"I've learned that according to you, honesty is relative."

Oh, the webs we weave, I thought. Still, I shrugged, palms up.

"Business ledgers," Gardner prompted.

"Business ledgers? I don't know what the hell you're talking about."

"Your grandfather fired his accountant—"

"No, Walter fired him," I emphatically interrupted. "Pissed Grandpa off. Said Walter couldn't keep books for shit and had no business canning the accountant without talking it over first, even if it was to save money." I stopped, realizing I'd added more fuel to the fire against Grandpa.

"That would be Edgar Bryant."

"The accountant, yes."

"My Colorado colleagues are attempting to locate him to obtain his version of his dismissal as well as his insight into your grandfather and Walter Pierce's relationship."

"Sounds like a good idea."

"Do you know where he is?"

"Fishing in Hawaii," I replied. "Walter pink-slipped him the day before his trip, swore it was a mutual decision, which it wasn't. Grandpa hasn't heard from Edgar."

"Have you heard from him?"

Stupid question from a normally competent investigator, I thought. But I kept my composure by imitating his thin smile. "I've only met Edgar Bryant once, a few years ago. I wouldn't know him if he walked up to me on the street and slapped my face."

"Next time you see your grandfather ask him when Bryant's expected to be back," he stated casually.

"I'm sure you'll catch up to the old man long before I do."

Gardner grinned. "I'm sure."

"If you don't mind, Lieutenant, I have a lot of work to do."

"By all means, if you don't mind me escorting you inside."

"Better than to the station." As I turned I caught a glimpse of a Yellow Cab cruising over the broken pavement of the street. The car's lights were on under the overcast sky. Outwardly I paid it no mind, though I knew full well who was in the vehicle. With the uniformed cop standing bright as the flashers atop his car, however, I didn't expect the cab to turn in to the driveway. It didn't.

The yellow car coasted to a halt at the stop sign, hesitated, then hooked a right toward the freeway.

I'd missed the chance to meet with Christine Cooper.

My insides fell like a hastily prepared soufflé. But I pushed back the frustration and played it cool. After swinging the front door open, I extended an arm and invited the two policemen to enter first. They did, with Gardner politely lifting his hat from his head.

When I glanced back, the taillights disappeared like fireflies into a bank of mist.

In spite of the O'Hara philosophy I'd been raised on—*Tomorrow is another day*—I cursed my luck at missing Christine, at being little help to Grandpa, and at finding myself under Lieutenant Gardner's magnifying glass once again. I was growing impatient. Leave tomorrow for the dreamers.

I wanted today.

20

The first thing Claudia said to me was, "It's too soon to be trimming the lamb."

"The meat will be fine in the marinade."

"You should be roasting the ducks for tonight's job."

"Mattie's tending to the ducks."

"What about the sweet-potato dumplings?"

"The mix is made," I replied. "Mattie and Candace will finish them off on-site."

Claudia stood a little uneasy. Her skin was pallid and she moved in slow, exaggerated movements. I pulled up a stool.

"Sit down, double-check the work orders to see we've covered everything," I told her. "Then why don't you go home and rest."

"Don't want to go home. Sick of resting."

"Then sit here and bark orders."

"That's what I do best," Claudia replied, a broad grin dominating her face.

I finished the lamb racks while she grumbled, belly-ached, and snapped question after question. Fortunately, we were caught up and I had an answer to her every concern. And I also felt good I was there to deflect Claudia's cantankerous attitude from Mattie and Trisha—although Trisha, with her headphones on, continued to appear oblivious to the rest of the world. After close to an hour of Claudia's bitching, though, even I was wearing down.

"Well," I told her as I bundled up my apron and tossed it

in the laundry basket, "I'm going to run out and grab a bite to eat."

"Eat!" Claudia exclaimed. "This here's a kitchen. There's plenty for you to fill your gut with."

"I need a break, dear."

Perry, hearing my intentions, strutted from the office and offered to buy me lunch.

"I'll take a rain check, boss," I responded. "I made plans." I hadn't, but I wanted to run by C.J.'s office and chat with him.

"Oh," Perry said, and straightened his bow tie. "Very well. Don't be gone all day." Robbie, his usual luncheon partner, was serving veal roulade stuffed with feta cheese and sun-dried cherries to a handful of executives and their clients at one of the banks downtown. "Guess I'll have to brown-bag lunch," he muttered, and wandered off to pillage from the coolers.

Claudia raised an eyebrow. "Must be important to say no to the bossman."

"It's only lunch."

"And the next invite you get will be two months from now."

"Maybe."

"Maybe, phew! His mama done spoiled him to the core."

"Speak a little louder, I don't think Perry heard."

"He knows he's spoiled. I tell him all the time it's a good thing he's got me around to keep him honest."

"We all think it's a good thing you're around," I said.

"Don't mock me, Neil Marshall."

"Never," I said, and left. Being outside and on the road was freeing. There'd been a shift in the wind, and now it blew in from the south, creating a balmy afternoon. The warmth brought about as much Christmas cheer as an anorexic Santa Claus. It was highly unlikely the weather would hold. I only hoped a blue norther would slip in before the twenty-fifth. A Christmas Day that felt like the Fourth of July would do me no good.

Linda's truck was parked in front of C.J.'s office. McDaniels's red Mustang was absent, which meant Linda was probably up there alone. Ever since our flash-in-the-pan romance had burned out, we'd kept a wary distance from each other. I approached feeling nothing short of trepidation.

The bottom door was unlocked. I marched up the narrow stairs and checked the office door. It, too, was unlocked, so I let myself in.

A large overhead fan lazily swept the tepid air. The window facing Westheimer was open, allowing the steady sound of passing cars to roll into the room. On the front desk was a small artificial Christmas tree with little wooden ornaments. New since I'd brought Grandpa here. I wondered if he'd said anything, comparing the starkness of the office to my apartment. It'd be just like C.J. or Linda to dig something out in order to ride me on it later. There was a rustling in the back office.

"C.J.?" Linda called.

"Neil," I replied.

Linda peered around the corner. Her jet-black hair was tied in a ponytail, accentuating her thin face and olive complexion. Snug against her trim figure were black jeans, matching Tony Lama boots, and a white cotton shirt with dark pinstripes. Linda carried herself with the confidence of a Texas Ranger. And she could be just as tough.

"I hate digging around C.J.'s part of the office," she said, and stepped into the front room. She wiped her palms together. "Feel like I'm taking my life in my own hands."

I smiled.

"But you didn't come here to talk about C.J.'s organizational skills," Linda continued.

"You hear that Rats Kern was bailed out?"

"Yeah, Vic called."

"How is Sergeant Hernandez?"

Linda set her eyes on me. "Fine. He knows a good thing when he sees it."

Meaning I didn't, of course. Still angry, huh? She

wasn't used to rejection, usually did the rejecting. I let it go.

"Hernandez's a good man," I agreed. "He say anything else?"

Linda sat behind her desk, intertwined her fingers, and stared at her hands a minute. "Kern swore he wasn't shooting at the cops but trying to control his partner, which is why he accidentally shot him in the ear."

"That's bullshit." I paced to the window.

"Of course it is. But since you and your grandfather took off and didn't give a statement, and Kern's main shot was at his partner's head, there wasn't much to hold him on. Add the appearance of a high-priced lawyer and, well . . ." She flattened her palms in the air like there was a transparent wall between us.

"Cops try to play that off Corbett?"

"Tried, but he's tighter than a horse with colic. Only way they tied them to Albright Cooper was a business card with his private number."

"A business card?"

"No one ever accused hired muscle of being brain surgeons."

"I'd have thought C.J. sent the authorities in that direction."

Again the palms raised.

"Anything else?"

"Not that I've heard. Walter Pierce remains dead, and your grandfather is a wanted man." Linda picked up a Red Delicious apple from the corner of the desk, opened up a pocketknife, and began slicing the fruit into wedges.

I sat opposite her. "What about Albright Cooper?"

"The man's batty as a june bug but has enough money and influence to be considered eccentric." I accepted a piece of apple from Linda and crunched it down in two bites.

The downstairs door opened and closed.

"The old man's back."

"C.J.'s going to hear that someday," she began, then stopped and sat upright.

"What?"

She placed a finger to her lips and set the apple and knife down. Quietly, Linda drew open the top desk drawer, tucked a .38 in her lap, and leaned back.

I realized there were two sets of footsteps ascending the stairs. And no talking.

The office door was ajar. The climbing was slow and deliberate, as if they didn't care to be heard. I fumbled with an open pack of cigarettes C.J. had left on the desk.

"You're not going to start smoking again, are you?" Linda asked, voice normal. "I've been trying to get C.J. to quit and you beginning won't help."

"Too hard to quit," I replied as calmly as I could. "Doesn't mean I don't miss it, though." I fumbled the package and a slew of cancer sticks slipped out and fell on the desk and floor. Linda rolled her eyes.

"Nic fit," I joked, and was picking them up, hands and knees on the floor, when they pushed into the office.

Scrawny Rats held the door open, arms folded, and grinned. Actually, he leered at Linda, then caught my eye. The glare I emanated must have caught him by surprise, because the grin faded. And then entered a trim, moderately sized man with white hair and pale blue eyes. He was clean-shaven, wearing a blue Armani suit, and carrying a hickory cane.

I stood.

"You're not McDaniels," he said.

"No."

"And you're too pretty to be a tired old shamus," he directed toward Linda.

She said nothing.

"You sure this is the right place?" he snapped at Rats. "I want the bastard who called me on my private line."

"That's Marshall's grandson," the thug replied, pointing at me.

"Really?" He came within a couple of inches of me. I smelled the cologne. Nice. I was a head taller.

"Where's dear old Grandpa?" he asked.

"I don't know, Mr. Cooper."

"So you know me?"

"Of you."

"I have power, boy."

"I hear you do. Enough to have someone murdered, probably, then point the blame at an innocent man."

He tossed his head back and laughed. "If that's what you think, then you're a fool. I don't kill men." He raised a fist and squeezed. "I crush them until their spines break and they wish they were dead."

"That's about how Grandpa characterized you."

"Then he understands."

"Perhaps more than you realize." I paced to the window and back. "Did you stake Buster Ledbetter's operation into Grandpa's land?"

"Ledbetter is a buffoon, but even buffoons can be useful if trained correctly."

"I guess that's a yes, and what Grandpa figured before he left town."

"With my wife!" he accused. A hiss slithered between his teeth.

"You're crazy," I blurted.

Rats shuffled. Linda shifted forward.

"What'd you call me?" The wild look in Cooper's pale eyes showed me my mistake.

"My grandfather didn't—"

"I am not crazy!" he bellowed, and slammed his cane down on the desk, just missing the little decorative tree. "Your grandfather's crazy!"

Linda didn't flinch or yelp or, as I wished, raise the gun from her lap and shoot them. I tried to take a lesson from her calmness.

"My grandfather is not with your wife," I told Cooper, and stood my ground, hoping not to get swatted on the head again.

"Of course he is. Why else would she follow him to Houston?"

"I don't know."

"You don't know," he mocked, and paced the length of the room, his cane striking the wooden floor hard with each step. "You idiot. Next you'll tell me you didn't know that Walter Pierce was embezzling money from the company."

"No, I didn't," I said, caught off guard. Though, from all that was unraveling, the revelation shouldn't surprise me. But why didn't Grandpa say something? "You sure of this?"

"Am I sure?" He laughed an unnatural, forced cackle, and slammed his cane down as he stopped pacing. "God gave me a gift, boy."

Now he was making me nervous. I waited.

"A wife with a big mouth," he continued. "Given time, everything in that tiny mind of hers spews out like a drunk who can't hold her liquor." He cackled again. "That's how I knew the old bastard was plotting to kill his partner. Revenge. And the accountant knows the big picture, too. He can't hide in Hawaii forever. I'll find him and show everyone. Your grandfather was out for revenge, boy, and to steal my wife."

Again he was inches from me, leaning up. "Where'd that murdering bastard take my wife?" he demanded.

Logic told me the man was a fool. I'd seen Grandpa send Christine away. But staring at the psycho before me sent me into a different realm. For all his idiocy, culminating with his attacks against Grandpa, I wanted to knock him upside the head. I took a deep breath.

"Your wife is not with my grandfather," I stated calmly.

"Liar!"

I forced a thin smile and rubbed my hands together so they wouldn't ball into fists. "I don't know where your wife is," I told him, then added, "but if she has an ounce of sense she's a long way away from you."

I stepped back from his red face. The old man stood

there a moment, shaking with anger, then, without warning, he swung the cane at my head.

Instinctively, I ducked and backpedaled some more. Cooper, in his rage, lost his balance and stumbled to the floor. Rats was caught totally by surprise, but when he tried to draw his piece, Linda already had the .38 leveled on him.

Cooper, stunned for a moment, rose surprisingly quick, cane brandished high. "You son of a bitch." Again he swung wildly. This time I turned and took the blow on the back.

"Mr. Cooper," Linda yelled, "in a minute I'll tell Neil to hit back."

The warning fell on deaf ears. He swung again. This time I caught the cane with my right hand. With a sharp jerk I broke his hold on the improvised weapon. "Enough," I said.

He was gasping hard, but fury still colored his eyes.

Rats began to move. Linda cocked the gun.

"Before you bloody up my office," a voice bellowed, "I've got something to say." C. J. McDaniels entered the room like a Brahma bull. "First, I don't like vermin." He backhanded Rats in the nose. The scrawny thug winced and cupped his face, blood seeping through his fingers. C.J. patted him down. On finding Rats's gun, the big investigator tossed the piece on the desk then unceremoniously grabbed the thug by his collar and belt and threw him out of the office and down the stairs. The thuds and yelps made me squirm.

"You're getting too violent," he added, pointing a big finger at me.

"Sorry, it's the company I keep."

C.J. yanked Cooper by the lapels. "You get out."

"My cane," he gasped.

McDaniels let go of the man, eyed the hickory, then picked it up and snapped the polished wood over his knee. He tossed the pieces aside.

"The governor gave me that."

"Then you'd better ask the governor to get you another," C.J. growled.

"You'll pay—"

"I'm sure." He tugged Cooper to the door. "You can leave one of two ways. As your associate did, or on your own free will."

Cooper's eyes were wide and wild, but his voice was cold and steady. "You don't know who you're fucking with."

"Tell me later."

Cooper pulled away from C.J.'s grip. "I'll—"

"Don't even start," C.J. warned. "Because if I see you again, you'd better have more protection than that yahoo down there. And if you threaten my friends again, I'll kill you."

"You can't say that to me."

C.J. shoved him to the landing and Cooper slipped a couple of steps down. "I said it, and I meant it. Now git!"

Cooper scrambled to where Rats was dizzily pulling himself up, grabbed hold of him, and they burst out into the afternoon. C.J. slammed the door.

"You know, Dad," Linda said, and eased the hammer of the .38 down, "we had the situation under control."

"Under control? Neil's whooping up on an old man in my office and you call that under control?"

"Wait a second," I interjected. "Who was whooping up on whom?"

"You could've broken that man's neck," Linda continued.

"You'd rather he emptied his gun?" C.J. eyed the rubble of cigarettes on the desk and took one without questioning their position. "It'd have happened sooner or later," he added, and lit up.

"Aren't you the least bit curious why he chose to visit you?" Linda clicked on the safety and set the gun back into the drawer.

"Besides me antagonizing him, Cooper's looking for his wife, who, if she has half a brain, is a million miles from Houston by now."

"Then she doesn't have half a brain," I spoke up. "She buzzed by The Kitchen in a cab this morning. Unfortunately, Gardner and a couple of blues were outside questioning me again, so Christine didn't stop."

"Damn." C.J. flicked ashes into a ceramic dish on the desk.

"Now what?" Linda asked. "Seeing as you two have made a great enemy of a lunatic who likes to crush spines."

"Watch your back," C.J. told me.

"Funny."

"Who's laughing?" He stubbed out the cigarette.

"Good question. Who would be laughing at this whole episode?" I asked.

C.J. caught my eye. "You ain't so dumb for a college boy."

"Albright Cooper wasn't very amused."

"Hardly."

"I'd think he'd be enjoying every minute of this if he were the driving force."

C.J. picked up another cigarette. "Still could be the driving force in his own warped way, but wandering down another path won't hurt none."

"What are y'all talking about?" Linda asked.

"So what other path?" I asked.

"One we've not paid much mind to," C.J. agreed.

"The accountant?"

"Why not?" C.J. told me.

"Is he the man Cooper's after, too?" Linda asked.

"Crazy Cooper." I shook my head. "Wouldn't you take anything he says or does with a grain of salt? But, yes, Edgar Bryant is the man Cooper's after. Even the cops haven't been able to find him, though."

"How hard have they looked for the accountant?" C.J. asked.

"He's supposed to be fishing in a remote region of Hawaii. But what if he's skipped the country?" I asked. "Weeks could pass before anyone realizes he's not on vacation."

"What if he's right under our noses?"

"Okay, we won't know until we look."

The phone rang. Linda answered. She muttered into the

mouthpiece, paused, then placed the receiver on her shoulder. "Ah, Houston, we have a problem."

The cliché stopped us in our tracks.

"This is the professor," she said to me.

"Keely?"

"Seems she's lost something."

"Oh, no—"

"Or rather, someone."

"Don't tell me—"

"Your grandfather's missing."

21

Driving away, I thought of how I'd assured C.J. I'd find the old man, of how I *knew* where he was. Neither he nor Linda believed me, though they didn't challenge my word. This left me bobbing through traffic like a confused reindeer that'd lost his leader. Unsure which direction to turn, I simply went with the flow. The whole time I mulled one question over and over as if it were prayer and subconsciously I expected an answer:

Why in hell did Grandpa leave?

Keely had taken a shower. When she'd finished and gone for coffee, she found his note, which she read to me:

Keely—
   Have promises to keep
   and miles to go before I sleep.
   Thanks for the delightful company!
                              A very merry Christmas,
                                          Stephen

Why the Frost? we'd both wondered. What promises? I hadn't bothered to go into the specifics of the note with C.J. or Linda. I'd simply made my declaration and hit the road.

What also bothered me was that the old man hadn't taken his overnight bag or the presents he'd bought with Keely. She was particularly surprised he'd left the gifts, though she wouldn't elaborate. Did that mean he was returning? Not from the sound of the note. Then would he send for his stuff? And from where?

With a city as large as Houston, it would be futile to simply drive around searching, even with someone as conspicuous as Grandpa lumbering about. The first logical stop was my apartment. I pondered the old man's love for food, however, and rashly made a few wild side treks to restaurants we'd frequented in the past.

At The Stables, a rustic, old Houston steak house, the hostess giggled when I asked if anyone resembling Saint Nicholas had come in for lunch.

"No," she replied, "but a couple of his elves wandered in about half an hour ago." She nonchalantly pointed out a city councilman sitting with the superintendent of the Houston school system.

"Not even close," I replied.

Next I swung by the original Ninfa's. A neighborhood business that she'd founded in order to make ends meet after her husband had died, Mama Ninfa had built a multimillion-dollar empire. Her roots, however, were over here on Navigation, in a strongly Hispanic section of town, and this was generally the restaurant of hers I patronized. Grandpa loved it.

In luck, Teresa, a friend of mine, was busily seating people when I arrived. And she didn't giggle when I asked my question. Instead, she directed me to the back of the small place. The smell of corn tortillas filled the room, along with the light smoke of sizzling beef and chicken fajitas. Baskets of crisp tortilla chips donned each table, accompanied by their homemade red and green salsa. The delectable odors made me dizzy as they reminded me I hadn't eaten a thing all day.

Then surprisingly, sitting with his back to me, was a large gray-haired man wearing a baseball cap.

"*Éste es el hombre, Señor Neil?*"

"*Gracias.*"

Teresa curtsied and went back to work.

"Why'd you run away, Santa?"

The man turned. Before he faced me, I knew he wasn't Grandpa from the size of the man's belly. "Damn right I did," he grumbled. "Those kids are driving me crazy. Brats crawling on me all day, pulling my beard to prove it's real. Don't this look real to you?"

I nodded, thinking it wasn't as thick as Grandpa's, but sufficient.

"How'd you find me? Bet it was that little bitch elf who complains I smell like booze. Hell, I only have a margarita or three with lunch." He drank.

"You're scary," I said.

"Oh, lighten up and have a snort." He lowered his voice. "I put them on my expense account. Don't you tell no one."

"What's your name again?"

"My name? All you college boys think you're so damn smart, but you can't even remember a name."

"Fine, Mr. I-Can't-Remember-Your-Name, you're fired."

He slammed the margarita down. "I'm what!"

I began walking out.

"You can't fire me," he slurred.

You're right, I thought. But I suspect you believe I just did.

Winding toward my apartment, my last stop was one of my hangouts—The Flower. Juanita, the owner, welcomed me warmly and asked if I was eating alone today.

"Actually, I'm looking for a man who strongly resembles Santa."

Her eyes widened, then she laughed. "You mean your grandfather. Remember, you brought him to my place a few years ago."

"Oh, yes, that's right."

"So Stephen is in town?" she asked, and nudged close to me. "He is a fine-looking man."

"I'm sure, but I guess that means you haven't seen him."

"Too bad, no." Juanita was twenty years Grandpa's junior and a good-looking woman. "Bring him by," she added, batting her long dark lashes.

"I might just do that," I replied, and thought, *You, my dear, may be the only person in the city who can keep him in one place for any length of time.*

Finally, I puttered down through the neighborhood to my apartment. No one was there. Jerry's house was locked and dark. No one waited on the back porch, or in my hall, or in my place. And there were two hang-ups on my machine. Now what?

I called The Kitchen and got Robbie.

"How'd the lunch go?"

"Divine," he said. "Excellent service. But where the hell are you?"

"Home."

"Home? You went home and sent your grandpa to cover?"

"Did I hear you right?"

"He's back there just annoying the hell out of everyone. Cutting the beef tenders into steaks so thick I thought Perry was going to have an apoplexy."

"Don't let him leave," I ordered, and slapped down the receiver. In less than ten minutes I was parked in front of The Kitchen and limping quickly up the driveway. My knee really needed ice and a good soaking. I swore I'd never tackle anyone again.

"Where is he?" I demanded as I sailed through the door.

"Perry left," Robbie replied.

"Not Perry."

Robbie grinned, jerked his head toward Mattie's station.

"Neil," Grandpa greeted. He was decked out in an apron and holding a large chef's knife. "Aren't the steaks biggest in Texas?"

"I think only headaches are biggest in Texas, Grandpa."

"Well, come here. That little boss of yours seemed to think these are too big." He held up a portion of beef that against his large frame appeared small but in actuality probably weighed as much as Rhode Island.

"I don't understand why he'd think that," I stated dryly.

"Exactly," Grandpa agreed, not picking up on my tone, and placed the meat on a tray.

Mattie rolled her eyes and muttered, "Be glad Claudia's not here. She'd be knocking him upside the head with a rolling pin by now."

I approached Grandpa. Mattie and Robbie were hustling around collecting the materials they needed for tonight's job.

"How many people you figuring to serve with this beef tonight?" the old man asked.

"Eight. And it's for a lunch tomorrow."

"Doesn't look to me like you have enough."

"Funny how five pounds of beef isn't enough for eight people."

"Isn't it, though?" Grandpa said. "Must be in the—"

"Carving?" I interrupted. "Imagine." I leaned close. "What are you doing here?"

"Helping, obviously."

"Grandpa, why'd you leave Keely's?"

"A lovely young lady, Neil."

"So you've said, and I concur."

"I fear I was overstaying my welcome, and my instincts told me to get out before the police closed in and caused trouble for her."

"The cops come here all the time."

"I can't keep running, son."

"You can suck it up a little longer."

He set the knife down and rubbed his hands on a white kitchen towel. We continued to speak in low tones to each other.

"Why?" Grandpa asked. "You any closer to cracking the case?"

"I learned today that Walter was embezzling from the company. Why didn't you tell me that?"

Grandpa's face grew stern. "I only found out today. Decided to do some research of my own and called T. R. Spence. He has a lot of connections, and I thought he might know a thing or two about Walter's death we didn't. Well, damn it, I guess he did. My last check to T.R. bounced. Should've been over a hundred thousand in that account. So I contacted the bank and sure enough, Walter sucked that water hole dry. Seems like another nail in my coffin."

"I'm not prosecuting you."

"It's getting so Mattie's little boy could prosecute this case. Walter steals from me, I get mad and plug him. Open and shut. Wham, bam, in the slam. At least not many people know Walt was stealing."

Revenge, Cooper's voice echoed in my mind. *Revenge.* Damn him. "If Albright Cooper knows about the missing money, you can bet the North Pole a lot of other people are aware, too."

He was quiet a minute, then he picked up the knife and trimmed a piece of fat off the beef. "Good thing I have faith in you," he finally said, "or else I might think the situation's hopeless. Wrong time of year for hopelessness."

I couldn't respond. Mr. Live-and-Breathe-Christmas clinging to his faith—placing his trust in me. Me.

My heart jumped a notch when I heard the front door open but not close. To my relief, it was Candace, not the police, but there was a tentative expression on her face.

"Some lady wants to talk to your grandfather," she announced, and wrinkled her nose in disapproval. "I don't like the looks of her," the girl added in a whisper.

Grandpa and I glanced at each other.

"She's the real reason you came here," I said.

"Had a gnawing in the back of my head that she might show."

"A promise to keep?"

"Promise to myself. Christine knows more than she first let on," Grandpa said, and took off the apron. "I intend to lift the old gal's veil."

22

Christine, wearing the same Lauren Bacall outfit, glided into The Kitchen. Candace avoided her and went to confer with Mattie on the function they were working together. I glanced up and down the street, but there were no cops in sight and no sign of Christine's husband. Robbie noticed I locked the door after closing it. Sensing the tension in the air, he suggested we'd have more privacy in the office.

I stood in the back, allowing Grandpa to break the ice.

"Why are you here?" he asked bluntly. Break the ice? He took a sledgehammer to it.

"Albright sent a couple of tough guys down to Houston to find me and rough you up."

"Already made their acquaintances. But you had to figure that, after they called you from jail."

Her back and shoulders tensed. "They were going to take us both back," she said. "Me to Albright. You to the law."

"Your husband's dying to pin the murder on me."

"So no one will think to blame him," she said quietly, and sat on an office chair.

Grandpa waited.

"The minute I heard Walter was dead I knew Albright had murdered him," Christine continued. "You see, Walter and I were planning to skip the country. Argentina. Brazil. Somewhere in the islands—"

"And you were going to use my money to get there," Grandpa stated.

She crossed her legs and folded her arms. "We were going to pay you back."

"Don't bullshit me." He paced to the front window, separated the mini-blinds with his fingers, and peered out. Apparently satisfied, he allowed the blinds to slide back in place and continued to pace.

"We needed—I needed the money to get away from Albright."

"So you take a chunk from a man's life savings?"

"You still had the mine, and when you wouldn't sell or develop it, well, we saw no other way out." She lifted her chin high. "You don't just leave a man like Albright. He's a badger that keeps coming and coming. And every time he catches you, it's worse." She raised a gloved hand. "Don't ask me why I didn't divorce him. You don't divorce a man like Albright, either. You kill him or run away. I'm not the killing type."

Sounded familiar, I thought. Your husband doesn't kill but crushes spines. I held the thought, though, and asked, "Can you prove Albright killed Walter?"

Christine stared at me, having forgotten there was someone other than Grandpa and her in the room. She shook her head. "No."

"Where's the money Walter took?" Grandpa asked, looking directly into her eyes. Proudly, she held his stare. I debated whether or not that was a technique she'd learned after all those years with Cooper. Could be. After a long minute, however, with her poise only growing in strength, I decided her answer would probably be the truth.

"I don't know," Christine replied. "If I did, I believe I'd have been on the first plane out of here after you declined to leave town with me." She tugged her leather gloves off one finger at a time.

I stepped up to Grandpa. "The thugs kept asking where *it* was. Think they were referring to the money?"

"Doesn't make sense."

"Look at it this way: They claim you murdered Walter to get your money back. Could be evidence against you."

Grandpa scoffed at the notion. "How would a man ever prove a thing like that?"

"A slick lawyer could wreak a lot of havoc. Besides, maybe they planted money in Jerry's house then tore the place apart so it appeared like they were searching."

The old man shook his head. "You're reaching for straws. Albright's men are on a seek, find, and destroy mission. If you were right, they'd have to be acting. And I believe a tree stump could act better than them. Saying they figure I recovered the money, I reckon Albright's biggest fear is that Christine sweet-talks me out of the dough." He paused.

"What *are* you going to do, Christine?" Grandpa asked. "You can't run from hotel to hotel forever."

"You're right, Stephen, I need money." Christine stood. She slapped the gloves in the palm of her hand and circled the room. Her matching purse blended in with her London Fog, which was the color of her fair skin.

"You done played this vein out, Christine. I've been bled until I'm anemic."

"It was Walter's idea—"

"Don't blame everything on a man who may be dead," I told her.

"I'm not—" She whirled around. *"May be dead?"*

"There's plenty of circumstantial evidence," I said. "Glasses fragments. A distorted ring. Fibers of his clothes. But the corpse hasn't actually been identified, the last we heard."

"Can't they use dental records for that sort of thing?" she asked.

"Absolutely," I replied.

"Walter had a bunch of work done on his teeth about a year and a half ago. Remember, Stephen?"

"He and I weren't talking much."

"Well, he did."

"I'm sure checking dental is the first procedure the authorities in Colorado did," I interjected. "If there's a problem, we don't know what it is."

Christine fell silent.

Grandpa took out his pipe and lit it up. I didn't even bother to argue. "So *do* you have any plans, Christine?" he asked her.

"I—I don't know what to do."

"Where are you staying?" I questioned.

She cocked her head, appeared reluctant to say anything more.

"We're not going to tell anyone," I said.

"He's right," Grandpa assured her.

Christine cleared her throat, looked at her hands. Grandpa and I waited.

She sighed. "Oh, all right, I'm checked in at the Renaissance. I'd rather be at the Four Seasons, but that is the first place Albright would look."

You must have some money left, I thought. I debated whether I should inform her that Albright was in town, but Grandpa answered that dilemma for me.

"Neil ran across your husband earlier today," the old man stated.

She dropped a glove. "He's here?"

Grandpa picked it up. "Easy, now."

Christine sat back down. "How could everything go so wrong?"

The old man dropped the glove in her lap. "I don't condone what you and Walter were going to do to me," he said. "In fact, I figure you put Walt up to the dirty deed."

"Of course you'd believe that. After all, I'm the femme fatale."

"You're still chasing me."

Her eyes narrowed. "Am I?"

"Or my money. But the joke's on you because even I don't know where most of it is."

Christine abruptly rose.

"I blame Albright for the way you've changed," Grandpa added, "and for that reason alone, I wouldn't wish any more of him on you."

"I knew you cared for me," Christine declared, pleased with herself.

"I would, however, wish you to prison," he said, jaw set.

She staggered. "Prison!"

"And I didn't murder Walter, but if he was here now, I'd have a thing or two for him, and they wouldn't be a pair of airline tickets."

"I warn you that you're being hunted by the law and you'd send *me* to jail? You ungrateful bastard." She took a wild swing at Grandpa, which he simply sidestepped. Christine lost her balance and ended up in my arms, which she fought against as if I'd assaulted her. I righted her, endured a couple of elbows to the chest, and scooped her hat off the floor. She was seething with disdain.

"Now I understand why Walter fired Edgar Bryant," Grandpa commented. "He must have uncovered Walt's thievery. What I don't get is why Ed took Walter at his word and didn't come to me."

"You've got it wrong. Walt and Ed were close," she said.

"You mean Walt tried to buy Ed Bryant off."

"I hate you, Stephen."

"I've heard that before."

"You're a fool," she charged. "You're the one going to jail, and it's for a murder you didn't commit. You can't beat Albright. He'll get you. And he'll get me, now, too, thanks to you." She put her hat back on, picked up her gloves. Grandpa didn't reply.

There was a soft knock.

"Neil?" Robbie called.

I cracked open the door.

"Lieutenant Gardner's outside wanting to talk to you."

"Oh, shit."

"I told him you were with a client."

"Thanks. I'll be out in a minute." I closed the door.

Christine grinned. "The police?"

"Yes," I replied coldly.

"Don't worry, dear. I'm not finished with your grandfather yet."

"Because the minute I'm gone, your options turn to dust," the old man stated.

"It's love-hate, give-and-take, Stephen." And she breezed out of the office, declaring, "Thank you for seeing me on such short notice, Neil."

I thought Candace and Mattie's mouths were going to bounce off the floor.

"Now call me a cab, please," she continued. "Alfred's getting the Mercedes tuned and I told him if it took longer than an hour, don't bother to pick me up."

The lanky Lieutenant Gardner leaned against the butcher-block table up front, a thin smile on his lips as he carefully observed everything that was going on. He chewed on a toothpick.

"Why, you're a handsome man," she told the lieutenant.

"Thank you, Ms.—"

"Houston, Amelia Houston."

"Any relation to our city's namesake?"

"Very distant. I don't live here."

"Really? But your chauffeur is having your Mercedes tuned?"

"We drove in from Dallas."

"I see. I often tune my car after making that drive, also."

"Oh, I don't know anything about automobiles," she said, smiling broadly. "My husband just told me to have Alfred get it tuned and I figured we could do it as easily in Houston as Dallas. And seeing I needed to talk to these lovely people about a New Year's Eve party my friend Bessy is insisting on throwing for us—oh, but you don't care about all that. Are you a client, too? Isn't the cuisine here marvelous?"

"I'm a police officer."

"Security. I didn't realize this was that bad a neighborhood."

"It is, but I don't work security here."

"Oh. Well, here's my cab," she said, and pointed out the blinds. "Good luck doing whatever it is you do."

"Good-bye, Mrs. Houston," I said.

"I'll be seeing you, Neil."

Gardner tipped his hat, and she was off.

"Attractive woman," he commented.

If you like them old and psychotic, I thought. "What can I do for you, this time?" I asked.

"Am I making a nuisance of myself?"

"Of course not."

"Excuse us," Robbie said as he, Candace, and Mattie began loading items from the front worktable into the van for the night's job.

"Perhaps we could step into the office?" Gardner asked. "Out of the way."

"Perry's in there," I said quickly. "Let's go outside."

He bought it, and we walked around the van and down the driveway. The air retained the warm humidity of earlier. It felt like the inside of a mitten drying over a radiator.

"I understand you had an altercation with Albright Cooper," he began.

I listened, having learned not to volunteer information and to answer only direct questions.

"Upset some very important people up north," Gardner continued. "Laid some heavy pressure on us to arrest you for assault, and maybe harboring a criminal and such until we find your grandfather. Wouldn't be surprised to see the feds involved before we're through."

"Are you here to arrest me?" But I noticed the absence of uniformed cops.

"Until a short while ago, I'd have said yes."

"And now?"

"And now I say you're still managing to do your Houdini escape act through the criminal-justice system. I've never seen a son of a bitch as lucky as you."

He was still angry, among other things, for my taking the rap for a homicide—justifiable homicide, as ruled by the grand jury—he knew I hadn't committed. And I hadn't, but when it came down to the nuts and bolts, I'd been protecting Candace.

"I know it's not the forgiveness of the season that's keeping me out of jail," I said.

"Don't underestimate my tolerance at this time of year, Mr. Marshall. Also, I have a growing suspicion that behind this fog of circumstantial accusations there is some semblance of truth. And that truth revolves around a slightly unbalanced millionaire. Your grandfather, while perhaps not the saint you believe him to be, might benefit should this truth be learned."

"How enigmatic. What *truth* are you talking about?"

"I don't know, and truth might be difficult for you to find."

I bit my tongue. "So you're giving us—me—space."

"Miles. But that's not your Christmas gift from me."

"There's more?"

"A good friend of mine called. A homicide detective up there. Seems McDaniels contacted them and suggested they run a different check. My name had been used as a reference. I told him the hunch was a valid one, and that McDaniels, though a pain in the ass, was honest and a good investigator. The detective said he wished he'd had that tidbit of information a couple of days ago, because it was too late now."

"Too late? What do you mean?"

"The remains have been released to the family. Walter Pierce was buried yesterday."

His words fell like the walls of Jericho. "Isn't that rather premature during a homicide investigation?" There was a rise of pitch in my voice I couldn't control.

"Could be viewed as such. Legally, though, he's no John Doe. He was identified as Walter Pierce."

"Was there a DNA test?"

"Same problem as with the missing dental records— and compare the test to what?"

"I don't believe this." *Missing dental records,* I thought. *Figures.*

"They went on the word of Pierce's nephew," Gardner said. "He identified the ring and glasses, and he even went so far as to swear the corpse was his uncle. Despite the damage, he *recognized* the man's features."

"That ne'er-do-well probably still thinks Walter had money to leave him. He'd swear anything to put his uncle in the ground. I just can't fathom any cop up there bought it."

Gardner said nothing. He wasn't going to speak ill against his northern colleague. Not for something his associate had no control over.

"I won't find you for a while," Gardner said, and turned away. "Least not until the day after Christmas. Best make good use of your precious little time."

"What do *you* make of all this?" I asked.

"Old Marley was dead as a doornail," he called over his shoulder. "But is poor old Walter Pierce?"

23

I'm on a ski slope, but I'm not skiing. I'm carrying my skis over my shoulder. Poles, too. And I'm walking. Waving at Keely but suddenly she's so far away I wonder how I know it's her. And instead of the slope, I'm at the entrance of a cave. I set my skis down and walk inside. I'm walking for a while before I realize that the cavern is getting narrower and narrower, shorter and shorter. But the air is white. Luminous. Folding around me like fog, only thick, like meringue. Then I'm on my belly crawling, clawing webs of white from my face. Spiderwebs, sticky, that suddenly turn to strands of hair. In panic, I shake them from my fingers.

Finally, I see an opening and I slither through it, skid down the length of a small hill, surrounded by children and their sleds. I'm inside a building, like a department store, and there sits Grandpa on a throne, a line of children waiting to see him. A castle behind the grand old man. Lights and candy canes mark the gates. Elves in green outfits assist.

Then Grandpa spots me, beckons me over. He lets a child go, pats his lap for me to sit. I am young enough, again, to sit on his lap. He clears his voice. *There's something I've been meaning to tell you, Neil,* he says. Yes? I think and wait. I stare up at him. *Guess I shouldn't have kept it to myself so long,* he continues, a grin on his face. *I killed Walter Pierce.*

The old man pulls out a pouch and tosses teeth in the air. And he begins to laugh. A deep laugh that won't stop. Then I look down on myself. I'm inside a paperweight.

The laughter turns wicked. I freeze. Not Grandpa's voice anymore. The teeth flake apart, the swirling.

Marley was as dead as a doornail. Is Walter Pierce?

"No!" I heard myself say, and my mind tumbled awake. My heart drummed in my ears, accompanied by the sealike rasp of my breathing. The bedroom window was dark, and it took me a minute to realize I was in my own apartment. After Lieutenant Gardner had left, I'd driven Grandpa by Keely's to get his overnight kit—though he'd still left those presents at her house—then cruised here. If the police were cutting us slack, then there was no reason not to stay at my place, and if Cooper made a move, I'd be ready.

Often during a restless night I'd go for a run, but my knee was too stiff. My breathing slowed. I clicked on the light and tried reading. However, my powers of concentration wouldn't have lit a three-watt bulb. Over and over in my head I remembered C.J. muttering, "Damn!" after I told him about the burial. *Damn!* And he sent us home, saying we'd regroup in the morning. *Damn!* A sharp whisper. *Damn!* A bitter sigh of *What the hell do we do now?*

I closed the book and drew out a notepad and a pen. Normally, I'd play with a line or metaphor or tinker with a piece in progress, but phrases didn't come to me tonight, equations did.

$$\text{One dead body} = X \text{ (Walter Pierce)}$$
$$\text{Walter Pierce} + \text{Christine Cooper} = \text{embezzled \$}$$
$$\text{Embezzled \$} = Y \text{ (Missing)}$$
$$\text{Grandpa} - \text{Walter} = \text{Albright Cooper}$$
$$\underline{+ \text{Walter} + \text{Walter}}$$
$$\text{Grandpa} = \text{Albright Cooper} + \text{Walter}$$
$$\text{Christine Cooper} + \text{Grandpa} = \$ \text{ (She hopes)}$$
$$\text{Albright Cooper} + \text{Christine Cooper} = - \text{Grandpa}$$
$$\text{Albright Cooper} > \text{Buster Ledbetter} > \text{Grandpa}$$
$$\text{Grandpa} - \text{Buster Ledbetter} = \text{Mine } Or$$
$$\text{Albright Cooper} + \text{Ledbetter} = \text{Mine} - \text{Grandpa}$$
$$\text{Edgar Bryant} = Z$$

I rested my pen, examined the page. Looked good, I thought, but there wasn't much rhyme or reason. Guessed that was why I was a chef and poet and not programming computers for Compaq. The only conclusions I came to concerning my scratching were that I had three factors. X equaled the dead body that, according to official record, had gone down as Walter. Y equaled the missing money. And Z equaled Edgar Bryant because, lost on a mysterious Hawaiian vacation, no one knew how—or if—he fit into the big scheme.

And I couldn't forget Jerry's house. If the thugs were in Houston to find Christine, then why were they harassing Grandpa and tearing apart houses?

I tossed the notebook and pen down, folded my arms behind my head. Given Albright Cooper's mentality, Rats and Fats may easily have been ordered to shake down Grandpa on principle. If he thought Grandpa was out to take his wife, why he'd—

Cooper would kill him, I thought, and propped myself up on my elbows. I didn't care what Albright said. Perhaps one warning—like a ramshackle house—then he'd get serious.

But what did the thugs say at the Galleria? *Where is it?* Where was what? I tugged off the covers and put my robe on. The floor was chilly against my bare feet, and I realized the wind had shifted down from the north and a cool front had blown through. As quickly as that, the weather had changed—from sweating to shivering. It was a wonder half the city didn't have a permanent case of pneumonia.

I turned the living-room light on and threw myself into the chair by the couch where Grandpa was sleeping. His eyes shot open and slowly he turned his head to face me.

"What the devil are you doing, Neil?"

"I can't sleep."

"I was doing right fine, myself."

"What did those boneheads want from you at the Galleria?" I asked.

"Do we have to go through this again? And at this hour?"

"There's either something you're not telling me or something you've overlooked."

"I reckon by now you've heard everything." The old man pulled the covers to his neck and turned his back to me. "Did you tell McDaniels that Christine was at the Renaissance Hotel?"

"Yes."

"What's he going to do about it?"

"What is there to do about it?"

"Oh, he's useless."

I wasn't going to argue with Grandpa over C.J.'s abilities. "They wanted more than Christine and you," I thought aloud.

"I told you—the deed or the will."

"Nothing else?"

"Good night, Neil."

I sighed and stood. "By the way, how could Walter withdraw that money without your signature, too?"

"It was our daily-operations account. Often we were in two different parts of the state, or country, and getting the other's approval was a pain in the ass. So we changed the access to the account years ago then kind of forgot about it."

"With that much money?"

"I'd cashed some certificates of deposit. I was going to pick up some heavy machinery cheap and resell it. My fool mistake was not to think Walter could get into the dough, first."

"How do you know Walter had his hand in the cookie jar, not Bryant?"

Grandpa reluctantly faced me. " 'Cause Walt needed the cash more. And I *wasn't* certain until I talked to the bank manager."

"How reliable is he?"

"You're going to extremes again, Neil."

He was probably right. I went into the kitchen and fixed a glass of ice water. "My gut reaction says Cooper killed

Walter, is trying to pin the rap on you, and sent the thugs to Houston to retrieve his wife—and you for trial. I also wouldn't be at all surprised if Walt's nephew took money for his testimony. The only thing that bugs me is that I don't know what else the muscle heads were looking for."

"Brilliant theory, Watson," Grandpa grumbled.

"Then you agree?"

"Will it shut you up?"

"That's no reason—"

"Then I agree."

"All right, I'll let you get back to sleep."

Grandpa snuggled down. "Guess there is one more thing I should tell you," he said.

"Pray tell." I steadied myself as the dream washed back over me. *I killed Walter.*

"Christine was lying."

"About what?"

"She has access to money."

I almost dropped the water glass. "How do you figure?"

"She's waiting until the situation gets so bad I have to join her."

"You were ready to send her to jail this afternoon."

"I said that to irritate her, let her know you just can't steal a man's money. But, I tell you, Christine wouldn't have left alone, like she'd said. The woman can't do anything by herself."

"You're not giving her much credit."

"She needs a man."

I saw no sense arguing with his old-style values.

"Christine wants someone to protect her from Albright," he added. "But staying at the Renaissance—"

"I wondered about that, too. Might she not have money of her own, though?"

"Albright doesn't give her a long chain. No, Neil, she has access to money, and she's biding her time."

"If she's waiting for you to come to your senses," I added on my way out, "then she'd better take a suite by the month."

"What's it going to take for you to get out of the holiday blues?" he growled.

"You to get out of your holiday mess—"

"What else?"

"A damn snowstorm in Houston."

"That's the problem with you, Neil, you expect too much out of life instead of enjoying what's already on your plate."

"Can't help it if I favor my grandfather—I want it all."

I shut myself in my room, and shut out everything from my mind except Christine. Biding her time at the Renaissance, I thought. Bet she wouldn't wake up with a welt on her head and facing a pit bull named Nixon there. Then I caught myself. No, she was in worse shape. Amid the room service, cut crystal, and polished silver, Christine was liable to awaken with a broken arm and staring through a black eye into the demonic expression of her power-monger husband.

And it didn't sound like Grandpa would be there to protect her.

Two Days Before Christmas

24

The smell of bacon lured me from my lair. I hadn't even known I had any bacon left in my refrigerator. The apartment temperature was brisk, and I wrapped myself in a red flannel robe Mom had sent me that'd belonged to Dad. After strapping on my glasses, I hobbled into the other room. Damn knee had stiffened good once I'd finally fallen deeply asleep.

Grandpa was at the stove again, working his wonders. "Coffee?"

"Please."

He poured, handed me a mug, then flipped the bacon.

"You go to the store?" I asked.

"Took a long walk after my dream."

"Dream?" Hoped it was better than mine.

"Hawk visited me last night."

"Who?"

"The hawk. Messenger guide, according to the Native Americans."

"Oh?"

"Showed me the answer to all this centers on Christine." He placed the strips of bacon on a plate covered with a paper towel. I sat at the kitchen table.

"I'm giving you the lay version of the dream," he added.

I nodded.

"My fourth wife, Victoria, was a Ute scholar. She left me to become a shaman among her people."

189

"I thought she was an environmentalist and left you because of your mining."

"That's what I told everyone. Victoria didn't like mining," he said, and turned the stove off. "And I accused her of being a tree hugger. I didn't know, then. She has her feet on the ground much firmer than any tree hugger I ever met. We're still friends."

I pinched myself. Was I still dreaming?

He opened the oven and took out a stack of pancakes. "Want some?"

"Hell, yes, I want some. But once my knee gets better, I'm going to have to run ten miles a day to work your trip off."

"Still hurting?" he asked, and pulled two plates down. "Guess I shouldn't be so hard on you trying to protect me. You ended up hurt, and you were right."

"Haven't been much else help to you." I accepted a plate. "Tell me about Hawk."

"I did," he said, and sat with a full plate of flapjacks and bacon. He pulled out the bottle of real Vermont maple syrup, since I was out of the cheap stuff, and doused everything.

"Mom sent me that bottle," I said.

"Nice. I didn't see the good stuff when we had Finnish pancakes. Want some?"

"Yes." I was saving the syrup for a special occasion, and I guessed Grandpa had decided this was it.

"We have to keep an eye on Christine," he said.

"Why? Protect her from her husband?"

"We'll know why when the time comes."

I wanted to whistle *The Twilight Zone* theme, but I supposed deep down his plan was as good as any. And if he had any connections with hawks or doves or spirits of Christmas past, for that matter, then who was I to question?

"But we need to get another car," he said in between mouthfuls.

"What's wrong with the Bug?" The pancakes were light, fluffy, and delicious.

"Besides everyone on the Gulf Coast knowing it, what's not?"

"You want to take a cab?"

"No, we'll rent a car."

"I don't have any money, Grandpa."

"I know. I do."

"But you told Christine—"

"Oh, Neil, you really are a fledgling. You think I'm going to give her my financial statement?"

"But Walter stole all that cash from you."

"I have a lot of money, Neil. Many times over what he pilfered." The old man cleaned his plate, rubbed his belly.

"I didn't know that."

"I don't broadcast it because then every nut comes out of the woodwork asking for money."

"I've never—"

"Don't get your dander up, son. Neither you nor your mother has, though I send the old gal money every once in a while. Don't want her to lose that place your father worked so hard for."

"You send Mom money?" I set down my fork, dumbfounded.

He winked. "That's our secret. I mail a check every quarter and say it's from your father's share of the mine."

"But the mine's not in operation."

"It's the only way I could think she'd take money from me, and if you say anything, I'll switch your ass."

"Now don't you get *your* dander up. I won't say anything. You're brilliant, Grandpa," I said in admiration. "But you do this to me, always throw me off balance."

"Years of practice."

"I almost buy the hawk thing, now."

A twinkle sparkled from his eye. "I believe I'm finally getting through to you."

"Well, don't let it go to your head," I said and stood. "We have work to do."

* * *

At Zeke's Superior Used Cars and Rentals, Grandpa went directly to a red Mustang. I couldn't believe it. Just like C.J. And he'd love the comparison.

"How about this baby, Neil?"

"Yeah, she's got balls," Zeke started to say. "The perfect sled for a New Age Santa. Stick shift, eight cylinders—"

Before he got into what was under the hood, I cut him off. "Not bad for a McDaniels wannabe."

"What?" Grandpa said.

"We need something more discreet."

"I'm paying for it."

"Fine, you pay, and I'll take my Bug. Discreet means something not red and not sporty. We're not going to Daytona Beach."

Zeke's long blond hair fell over his eyes as he jerked his head from Grandpa to me. "Daytona Beach? Hey, can I come along?"

"A sedan," I said.

Grandpa's shoulders fell.

"He your kid?" Zeke asked.

"Grandkid."

"And he wants a *sedan*?" Zeke leaned way up to the old man. "Dump him. I'm usually telling this to the kids."

"He's right," Grandpa told Zeke. "A sedan."

"Brown or green," I added.

They both cringed.

Grandpa nodded.

"Well, I've got this four-door number," Zeke announced, and showed us a Ford. "Only driven by a little old computer geek on Sundays."

Two cars down I noticed a Camry, blue. "How about that one?" I asked.

"I like it," approved Grandpa.

"That's for sale only," Zeke told us.

Grandpa pulled out a wad of bills.

"What the hell are you doing?" I asked.

"Five hundred bucks for three days," Grandpa offered.

"You've got it, Santa," Zeke replied.

"And we leave the VW here," Grandpa added.

"Want me to try to sell it?"

"No!" I barked.

"You sure you want him along with you?" Zeke muttered to Grandpa.

"Just do the paperwork," the old man answered.

In half an hour we were out of there.

The Renaissance was an upscale hotel across from the Summit, home of the Houston Rockets. Had the basketball team been playing in town, we might've bumped into players of the opposing team, as they often stayed there. That is, if we were inside enjoying the warmth. Instead we sat outside in the car beneath a sky the color of an army blanket. It was a good bet we were under a severe storm watch. Just what we needed. Parking was limited, so we had pulled into a small driveway nearby. A stern wind shoved against the car at irregular intervals, and I noticed the doorman and valet parkers clutch their hats and dip their heads each time they left the shelter of the building.

"See, the Renaissance has plenty of Christmas decorations," Grandpa observed.

"Plenty," I mimicked.

"Even old Zeke had lights up."

" 'Have a four-on-the-floor Christmas,' " I quoted, "is not my idea of a season's greeting. Sounds more like a holiday special at a brothel."

Grandpa laughed. He sipped a steaming cup of coffee we'd just picked up at McDonald's. "You shouldn't shut out Christmas because your dad's no longer with us."

"It's not just Dad. I lost my best friend about this time a year ago."

"Sorry. I forgot."

"And the season's become nothing but one long stretch of work—a chef's nightmare," I added.

"Get another job."

"May have to after this. 'Where were you, Neil?' asks

Claudia. 'Sitting outside the Renaissance admiring the lights,' I respond. Lovely."

"I'll help you later," Grandpa assured me. "Between the two of us, we can boil, bake, or burn anything."

"Double lovely."

"When I say get another job, though, I mean a whole different profession," Grandpa followed up. "If you're tired of food—"

"But I like—" I cut myself off.

"You like your job. I thought as much." He adjusted his 49ers cap, rubbed at the condensation filming the window. I ran the car a few minutes to clear the air.

"Just because my job's all right doesn't mean I can't burn out on it."

"Very true," he replied. "So after we clear my good name, why don't you come up to the mountains with me? Maybe we'll do some hunting, a little ice fishing if it doesn't get too cold. And if it does, we'll go down to Cripple Creek to gamble."

"Might take you up on that. Especially if Keely decides to take the job in California."

"Don't be surprised if she does. Be a good chance for her to put some distance from here and think things through."

I looked at Grandpa. He was slouched down, sipping his coffee. "You two have talked about it?"

"Yes."

"And?"

"And what I said."

"You're not going to tell me any more?" I asked.

"Nope."

"You're not cheering me up."

"Sorry. Cheering you up could be an all-day effort, and like you said, we have work to do. Look." He pointed a gloved finger at the entrance to the hotel.

"Where's she going?" I wondered. "No luggage with her."

"Christine's comings and goings seem rather arbitrary,"

Grandpa said. "Albright will eventually bump into her out of dumb luck."

"Is that what we're waiting for? Him to find her?"

Grandpa shrugged.

"Should we follow?" I asked as Christine climbed into a cab.

"Can't hurt," Grandpa said.

I started the car.

"Wait!" he ordered, and grabbed my wrist as I was to shift into drive.

"She's getting away," I protested, and watched the cab roll down the street.

Grandpa's eyes were on the hotel, though, and suddenly he jumped out of the car and jogged toward the entrance.

"Jesus Christ!" I snapped, turned off the engine, and followed.

A honking car chased me back to the curb before I was able to half-skip and hobble across the road. The old man had disappeared into the hotel. A group of businessmen came out. Then a family. By the time I reached the entrance, Grandpa was back outside, peering at cabs as they pulled away.

"What the hell are you doing?" I asked.

"I saw him. I swear I saw him."

"Who?" I caught my breath.

"A tall, lanky man wearing a tweed suit."

"Meaning?"

"Edgar Bryant, Neil. I swear I saw the man, and he went into the hotel."

"Your accountant?"

"He wasn't checking in."

"Perhaps he already had."

"He's not registered. At least not under his name. No one could tell me if they'd seen a man fitting that description. He probably saw me coming and did an about-face."

I thought hard about the businessmen and family that had exited as Grandpa had entered, but their images were nondescript. I hadn't paid enough attention.

"From where we were, how can you be sure the man was Bryant?" I asked.

Grandpa looked at me, shook his head. "I swore it was, and not just from the clothes. There was something familiar."

"What would he be doing here? Besides obviously looking for Christine—why looking for Christine?"

"Damn it, Neil, I don't know."

"So let's go back to the car and wait," I said. "Let Christine do her thing." Not that we could catch her now, anyway.

"I probably spooked him." He teetered between facing the doors, me, the parking lot, and the cabs.

The valet parkers, doorman, and customers coming and going were all eyeing Grandpa. "I think you're spooking everyone," I joked.

"He won't be back."

"You know, I have a better idea," I said, and patted Grandpa on the back. "Let's go inside this swanky sleep-over and have a drink. Do a little people gazing. What do you think?"

"All we'll get is an overpriced bar bill."

"Hell, you said you had a lot of money." I wasn't sure what he saw, or if he saw anything. Or rather, if he'd manifested it in his mind. The big guy was under a lot of stress. I figured we'd hang around, see if Christine returned or anyone else showed up. Hopefully, we wouldn't be too tanked up for me to work later. But on the off chance Grandpa had spied Edgar Bryant—

We went inside, out of the cold.

25

All I hoped was to calm Grandpa down and warm up. I'd felt a turn of weather in Houston a thousand times but rarely as distinct as this. From a balmy afternoon to a Yankee cold spell. I hadn't anticipated it. Nor, after about an hour, had I anticipated the return of the tweed man in the lobby. I saw him before he saw us. And also before Grandpa spotted him. The old man's back was to the entrance of the hotel.

A man dressed in a black tuxedo with tails sat at the piano in the lobby bar and began to play a medley of Christmas carols. He ignored a request for "Grandma Got Run Over by a Reindeer."

"So what does Edgar Bryant look like?" I asked.

Grandpa was cupping his third hot toddy with both hands.

"Besides the tweed, he has a round face and pug nose. Hazel eyes. Gray hair that curls around a prominent bald spot. You know, like a halo that some devil's shoved over the crown of his head."

"Uh-huh," I encouraged, catching glimpses of the tweed man. He was wearing a hat, so I couldn't check the hair or bald spot. And his collar was turned up on his face. He had also donned a pair of sunglasses, making his features impossible to see from here.

"He big?" I asked.

"I told you tall and lanky."

Possible, I thought. This guy looked six-foot-something,

and I didn't sense much bulk beneath the overcoat. "You sure he spotted you earlier?"

"I thought so."

"What if he was too busy looking for someone else, and didn't?"

"Seems unlikely."

"Christine was leaving. What if he was trying to catch up to her?"

Grandpa perked up. "You see him."

"Sit still," I directed. "You're not exactly inconspicuous." He was out of view now, going toward the front desk.

"And if he takes off, you don't exactly have the get-up-and-go to outrun him."

"I won't let him take off on me."

Grandpa pulled the bill of his cap down lower. He'd tucked his hair under the collar of his down vest, but he still looked as if he should be sitting at a diner off I-10 and not in the lobby bar at the Renaissance. "You distract him, I'll come up from behind," he suggested.

"Just be cool. We're not even sure the man is Bryant."

"How'd someone so naive fall from my lineage?"

I stood.

"Don't let him get away," Grandpa said.

I took a circuitous route, walking through the lobby bar and out by the elevator banks. The tweed man finished talking to a desk clerk, then tried a lobby phone. After no apparent answer on the other end, he hung up. He then unfolded a morning newspaper and was about to sit on a cushioned bench when I approached him.

"Mr. Bryant?" I asked.

He hesitated. "You talking to me?" His voice was low and raspy.

"Edgar Bryant?"

"You got the wrong guy, kid."

"I'm Stephen Marshall's grandson, Neil."

"Nice." He folded the newspaper and tucked it under his arm. "But my name's not Bryant."

I couldn't read his eyes beneath the mirrored glasses. "That voice," I commented.

"Goodbye, kid."

"You mind me asking your name?"

"Are you a cop?"

"N-no," I stammered.

"Then beat it before I get a cop."

Tough talk for an accountant, I thought. Too tough. I raised my hands and backed off a couple of steps.

"Sorry, I thought you were someone I should know." I glanced toward Grandpa, but he'd left his seat.

As the stranger turned I caught sight of Grandpa over his tweed shoulder and across the room.

Grandpa stopped, lowered his head, and squinted. The tweed man's shoulders stiffened. And then a hand clutched Grandpa's arm from behind.

"Stephen," I heard Christine say, "what are you doing here?"

The tweed man took the opportunity to duck to the escalator to his left. Instinctively, I followed.

"Do you know him?" Grandpa was asking Christine.

"Who? Your grandson?"

"No, him."

They were above us, looking down.

"I have no earthly idea."

Banks of mirrors and reflective metal lined the escalator and the balcony we passed underneath. The tweed man would have to be blind not to know I was behind him. When he reached the bottom, he walked off briskly. I kept up with him, trying to decide what to do, hoping he didn't have a gun or wasn't a fresh face Albright Cooper brought on the scene.

The tweed man shoved open a set of downstairs doors and entered the shopping pavilion beneath Greenway Plaza. The cavernous area was bustling with mostly office workers buying last-minute gifts, or getting together for lunch in the rotunda. Decorations sparkled and music echoed raucously. A Salvation Army Santa rang his bell on one of the corners.

At first, staying with the tweed man wasn't difficult. I kept with the flow of the crowd, and watched for the tweed, which stood out like fox fur catching the gentle blue light of the moon. Then he tried doubling back and I almost missed him except for the newspaper tucked under his arm. He ducked inside a pipe-and-tobacco store. I hovered nearby. He slipped out, having discarded the newspaper. Then a rush of ladies emerged from a bath-and-perfume shop, cutting me off from him. As politely as possible—meaning I didn't throw any elbows—I circumvented them. When finally I hobbled down the hall I'd thought he turned in to, I found myself pushing through a door and entering the parking garage near the theatres. The garage, too, was packed, and I circled the lot a couple of times, but it was no use. I'd lost him.

On my way back to the hotel—while muttering over how I was going to explain to Grandpa I'd let the man get away—I took a quick detour by the pipe shop. There was only one salesman inside, and I described the tweed man and asked if he'd purchased anything, feigning that I was looking for a gift for him. The clerk confirmed that I'd been following the right man and told me he'd bought some Turkish cigarettes. I thanked him and returned to face Grandpa.

Christine and Grandpa were sitting at the table in the lobby bar we'd occupied. I caught Grandpa's eye after stepping off the escalator, and for a second I had the urge to pull a one-eighty and take the stairs back down.

"Where is he?" Grandpa demanded.

"What was I supposed to do, hog-tie the man, sling him over my shoulder, and cart him up here?"

"If necessary."

"Who is he?" Christine asked.

"I don't know," I replied. "He denied being Edgar Bryant."

"Because he's got my money," Grandpa grumbled.

"So you're sure that was Bryant?" I pulled up a chair, watched for Christine's reactions. Her face was deadpan.

"I wasn't close enough," Grandpa replied, "but he recognized me, that I could tell. And there was a familiarity about him in spite of the hat and dark glasses."

"But why the hat and glasses?" I asked.

"So he wouldn't be easily recognized," the old man retorted like I'd asked the king of simpleton questions.

"Then why not change from his trademark tweed suit?"

Grandpa started to say something, then stopped. He turned to Christine. "He was here to meet you, wasn't he?"

"He didn't make an appointment."

"Probably fulfilling Walter's last request and supplying you with my money."

"Why would Bryant do that after Walter fired him?" I asked.

"Maybe the firing was for my benefit. After all, no one's been able to track the man down."

"You're saying they were in it together?" I asked.

"Could be."

"You said yesterday he must have uncovered Walt's thievery."

"And I also wondered why Ed didn't tell me. Conspiracy."

"With the access Bryant had to your finances, he sure didn't steal much," I commented.

"A hundred grand isn't much?"

"Not divided three ways."

"Hey, wait a minute," Christine spoke up. "I haven't seen a dime of that money."

"Much to your chagrin," Grandpa said.

"I don't have to take this." She stood.

Grandpa grabbed her by the wrist and yanked her back into the seat. "You do have to take this, and you do have to tell me what you've been holding back, or I'll take you to Albright myself."

"Then you'll be taking yourself to a murder charge!"

I held my head in my hands. "Speak a little louder, you two, they didn't hear you at the front desk."

"I don't care!" She pulled herself free, then leaned within inches of Grandpa's face. "I came here because I want to get away from my asshole husband," she said low and slowly, emphasizing each word as if she were shooting them from a gun. "I thought Walter was going to free me. Albright killed him. Now I want you to free me, Stephen! That's what I know!" She straightened.

Grandpa sat solemnly.

"And I'm running out of time," she added, not pleadingly, but there was a touch of desperation in her voice.

Grandpa said nothing.

"Oooh," Christine grumbled, and walked away.

Oooh for two, I thought.

"We might as well leave," said Grandpa.

"Christine will bolt again."

"Not right away. She'll want to know who the man in tweed was, first. And he only knows to reach her here."

"He found her before. He could find her again."

"Like the lady said, she's running out of time."

"What if he's working with Albright?" I asked.

"He wouldn't have run from you."

Or he'd have plugged me in the parking garage, I thought.

Grandpa rose and located the waiter to clear the bill.

I drummed my fingers against the table. Time wasn't running out for only Christine. Then it dawned on me we'd been focusing on the wrong person. And a plan began to form.

A plan even C. J. McDaniels might agree to.

26

I drove back to the sanctuary of The Kitchen feeling weary and beaten. The energy that had started the day was at a lull. Even Grandpa had that pounding-his-head-against-a-wall look.

"I'll call C.J." I tried to comfort the old man. "I'll work and you relax."

"Said I'd help."

"So you did. Up to you." I made sure to lock the Camry's doors. Not that Perry had ever had trouble with his Lexus in this neighborhood—a neighborhood that fringed on crack houses and entertained ladies of the evening—but then I wasn't used to worrying about a nice car parked out front. A very nice car. I was going to hate going back to the Bug.

"The damn vehicle will be fine," Grandpa grumbled. "Stop fussing."

"I'm not fussing."

"Christ, you'd do well to worry about me as much."

I almost spat. "I've done nothing but worry about you since you showed up breathless a few days ago."

"Hell if I've known that."

"I didn't want to worry you any more than you already were. And you've known it. Damn, I don't know what else to do for you."

"Whatever it is, be careful. You might hurt yourself again."

"Shut up." I limped past him, trying my best to walk normally. Which wasn't a very good effort.

I swung open the door.

Trisha's eyes widened. She was working on the last of the gingerbread houses. "You're having a bad Karma day," she said, and pulled off her ear phones.

I pictured my hands around her throat. Instead I picked up the phone and punched in C.J.'s number.

"Boy, a real bad Karma day," I heard Trisha tell Grandpa.

"Is that like a bad hair day?" he asked her.

"Worse."

"He's always been like this," Grandpa said as if I wasn't present. "Even as a baby he had a nasty temper once a burr got in his diaper."

Thankfully, Linda answered the phone. I informed her about our latest encounter.

"But I have an idea," I said. "I need y'all's help."

"Don't we already know that?"

"Yes, dear, everyone seems to. Would you have C.J. call?"

"Calm down, Neil. I'll leave word, and then mosey on over to the Renaissance and keep an eye on things for the hell of it. Might even have lunch there. Your granddaddy's treat."

"He's got the big bucks. Go for it, thanks." With great care, I gently replaced the receiver.

I took a deep breath, looked at Trisha. "I feel better now."

"Wow, you can turn it on and off."

"As the spirit inhabits me."

"No, guides you, Neil," Trisha corrected.

"I get inhabited," I stated, and went to check on the progress of the work orders.

"Makes him sound like a domicile," Grandpa quipped. "And sometimes I think it's the Bates Motel."

"Mattie!" I called. "Don't we need sourdough toasts for the Gilcrest party?"

She edged up to me. "They're done."

"We need more," I said, then hissed under my breath, "Won't you show Grandpa how to do them?"

Mattie frowned at me.

"Please? He wants to help," I pleaded.

"I see," she said, and scurried off. "Why, no, Neil, the toasts haven't been prepared yet," she added rather loudly. "Mr. Marshall—"

"Stephen," he corrected as he put on an apron.

"Right, Stephen." She placed a cutting board on one of the stainless-steel tables and pulled a round cutter out alongside a half-dozen loaves of sourdough French bread. "First we have to melt butter," I heard her explain. "Now, this isn't the most exciting project, but then a lot of prep work isn't."

"Don't worry about me, young lady. I'm here to help. By the way, have you done anything about getting that little boy of yours a puppy?"

I stepped into the office before hearing the answer. Robbie was working on a couple of bills at the computer.

"Where's Perry?" I asked.

"Talking to Mrs. Gilcrest with Claudia."

"That's my party."

"You weren't here."

I sighed. "Well, if Claudia wants the job—"

"I don't think she does." He hit a series of keys on the computer then got up to fetch the bill that was being etched out on the printer. "She's tired. But you'll have to be diplomatic if you want it back."

I shrugged. "All I want for Christmas is my grandpa cleared."

Robbie lowered the bill he was examining. "About time you told me what was going on."

And so, in my convoluted way, I did.

By the time I was finished, he was sitting in one of the rolling chairs, shaking his head, the bill having fallen to the floor.

"That explains the cosmetic surgery someone did on the side of your head. Is that why you're limping, too?"

"I don't want to go there."

"Where are you going from here?"

How about Canada? I thought. If Christine Cooper was flying south, I was going to head as far north as possible. But I said, "I'm going to talk to C.J. He should be calling this afternoon."

"Why aren't the police helping you?" Robbie asked.

"Gardner is. He's buying us time. Best he can do seeing as his hands are tied."

"Lord, sounds like you're walking in front of a bull wearing red britches."

"Or a Santa Claus suit."

"You're talking cryptically again."

"If I have my way we're going to give Albright Cooper the perfect Christmas present."

"I sure hope you live long enough to make a New Year's resolution," he muttered.

"Is that a hint?"

"It's a clubbing."

"Fine." I raised a hand. "I swear never again to help a relative who comes to me in trouble."

"You're missing the point."

"Am I?"

Robbie clicked over to a new listing on the computer and printed out another bill. "You don't have to carry everyone's burden. There are enough martyrs in the world."

"But not enough who know how to do things correctly."

"You're impossible. Stubborn and impossible."

"It's the stock I come from," I replied, unable to keep the grin from my face.

The front door opened and closed. "Where is everybody?" a woman's voice asked. Definitely not Christine, since her words boomed across The Kitchen.

"Neil and Robbie are in the office," Trisha responded.

"What a delightful house," the woman said. "Is that mine?"

"Yes, Mrs. Stein."

"Wonderful!"

"What are we doing for Mrs. Stein?" I asked, and poked my head out.

"New Year's Eve party," replied Robbie.

"And look," said Mrs. Stein, "Santa's a little helper today." She wandered back to where Grandpa was dutifully cutting out toast rounds and buttering them.

"A pleasure, ma'am," said Grandpa.

"Oh, call me Rhoda."

"Stephen Marshall, Neil's grandfather."

"Family comes to town and gets put to work, huh?" Her large dark eyes sparkled. She was an elegant, stately woman, tall and wearing a slinky black suit.

"Neil's a terrible slave driver," said Grandpa.

"Where is old Simon Legree?"

"Good to see you, Mrs. Stein." I approached her from the office. I noticed that someone had switched stations on the stereo. Instead of classical, the music was now country and western. I glanced at Grandpa.

"Putting your own grandfather to work—shame on you!" Mrs. Stein scolded.

"And without pay," the old man piped in.

"Scrooge!" A smile as broad as a crescent moon dominated her face, and she playfully backhanded me in the gut. "You know, Mother and I are taking a trip."

"Where to?" I began to lead her back to the office, but she paused so Grandpa could hear her story, too.

"Egypt. I've always wanted to travel the Nile. And Emma's going to join us from Greece. Say, you married yet, Neil? Emma's awfully smart and rich."

"And beautiful like her mother?" I asked.

"Ah, you're sweet."

"Mrs. Stein, I'd say you are indeed a beauty," Grandpa put in.

"Max'd better watch out for you—" Mrs. Stein joked.

"And you'd better watch out for my grandpa," I warned.

Her laugh was rich as she continued, "But you know what Max says about the trip? While I was making plans he watched the Michael Douglas movie *Jewel of the Nile*. Ever since then he says I'm going to be the Jew of the Nile. Says the river will never be the same once I've been on it. What do you think he means by that? I think he's jealous because he's not going."

"I know I'd be;" said Grandpa.

I returned Rhoda Stein's smile. "Would you like to go over your menu?" I asked.

"The little guy's not here?" she responded.

Perry would cringe at the reference, I thought. "He's at another job site."

"How dare he right before Christmas?"

"I'd be glad to help you," I offered.

"No, you people have real work to do. I just stopped by to harass the boss. We all know who makes up the backbone of this operation, and it isn't Mr. Bow Tie and Grins."

"Oh, God, don't let Perry hear you say that."

"Why not, it's true," she said with a grin. "No, just kidding. I wouldn't whisper a word of it."

I knew she picked on Perry because it was so easy to get his dander up, and he'd never complain about the way she treated him—at least not to her face. Max and Rhoda Stein had more money than Israel.

"Well, I'll be off," Rhoda announced, breezing out as energetically as she'd breezed in. "Tell Perry I'll talk to him after Christmas. Nice to meet you, Stephen."

"Likewise, Rhoda."

"Happy holidays, everyone!" And she was gone, the air crackling in her wake.

"What a delightful woman," Grandpa observed.

"A handful," I added.

"Now, there's the spirit of the season," he said. "The spirit we should all embrace."

Of Christmas? I thought. *She's Jewish.* But Grandpa only eyed my confusion, grinned, and continued cutting out toasts. The phone buzzed, and Robbie paged me. I took the call in the office. Robbie slipped into the other room.

"Why the hell did you approach the man?" C.J. barked before I'd finished saying hello.

"Grandpa was certain he was Edgar Bryant, and I saw no reason he'd run from us," I explained.

"Your granddaddy hasn't seen the man since his partner fired him and you saw no reason he'd run from you? Just when I think you've earned some smarts, you pull a bone-headed stunt like that. And to think the old man went along with it."

"He was going to approach the man himself. Grandpa's getting desperate," I said quickly. And so was I.

"You may well have scared off his only clear chance of beating the charges," he barked.

"The man will be back."

"Even if you're right, nabbing him won't be so easy the next time. He'll change clothes, change the way he'll meet Christine. He won't walk right into our welcoming arms." I heard him light a cigarette.

"So we tail Christine."

"And that's been an easy chore," he muttered.

"Linda's over—"

"I know where Linda is. She left a note indicating you have an idea. Do I want to hear your plan?"

"You're probably going to think part of it's crazy."

"I'll probably think it's all crazy."

"To begin with, let's slip Christine's whereabouts to Cooper."

"You really don't like that woman," he said bluntly.

"No, I'm trying to mix things up, keep watch at the hotel, perhaps send Grandpa into the fray and confront Albright. We'll be there to protect Christine."

"Oh, we will."

"I will."

"Then be ready. Cooper's no doubt fuming over that tussle you and he had. I'm quite sure he'll have a shot or two awaiting you," C.J. cautioned me.

"You have a better idea?"

"Sadly, no. I suppose throwing a monkey wrench in the works is better than nothing."

"Well, then, you want me to call Cooper's office and leave the message or do you want to?"

"You still have his number?"

"No."

"I do." He dictated it to me. "This is your idea, your pleasure. One thing, though. Cooper's a dangerous man. Don't put yourself in a stupid position."

"Spoken eloquently."

"I use simple words so maybe they'll sink into your thick head."

Thick head. Another reference to stubborn. Was this the Neil Marshall tag of the season?

"Hell, I'm wasting my breath," C.J. muttered, and hung up.

Guess so, I thought, and switched over to another line. I then tapped in Albright Cooper's office number. There was a slight tremble to my finger as I did. And as his machine picked up, a wave of self-doubt left me momentarily speechless before I was able to drone half a dozen words.

"Your wife's at the Renaissance Hotel."

I slammed the receiver down. A layer of sweat covered my forehead. Now, how was I going to tell Grandpa? I wouldn't. I'd say I learned through C.J. that Cooper knew where his wife was. That'd put the old man on the alert, and get us moving.

I wondered when Cooper would get the message. His wife was now dangling out there like tiger bait.

God, I prayed I'd done the right thing.

27

Perry returned and The Kitchen hummed with the efficiency of Santa's workshop. Not that Perry's appearance actually created the efficiency. It was more that the eccentricities of the day had exhausted everyone—or at least exhausted me—and a return to some form of normality was the medicine needed.

"Where's Claudia?" I asked.

"She went home to rest up for tomorrow's dinner party."

"I see."

"I want you both to work the job," Perry said. "She knows the layout. You have the energy to make it work."

"All right," I responded, though I had my doubts I'd be readily available. I kept my reservations to myself.

I completed the jalapeño-corn pudding and helped Mattie put the finishing touches on a cocktail party she, Robbie, and Candace were working this evening. She deep-fried strips of lemon-chili-pepper chicken while I whipped up the basil-garlic dressing that would accompany it as a dip. Grandpa had graduated to prepping the baked Brie. I'd shown him how to slice the wheel of cheese into two thin circles as if it were a cake to be filled. Next I explained he needed to spread the bottom portion with jalapeño jelly and sandwich the top back on. The final, and most important step, was to wrap the whole wheel in phyllo dough, brushing each delicate layer with butter in order to seal it and prevent the dough from drying out. Later the wheel would be baked in a hot oven to melt the cheese, which would be held intact by the golden phyllo dough.

Perry eyed Grandpa carefully as he worked on the second of four wheels. "You ever have one of these things melt everywhere?" the old man asked.

"Absolutely not," said Perry.

"Guess the pressure's on me. 'Course, I view cooking as a hobby," he continued. "Keeps my hands occupied and gives me time to think. And if what I'm fixing's not perfect, what the hell, it'll still taste good. It's not like I'm performing a heart transplant, where an *oops* really means something."

"Presentation is very important," Perry told him.

"From where you're standing, I guess it is. You charge a lot of money for this stuff, and I wouldn't want to be the one to disappoint. So don't you fret, these stuffed cheeses will be perfect, unless you think they're too big," Grandpa said, and shot Perry a sideways glance.

Don't get back on the tenderloin steaks, I thought.

Perry shot me a *When is he going to leave?* look, then marched off into the office.

"Sensitive little fella," Grandpa stated. "You really never had one of these wheels melt apart?"

"Absolutely yes," I told him. "In fact, one time we did a job downtown in Houston House for the youngest daughter of one of the more well-to-do families in town. She and her new husband had rented three units near the top floor of the high-rise and renovated them into a beautiful, spacious apartment. Well, they wanted to show all their young friends the new place, so they had a party. As we'd always catered for her daddy, they used us. To make a long story short, their maid wasn't familiar with our food, and while no one was paying attention she took the phyllo dough off the Brie, thinking it was the wrapping, and put the wheel in the oven. Needless to say, the cheese spread all over the baking pan like a snowman melting in a March thaw.

"We had to run out to the store," I concluded, "and buy a regular block of cheese to fill in the gap. The hostess was irritated with us for not properly instructing her maid.

Bless the servant's heart for trying to help—we just weren't used to such assistance. Usually domestic staff did nothing but act as overseers."

Grandpa chuckled and completed the third wheel. "The pressure's lifted."

"Good. I was so worried." I winked.

Candace bounced in a few minutes later. She greeted Mattie and politely acknowledged Trisha—Candace didn't cotton much to this guiding spirit of Trisha's; all that talk of being *moved* to work, the girl had told me, was just a fancy cover-up for laziness. And she knew what kind of spirit encouraged sloth.

"Everything back to normal?" she asked me.

"Now that's kind of a relative question. What's *normal*?"

"You mean your granddaddy's not out of the woods?"

"Have no fear," Grandpa said, and leaned toward Candace. "Neil has a secret plan."

"Yeah, the same way Nixon had a secret plan for ending Vietnam," I said dryly.

Candace looked at me blankly.

"Never mind," I told her.

"I don't find the plan encouraging, either," Grandpa said.

"Why are y'all in here cooking?" Candace asked.

"Part of the plan," replied Grandpa.

"Because the work needs to be done," I offered.

"I hope you know what you're doing." Candace shook her head and began to help Mattie gather what they needed for tonight's job.

I was getting tired of people saying that about me.

C.J. didn't call until after we'd packed Mattie, Candace, and Robbie off for the cocktail party, and Perry was preparing to leave for the day.

"Sure hope the Bries hold together," Grandpa stated loud enough for Perry's benefit.

Perry had one arm in his overcoat and missed slipping the second one in on the first try. A genuine expression of concern washed over his face as he started to say, "What do you—" Then he caught himself.

Grandpa laughed cheerfully.

"You're an evil man, sir." Perry finally found his way to the sleeve for his second arm then buttoned the front of the coat.

"Oh, no, not evil, sir. Don't you also brand me as such."

The phone rang and Perry grabbed the extension in the front workroom as he passed by. He stretched the receiver out toward me. "Sounds like your grandfather's evil twin," he said.

"I heard that," called Grandpa.

"So did I," C.J. grumbled into my ear.

"Gentlemen," Perry said, nodded, and was out the door.

"What's going on?" I asked C.J.

"Linda lost Christine."

"How? Did Cooper show up?"

"According to Linda, Christine got off the elevator around three-thirty and bolted for the front door. Her coat wasn't fastened. She wasn't wearing her hat. Her mannerisms were exaggerated as she hopped into a cab. Linda had paid off one of the valet parkers so she could keep her truck right out front, but she said Christine left so abruptly she never had a chance to catch up. The cab was around the Summit and onto the freeway—she guessed the freeway, at any rate—before Linda saw it again."

"Running scared?" I mused. "And Cooper wasn't at the hotel? Doesn't figure that he'd call and tip her off."

"Unless he's hoping she'll lead him to your grandfather," C.J. pointed out. "Then he and his thugs would have the whole pot—his wife and the old man to drag back for prosecution."

"That's something he'd do," I said. "Play a little cat and mouse."

"And I bet he wouldn't mind another crack at you. Watch yourself. Linda's going to hang at the hotel a while longer to see if Christine returns. I'll be in touch."

We disconnected. I sat on a stool and wiped my forehead with a kitchen towel. Trisha was long gone, but Mrs. Stein's gingerbread house sat on the table as a reminder of the maker's presence. The candy structure was really quite remarkable. Based on the photograph Trisha worked from, it was a two-story facade of the client's house. The frosting was piped on in painstaking detail—there were even curtains on the inside portion of the windows as well as shutters etched around the outside. Peppermints, chocolate kisses, cinnamon drops, licorice, and the like were arranged like notes on a sheet of symphonic music. A candy-cane chimney was attached to the peak of the roof, and little jelly beans were lined around the perimeter like Christmas lights. There was a method to this little gem, unlike some of the tossed-together, candy-cluttered pieces I'd seen elsewhere.

"That young lady's flaky, but she can put together a mean house," Grandpa commented.

"You're right. Trisha outdid herself," I agreed.

"It's craftsmanship. But that's what's nice about this whole business." He opened his arms to the renovated ranch house that was The Kitchen. "You tailor to your clients. Do most everything from scratch. It's culinary craftsmanship, the way things were made a long time ago. Not prefab. Created with quality in mind. Y'all should be proud of yourselves. I like it so much I'm thinking about coming to work for you. Beats a drafty old mine any day."

I forced a smile. "I want to be here when you ask Perry for a job."

"Hell, I wouldn't ask. I'd just show up every day and see how long it took for him to feel guilty and start paying me."

I shook my head.

Grandpa laughed and untied his apron. "What's wrong, son?"

I told him about Christine.

"Could be Albright," he agreed. "And it could be the man you followed."

"Edgar Bryant."

"I know Ed Bryant." He slid a stool up next to me.

Conrad appeared from the back, flicked out the lights on that half of The Kitchen, rolled his apron in a ball, and tossed it into the laundry bag. He muttered goodbye. I gave him a short wave back and he left. Conrad and I hadn't been on the best of terms since he'd tipped off a less-than-reputable private investigator about me while I was trying to help Mattie out of some trouble. He'd done it for a carton of cigarettes, but it wasn't my position to fire him.

"So what do we do?" I asked once we were alone again.

"Your great detective going to find her?" Grandpa asked.

"I imagine so."

"*Imagine?*" he muttered. "You sound like one of those mop heads you used to listen to."

"Still do. And I never did get my bootleg Beatles album back from Susan after the divorce."

"Pity. *Imagine.* Guess that'll have to do, though. We're going to go out and have us a nice dinner."

"A nice dinner?"

"And then a good night's sleep. I have a lot of work to do tomorrow."

"Of course, Santa, it's Christmas Eve tomorrow."

"You're damn right it is, and I'm going to tell you something, Neil." He twisted around on the stool so he faced me. Even sitting, the old man towered. "You know, I've been watching you the last few days, all your griping about Christmas and commercialism, and the work you have to do. Well, what I see from these old eyes is that you're the one caught up in the commercialism of the season."

I started to respond, but he raised a hand.

"Yes, sir, and you're going to listen and let me finish. You see products—food or presents or what-have-you—and not the gifts behind Christmas. Maybe the season's too old-fashioned for you artists today, or maybe I'm too old-fashioned to change. But I do know what you've forgotten is the reason of the season, son—and that's the man who, as the little kid in the story said, made lame beggars walk and blind men see. Christmas is the time for me to refill my spiritual cup for another year. That's how I embrace it. Peace and goodwill. Not empty words. Not words restricted to one religious belief. Why, your Mrs. Jew of the Nile, a most delightful and refreshing lady, has more goodwill in her than most people will come across all year.

"Open yourself up to the spirit of the season, Neil, and see what happens."

My cheeks flushed. Who was he to talk to me like that? Me, the poet whose words were meant to bind flesh to soul? *Spiritual.* I knew spiritual. I hadn't been lectured to in such a way in years. *Spiritual,* from a man who talked to hawks. But his words hit me hard, like sparks from a fire meant to warm your bones after a cold day in the mountains. I couldn't speak.

"You still hungry?" he finally asked.

"I at least need to sustain the body," I managed.

He smiled. "I was thinking steak. Thick, tender, grilled."

"As good as anything."

Grandpa buttoned his vest. I hit the front lights, opened the door, felt the sharp wind that was whipping cold and wet in the dimming day, and put my jacket on, too.

"We could run across Cooper and his goon ourselves." I secured the door, then shut the outside gate and locked it.

"I'm not worried," Grandpa said matter-of-factly. "I have Neil the avenger to protect me."

I smirked, but said nothing.

"You have your problems, but you're one tough bastard. Worse comes to worst, throw one of your patented blocks," Grandpa suggested.

"Your humor is outdone only by your kindness," I noted.

"You got that right, kid," he said, and chuckled.

I hesitated before unlocking the car door. Something beneath the laughter in what he said rattled the door of my memory. Exactly why, I couldn't say.

And I didn't figure it out until it was almost too late.

Christmas Eve

28

Shortly before four o'clock in the morning, I felt a hand firmly shake my shoulder. I'd been dreaming about The Stables, where we'd chowed down on steaks earlier, and following men in tweed. A lot of men. It was like one of those old comedy chase scenes where a character goes into one room in a hallway and comes out of a totally different room on the other side of that hallway. But I was sitting in the middle of the hall with Grandpa, trying to eat, and these men in tweed were coming and going from room to room, orbiting me like so many moons around a slow planet. Grandpa appeared oblivious to the situation.

Then there was another shake.

"Neil," Grandpa whispered. "Someone's trying to break in downstairs."

"Oh, Lord!" I shot out of bed, my heart speeding from slumber to seventy in a millisecond, and grabbed my glasses and the .38 from the nightstand. Checking the chamber, I saw that it was fully loaded. I snapped the piece closed and released the safety.

A strong wind peppered the living-room window. Grandpa had left the area dark. Only the milky glow from outside lights seeped into the small apartment. Slender strands wavered through twisting trees and clutched the ceiling like bony fingers desperately clawing to get out. The wooden floor creaked beneath my bare feet and my knee was stiff as I inched close to the door, steadied my breathing, and listened.

The old man leaned close to my ear. "The doorknob's been clattering, and there's a scratching like someone's doing their damnedest to pick the lock."

"Sure it's not the wind?" I asked softly.

"I've listened carefully the last few minutes. The noise isn't the wind."

Then we both heard a click.

"You're right," I said. "Definitely not the wind."

There was a rush of wind sandwiched by the gentle opening and closing of the door. Then footsteps, a hair above silent, ascended the stairs. No voices. I pictured Albright Cooper and his thug muscling toward us.

I motioned for Grandpa to step back to my bedroom while I edged over and stared out the peephole. The stark lightbulb blazed harshly on the small landing. Then an image came into view. Trim, shapely . . .

"What the hell?" I said aloud, and flipped on the lights.

I lowered the gun to my side, then unchained, unlocked, and swung the door open.

"Lady, you almost got yourself killed," I said as Christine Cooper breezed into the apartment.

Grandpa's eyes narrowed.

Suddenly I realized I was standing there in only my green boxers and ZZ Top T-shirt.

"Didn't realize you also had the talents of a cat burglar," Grandpa stated. He wore gray sweats.

"I need your help, Stephen." There was a quiver to her voice, and she rubbed her hands together as if to warm herself.

"Your husband find you?" I asked, guilt striking me.

"Stephen?" she repeated, ignoring me.

I shoved the door closed before I ducked into the bedroom to put on my bathrobe. The gun was heavy in my hand. I glanced at it, started to set the piece down, then changed my mind. After clicking the safety back on, I shoved my hand with the .38 into my pocket.

"I'll bet my blind mule you want me to give you money," Grandpa said to Christine.

Her jaw was set firmly. "I don't want you to simply *give* me money. Not without compensation."

"Compensation?"

"Yes. Your freedom."

"Speak plainly, Christine."

"I can prove you didn't kill Walter." She spoke rapidly and in a high tone.

"I know I didn't kill Walter—"

"You're right. You know it. I know it. Junior, here, knows it. Added together that information's not worth the quarter it costs to call your lawyer."

"What kind of proof are you talking about?" Grandpa demanded.

"Not so fast, Stephen," she warned.

"This is extortion," I objected.

"No, this is business." Christine paced to the window and crossed her arms, trying to calm herself. "I learned well from Albright."

My head spun. "Wait a minute. In the not-so-distant past you wanted to run away with Grandpa. Now you're blackmailing him?"

She shrugged. "Things change."

I fought the urge to brandish the .38 and shoot her. At any rate, her latest shenanigans erased the guilt I felt for tipping off Albright.

"You can't have the deed to the mine," Grandpa said.

"I don't want your precious mine. Albright's going to end up with that hole in the mountain sooner or later, anyway."

Grandpa's back stiffened.

"All I want is a hundred thousand."

I pulled the gun out. "Lady—"

"Neil, put that thing away," the old man said.

"But, are you listening—"

"Neil! Are *you* listening?" he insisted.

Reluctantly, I walked into the kitchen, set the gun on the counter, and drew a glass of tap water.

"Christine, I'm calling your hand before I call the

cops," Grandpa stated. "So lay your cards on the table and let's see what you've got."

"That's not much money to pay in order to ensure your freedom," she persisted. "You're too old for prison, Stephen."

I drank, then set the water glass beside the gun. *Things change,* I scoffed, but suddenly realized what she meant.

I approached her and said, "You met with the man in tweed."

Christine threw up her arms. "You're impossible, Stephen," she cried, still ignoring me, and stepped away from the window. "A priceless chance—"

"It's not priceless," Grandpa said curtly.

"Damn you." Abruptly, she whirled around and stomped out of the apartment.

"You can't walk away this time," Grandpa called, and went after her.

Quite a performance, I thought, and limped after them both.

"You're going to the police with your evidence, aren't you?" the old man demanded.

Christine picked up her pace and disappeared into the early-morning darkness with Grandpa closing in. When I hit the driveway, the air that curled around me was a brisk reminder of what little clothing I wore. I heard voices in the shadows.

"I'm sorry, Stephen," Christine was saying.

"I should've known," Grandpa answered.

Something in his voice caused me to pause. Then I noticed there were three figures in the blackness, not two. And one was smoking a cigarette. What the hell was C.J. doing here? I wondered.

"Tell your grandson not to come any closer," I heard Christine say. "It would be dreadful to shoot someone so young."

"Stay where you are, Neil. He has a gun."

"I know he has a gun—" Then I stopped as a terrible mix of fear and understanding collided like storm clouds in my mind.

The third person wasn't C. J. McDaniels.

"Stephen, honey, I truly believe he'll shoot the boy's golden locks off his handsome young head."

"Just stay put, Neil," Grandpa ordered.

Damn me for leaving the gun upstairs, I thought. Then again, I was in the light, out in the open, mobility impaired by my knee, while they were in the dark, close to cover, with Grandpa between us. Gun or no gun, it was a rotten situation. Hell, it'd been a rotten situation since day one of Grandpa's arrival. To top it off, now there was a serious shortage of help. Where was that cantankerous old detective when you needed him?

"What do you say, Stephen?" I heard Christine implore. "You see we can help."

"You're much too greedy, my dear."

"You'll never see us again," she said.

That could be taken two ways, I thought. I surveyed the area for an idea, a plan. But with the porch light blazing, I felt imprisoned, surrounded by shades of black. Somehow I was the one who ended up under the glare of the interrogation light. Alone and vulnerable. The three shadowy figures stood by the Cyclone fence that ran along the side of Jerry's property. Nearby a large car was parked in the driveway. The wind spiraled leaves off the pavement. The limbs of the massive pecan tree swayed like great rowing oars. The sky was a frigid blue-gray river against the blush of the city lights. Somewhere in the neighborhood a trash can blew over.

"You won't shoot me," Grandpa said, suddenly and loudly. "I'm no use to you dead."

"And little use alive," the third voice said. Gravelly. Familiar. The tweed man, but as I was not facing him, I caught an intonation to his tone I hadn't picked up on before.

You got the wrong guy, kid. He addressed me as kid. Only one person ever consistently called me that. And the cigarettes. I was a fool. The man in the tobacco shop even told me they were Turkish.

"Don't push him, Grandpa," I called. "He will shoot you. But he won't shoot me." I began to step from the light.

The sound of the gun cocking was as loud as a limb ripped from the pecan tree.

"Neil, don't," Grandpa shouted.

"You know, I'm cold and tired, right to the point of not giving a damn," I stated.

He fired. A thunderclap Zeus would've been proud of. The shot skipped off the driveway to my right and splintered the corner of the garage.

A dog began to bark. With any luck someone would call the cops.

I took another step. "You two best leave."

"Don't make me kill you, kid."

"Come on, honey," Christine pleaded to the third man. "It didn't work; let's just go."

"He owes me more!"

I saw the gun swing toward Grandpa's belly.

"He owes you nothing—Uncle Walt!" I cried.

"The boy's not stupid," Grandpa told his former partner.

I watched as he waved the gun from Grandpa to me and back.

The dog's barking grew louder, and I realized it was coming from behind me.

"Whose body was in the mine?" I asked.

"Edgar Bryant's, of course," Grandpa answered from the shadows. "He must have caught Walt skimming—"

"Shut up," he said. "You don't know the half of it. All I wanted was my rightful share."

"You gambled away your share," Grandpa said angrily.

I heard the gun cock again. And the dog, still barking fiercely.

"And so you had to implicate Grandpa," I concluded quickly. "Tensions between you and my grandfather were well-known, and of course there was the argument in the bar. After dumping Bryant's body in the mine, you staged the fire so identification would be difficult."

"But to misdirect the investigation, you dressed Bryant in your clothes along with your ring and glasses," Grandpa joined in. "It was a good bet that some cloth fibers would survive, as well as your ring and glasses. Christine said you'd had dental work done not too long ago. What'd you do, steal the records or burn the office down?"

"Either way you're free as a ghost," I added. "What a Christmas present for a dead man. Wander the earth in anonymity while your nemesis takes revenge for you on your own partner. Diabolical."

"Shut up!" the third man snapped.

The barking persisted. I finally realized it came from Jerry's house.

Christine backed away. "I thought you were dead, Walter." Her voice quivered. "And then you came alive. I'm still in shock, but I'm so happy. Albright's the killer—"

"No, he's simply abusive and greedy," Grandpa interrupted. "He saw a way to get rid of me and took it, thanks to Walt. But Walt's the real killer."

"I don't believe it," she objected. "Albright killed him! Walter?" She turned desperately to Walter.

"Albright doesn't know his ass from his elbow," Walt said derisively.

"No," Christine cried. "Tell them what you told me. How Albright ordered his men to murder you because of our affair. Except his men hit Edgar Bryant by mistake. Your only crime was to start the fire so no one could prove the dead man wasn't you, and then you could safely go into hiding."

"Christine, Ed and Walt might've been about the same size," Grandpa reasoned, "but they didn't resemble each other much. Albright's men wouldn't have mistaken Ed for Walt."

"Walter!" She stared at him, not believing Grandpa.

"What's the difference, Christine?" Walter said coolly. "I'm dead, Albright's gun was the murder weapon—thank you, dear, for giving me access to it—and Stephen's going to take the rap unless he comes up with some cash, quick."

"At four in the morning?" I said incredulously.

"He has stocks, certificates of deposit—"

"Is that what you were looking for when you smacked me on the head in the motel room?"

"You surprised me, kid. I didn't want to hurt you," Walt said.

"So now you take potshots at me?"

"Haven't hit you. Yet."

"Walter?" Christine said, voice low. "You killed—"

"Shut up!" he snarled. "Well, Stephen, what'll it be? You cleaned out the safe—"

"It was my property," Grandpa cut in.

"You killed him?" Christine's voice rose.

"You wanted to be rid of your husband," he stated calmly.

"That's the same way Albright would've handled it," she said, backing away.

The dog's barking grew louder.

"But I handled it better," Walter said proudly. "I played him for a fool the way he's been using people for years. I told him his gun was the murder weapon and I could prove it. And then I hid the piece where he couldn't find it or report it stolen without implicating himself. So he had to pay me, too."

"But you didn't deliver on your end of the bargain," I said, beginning to see the light. "You set Albright and Grandpa against each other, and took them both—or tried to take them both."

"I'm entitled to half the worth of the mine, one way or another."

"Never," Grandpa told his former partner.

"A shame, Stephen. May you rot in jail." Walter's voice was cold.

"You'll rot in hell first," Grandpa shot back.

"Everyone's getting hurt except you, Walter," Christine declared, "and you're the murderer."

"Then stay with Albright," he said dismissively.

"No, I didn't mean—"

"Trade one bastard for another," said Grandpa.

I heard Walter shuffle. Christine started to wail.

"This was all premeditated," I said, everything coming clear at last. "You waited for Ed Bryant's vacation, knowing if he was gone no one would think anything of it. And tracking down someone who's fishing in Hawaii isn't easy."

"You're thinking too much, Neil," Walter stated.

"Did you figure Albright would come after you so hard?" I asked him. "He had Christine followed to Houston hoping to find you. And they trashed Jerry's place, thinking it was mine, in case you'd sold Grandpa the evidence—or you told him you sold the evidence, again to play them off one another. If there actually is evidence," I taunted, "and not just fool talk."

"I didn't mean for you to get involved in this, Neil," he said coldly.

Christine's whimpers grew louder.

"Shut up!" Walter ordered.

The dog was still barking. Old Samson pulled through, I thought.

A sudden crash at the back door of Jerry's house caused us all to jump. There, weaving from inside the house to out, was my landlord, dressed in a V-neck T-shirt, blue striped boxers, and black dress socks. He was toting a shotgun.

"You came back for my dog, did you?" he slurred, snapping the shotgun closed. "Hell, I'll show you whose bite is bad." He hesitated, rocking from foot to foot. "Neil?"

Having noticed me, he had a look of confusion on his face.

The next few seconds lasted the rest of my life.

"Jerry," I hollered, "get back inside the house."

A flash from the darkness, and the porch light exploded. Jerry ducked, then turned and fired both barrels into the cold morning. The blast was enough to pound the wind into submission. Christine screamed. The front windows of the large car shattered into a million tiny tears. I ran toward the three of them. Grandpa wasn't standing. Neither was Walter. Then I heard grunting. They were struggling on the ground. Christine wept uncontrollably. Before

I could reach the two old men, the gun went off again. I froze. The wind whipped my bathrobe like a cape. I heard sirens over the ringing in my ears and Christine's shrieks.

One man stood. He turned toward me slowly.

"Well, Neil, I guess it's true now." Grandpa took a deep breath.

"I killed Walter Pierce."

29

Walter Pierce was not, in fact, dead as a doornail. But he was in serious condition. And therein lay the problem.

An onslaught of flashing lights torched the neighborhood like the front line of a forest fire. Grandpa and I drank coffee in Jerry's kitchen to warm up and calm down. Jerry paced the house and drank coffee to be an awake drunk. Christine sat at the end of the table in silence and stared blankly at her intertwined fingers in her lap.

The first investigator tried to separate us for questioning. He wasn't much older than me, and very aggressive.

"I want the old man first," he directed an officer, "then the woman and the drunk guy. Last the kid in the bathrobe."

"You'll talk to us all together," I said, and tasted the coffee. Too strong, and bitter.

"No, bubba, I run the show."

"We'll talk, but together." I wasn't going to let Christine out of my sight, and I wasn't going to give this yahoo a solo shot at Grandpa.

"You'll talk when and where I tell you to," he grunted.

"How Napoleonic. Then I'll put an end to this right quick," I said, looking up from my mug. "I'll insist on my lawyer being here. You know Alice Tarkenton? She's eaten Eastwood wannabes like you for hors d'oeuvres."

"Why, you—" he burst out, the veins in his neck bulging.

"There's no need for lawyers yet." Lieutenant Gardner entered the room. "I asked the station to contact me if anything happened in your situation," he added, looking square at me. From the bags under his eyes it was obvious sleep had not been his recent friend. However, he continued to maintain his calm demeanor and easy smile.

"But—" the underling began.

"But your ass." Gardner cut him off. "We're going to have ourselves a friendly fireside chat. Go wait outside."

The young detective choked, "Yes, sir," and stalked out of the room.

"I need to get him transferred," Gardner said absently. Two blues remained with him.

"Cup of coffee, Lieutenant?" I offered.

"Don't get too friendly, Neil," Gardner warned.

I raised my hands, glanced at Grandpa. He'd been quiet since the shooting. Couldn't blame him. He and Walter had known each other longer than some people lived.

"I thought your grandfather left town?" Gardner asked.

"He came back," I said shortly.

Gardner sighed. "Tell me, Neil, what kind of magic trick have we here? Your grandfather shoots the man he was supposed to have killed in Colorado."

I was about to explain the events of the night, when Jerry wandered in.

"He fired at me," Jerry said to Gardner. "It was self-defense. They were after my dog again."

Samson rested nervously on the couch in the other room. The wide collar that discouraged the dog from biting his wound did resemble a lampshade. From a face-on view Samson looked like a demonic daisy. He tried to get up when he saw me enter the house, so I hustled over to him to calm him down. Occasionally, though, a deep-throated bark still sprang from his direction.

"I thought old Santa did the shooting?" Gardner asked.

"I did," Grandpa replied.

"I wasted the car, man," said Jerry.

"That gave me the chance to jump Walter."

"Oh, man, so I am responsible."

"Accessory by blown windows," I joked.

"Go watch your dog, Jacoma," the lieutenant ordered.

Jerry scurried into the other room, and I returned to the kitchen. Gardner's attention refocused on us.

"I have two simple questions," he stated. "Whose remains are buried in Colorado? And what were y'all doing outside in the cold playing O.K. Corral at four in the morning?"

Christine didn't move. Grandpa and I looked at one another.

"The body resting under Walter's headstone is that of my former accountant," the old man said in response to the first question, "Edgar Bryant." He then recounted the tale of Bryant's discovery of Walter's embezzlement, Bryant's murder, and Walter's scheme to disappear with the money by posing the body as his own. He'd planned the murder all along to coincide with Bryant's fishing trip to Hawaii. By the time Ed was missed, Walter would've had time to blackmail Albright Cooper—as his gun had been stolen and used to commit the foul deed—and extort money from Grandpa.

Christine's original plan was to run away with Walter, so when she heard that the body in the mine was probably Walter's, she believed her jealous husband had killed him. She fled to Houston to warn Grandpa and to convince him to take Walter's place and leave the country with her. Then Walter reappeared, and in her eagerness to continue with their plan, she bought his explanation that Albright Cooper had murdered the wrong man.

Gardner nodded, waited. Grandpa shifted his gaze to Christine. "You can't go back to Albright," he told her.

Weariness shifted to scorn. "How dare you even try—"

"You don't need a man by your side in order to leave him. You're strong enough, and I *know* you have money to fall back on."

It didn't escape me that Grandpa had neglected to inform the good lieutenant that Christine was privy to, and supportive of, Walter's embezzling.

She sat stiff as a preacher's wife, gathering her poise, or maybe trying to hold it together.

Finally, Gardner, the gentle smile on his face a sight more forced, broke the long stretch of silence. "Okay, let's put this in perspective before moving on to my second question. We have a burned corpse in Colorado that is supposedly the remains of Edgar Bryant. Of course, proving the identity at this point is just a tad troublesome. And the person who allegedly murdered Mr. Bryant is, himself, in serious condition. So all that remains, for now, is hearsay from you, your grandfather, and, presumably, Mrs. Cooper."

Christine's stoic appearance didn't change.

"Three accounts of the crime aren't enough?" I asked.

"Did he actually confess to killing Bryant?"

Yes shot through my brain then braked to a halt on the tip of my tongue. "He—he murdered Bryant. Christine knows it, too."

"Let's talk hypothetical. I'm leading an investigation. Two hundred upstanding citizens swear the assassin is the man on the grassy knoll. They heard the shots coming from there. They all confirm it with each other. But no one sees it happen. A great theory. A sensational story. All hearsay."

"The potential in this situation," Gardner continued, "is that old Mr. Marshall's accused of taking vengeance on his former partner and accountant because they were stealing from him. Who's to say a Colorado DA can't make such a case?"

"That's ridiculous!" I snapped, and pounded my fist against the table. The commotion frenzied Samson again and I heard Jerry reassuring the dog.

"And now for my second question," the lieutenant said.

"Before that," Christine interrupted, "may I say something?"

"By all means," said Gardner.

With trembling hands, Christine opened her purse and pulled out a small package wrapped in brown paper. She handed it to Grandpa. "This is what I was supposed to give you."

"I thought he was bluffing," I said absently.

"Do you know what's in the package, Mrs. Cooper?" Gardner asked.

"No."

"How'd you come by it?"

"Walter gave it to me after we pulled into the driveway."

Grandpa loosened the wrapping. He came to a little white box and lifted the lid. Inside was a Baggie, and inside the Baggie was a small slug.

"Don't take it out of the bag," Gardner directed. He leaned over, picked up a corner, and lifted the plastic bag out of the box. He raised it to the light. "I believe I see flecks of blood."

"What good is that?" I asked. "There's no corpse to compare them to."

"They did an autopsy," said Gardner. "There are records to compare with."

"Even though the identification seemed railroaded through?" I questioned.

"If need be, there are grounds now to exhume the body," the lieutenant told me.

"Looks familiar," said Grandpa. He drew the slug from his pocket. "Remember this, Neil?" He set the bullet on the table.

"I sure do. You dug it out of your living-room wall after you were shot at."

"Lab work will show if they're the same."

"I can do one better," Grandpa responded. "I worked with Walter for years. I know where he'd stash the gun. He bluffed Albright. Walt knew the stakes were too high for Cooper to call."

"What are you getting at, sir?" Gardner asked.

"Check the gun Walter was carrying. I'll bet my gold mine it's Albright Cooper's and fits these bullets."

"And since Walter was *dead*, he reckoned he'd never be caught with the piece," I added, understanding.

Grandpa nodded.

Lieutenant Gardner perked up. "If you're right, then now we have a case."

30

Light tweaked the early-morning sky as the front door opened and a barrage of voices broke into our heated conversation. Lieutenant Gardner was informing Grandpa that when a new grand jury convened after the holidays, he'd have to appear for the shooting of Walter Pierce. In all likelihood, Christine would also have to testify. The lieutenant's voice rose until he could no longer talk over the ruckus in the other room.

"What the hell's going on?" Gardner yelled. Samson was again growling, and a groggy Jerry tried to relax him.

"Three men insist on seeing you," an officer replied.

"I want to file charges," I heard Albright Cooper say.

"Just get your ass in there," C. J. McDaniels grumbled.

I tensed, wondering if I'd identified the voice correctly.

Grandpa's eyes narrowed, and he clutched the edge of the table. I hoped he wouldn't jump over it in order to go after his old nemesis.

Christine's hand went to her mouth.

"Let them through," directed Gardner resignedly.

From living room to kitchen, first Albright entered, then a subdued Rats sporting a bandaged nose, and finally C.J.

"I want to charge this man with kidnapping," said Cooper, pointing to C.J.

Samson was in the vicious mode now. Jerry's voice grew louder. Rats's eyes darted nervously toward the living room.

"As if I don't have enough to deal with," Gardner groused. He rose and poured himself a cup of coffee from

237

the Mr. Coffee on Jerry's turquoise counter. "What are you doing here?"

"I told you—" Cooper began impatiently.

"No," the lieutenant said, cutting Cooper off. "Him." He looked pointedly at C.J.

"I heard about the activities here tonight and figured we needed to put closure to this episode," C.J. said mildly.

"You heard? From whom? Jacoma, calm that dog!" Gardner ordered.

"*Whom?* Hell, it's all over the police band. That's whom."

"You're listening to the police band at five-thirty in the morning?" Gardner was incredulous.

"I couldn't sleep."

"You lead a sad life, McDaniels."

"I want to file charges," Cooper repeated. "First this man throws my associate down stairs. Next he forces us against our will to drive here."

Samson wouldn't relax. "No," Jerry ordered ineffectually. "Stay."

Rats shifted his weight from foot to foot.

"That's your prerogative, sir," Gardner responded to Albright. "But since you are here, let's talk about murder."

Cooper's mouth hung wide open enough to house my VW Bug. Then he looked at Christine. And Grandpa.

"There's your murderer." He pointed at the old man.

"I have reason to doubt that," the lieutenant said.

"And you're helping him," Cooper accused his wife. "Wait until I get you home."

"I'm not going home with you, Albright," she said, straightening herself.

"What do you mean you're not going home with me? Damn hell, you are."

"No, we're finished." She was emphatic.

Cooper glanced nervously around the room. "We'll talk about this later."

"There's nothing to talk about," she said, and crossed her arms. Christine's determined facade was commendable, but seemed no stronger than one of those plywood Christmas cutouts Grandpa and I had run past a few days ago. Should Albright continue gusting, I could see her tumbling to the ground.

He took a step toward her. I stood up.

Cooper glared at me, and said to Gardner, "And I want to charge this low-down Santa's helper with assault."

"Then I'll charge Rats and Fats with attempted kidnapping," I countered. "On *your* order. Not to mention attempted murder, since Rats took a shot at us."

The thug was as uncomfortable as a mouse in a roomful of hungry cats.

"Gentlemen," Gardner intervened as his officers closed in. "We can sort out all these charges and countercharges later. I'm more concerned with a murder in Colorado and tonight's little fireworks."

Samson, unbelievably, was growling even louder. Rats took a step back. Cooper was sweating a little himself.

"Sit down, Neil," Grandpa commanded. "Christine doesn't need to hide behind men any longer."

Christine shot the old man an appreciative, almost loving look, then stood. "No, I don't," she agreed.

I backed off. Perhaps I'd read her wrong.

"A man used your gun and killed for me—no, killed for himself, and I was part of his bounty," she continued bitterly.

"So you know I didn't shoot the man." Cooper suddenly sounded happy.

"No, you bastard, you didn't." Christine swung behind her chair and gripped the top of it with both hands in order to steady herself. "*I. Me. Mine.* All these years you've been so concerned with yourself and what's yours," she spat. "But now I'm leaving and I'm taking half of what we have. I'm not running off any other man's money. I'm leaving with mine."

"You mean mine!" Albright yelled.

The dog's barking grew in volume with Cooper's tone.

"We'll talk in court," Christine replied.

"Yes, you will," said Gardner, and set his coffee cup down. "But what I want to know is, since you're not the killer, what was your role?"

Cooper hesitated. "I want my lawyer," he finally said.

"Again your prerogative." Gardner paced the floor.

"You were in cahoots with Walter," I pushed, judging Cooper's temper wouldn't hold him back.

"You little bastard—"

"You're great at abusing women and hiding behind your thugs when dealing with men. Come out alone, though, and you're not worth a shit," I said, my anger getting the best of me.

"Young Mr. Marshall, that's enough," said Gardner.

Cooper's face was red as a Santa suit and his whole body shook. Grandpa laughed. Samson still wouldn't calm down in spite of Jerry's efforts. Rats's head was bowed so low he could've buried it in the floorboards. Cooper kicked him. "A lot of goddamn help you are."

"Mr. Cooper, do you want to address the fact that your gun was used to kill Edgar Bryant, shoot at Stephen Marshall, and, finally, wound Walter Pierce?" Gardner inquired. He was jumping to conclusions, but I knew his purpose.

"I want my lawyer," Cooper repeated.

"Then we can talk at the station, and talk we will. About breaking and entering into this very house, for starters."

Samson had worked free of Jerry and pulled himself into the kitchen. The Doberman thrashed at the lampshade collar and growled and barked so ferociously the hairs on the back of my neck stood stiff.

Rats turned and collided with C.J. Caught by surprise and obviously feeling threatened, the big detective threw a short jab into the thug's bandaged nose. Rats squealed in pain and dropped to his knees, but he still tried to crawl away.

"You hit my broken nose," he whined.

"What the hell are you doing?" C.J. snapped, and shoved the man onto his side with his foot.

"Get that dog away from me!" Rats cried.

Samson inched forward, barking with possessed madness.

C.J. blocked the doorway and cut off the thug's point of escape. "That dog don't like you much, Rats."

"Keep it away from me!" he begged, and tugged on C.J.'s jeans.

"Don't get blood on me," the detective ordered, but couldn't shake him loose.

"Keep it away," Rats repeated, eyes bulging in fear. "That fucking dog almost killed me!"

"Shut up, you fool!" Cooper snarled.

"If Corbett hadn't put the knife in the dog, he'd have ripped my throat out. Get it away from me!"

I ran to help Jerry restrain Samson. The animal could barely walk, but his determination to tear his enemy apart was amazing.

"You heard that?" Gardner pointed to his officers. They nodded.

"Take him outside and read him his rights," Gardner ordered, then added, "We'll start by charging him with breaking and entering."

Rats shot up and skirted the long way around the table, never taking his eyes off the dog. I led Samson back to the living room with Jerry.

"I should've let Samson have that sleazeball for breakfast," Jerry said.

"The dog would've pulled his stitches out. Just keep him in here." I patted the Doberman. His deafening barks had turned to low growls. He could strike the fear of God into anyone.

"So now you have one, ah, associate in jail for shooting an officer, and another for suspected breaking and entering," Gardner told Cooper. "You talk to me or I tell the DA to put the screws to you. Got it, bubba?"

Cooper was a tough nut—there was no doubt. But now a tremble shook his hand, a quiver distorted his voice, and his arrogant confidence cracked like ice breaking on the surface of a lake.

"Walter took us both," offered Grandpa.

"We can work out a deal," Gardner stated.

Cooper looked slowly from one to another, then finally settled his gaze on Christine.

"For God's sake, Albright," she snapped, "just tell them the truth."

"She gave him my gun," he finally said, pointing at his wife.

"I most certainly did not. He must have stolen it," Christine objected.

"From my nightstand?" Albright shot back sarcastically.

Christine turned her back on him and walked to the kitchen counter.

Cooper's last flare of anger fell from his face, a dazed expression taking its place. He pulled out a chair and sat. "Walter Pierce blackmailed me. I had been to see Bryant the day he was murdered. But all I wanted to do was to convince him to talk Marshall into selling the mineral rights of his land. Bryant told me it would never happen. I left mad, but he was very much alive when I was gone. He was planning for his fishing trip. To Hawaii. He had a bungalow there.

"The next thing I knew, Walter Pierce was at my office threatening me," Cooper continued. "He claimed Bryant was dead and he had witnesses who saw me with him last. He said he knew my gun had killed Bryant. He said he had further proof.

"I was ready to throw him out on his tail, but Pierce said the murder victim was made to look like him so he could disappear. And if I paid him off, then he'd give me evidence to clear myself and prove that Marshall was the killer. I saw that option as the shrewdest way out. Of course, I didn't know he was running off with my wife, too. So I paid him," Cooper concluded glumly.

"How much?" Gardner asked.

"A quarter of a million."

"Jesus." I whistled.

"Walter's greed brought him down," said Grandpa.

"Then he left without giving me shit," Cooper stated bitterly.

"And you had your men shake down old Mr. Marshall in case Walter had sold him the evidence, correct?" Gardner asked.

Cooper nodded.

"One more question," Lieutenant Gardner said. "Did you help orchestrate the burial of Edgar Bryant?"

"It was part of the deal."

"We're going to have to exhume the remains."

"I think I can help there," said Cooper sadly.

31

Like old Marley, Walter Pierce died on Christmas Eve. I had no doubt his chains were long and burdensome. Dickens, I thought, had the right idea of hell. Wayward souls surrounding those earthly people in true need, mourning because they knew they should help—and could've helped in life—but no longer can.

By the end of our session, Albright Cooper, for all his earlier vigor, looked old and tired. Even with a plea bargain, he was still stuck in murky water. There was the matter of a cover-up followed by conspiracy against Grandpa. In the end, I had the sense that even if the man was visited by Walter and three other spirits soon, his fate was sealed, too.

After consulting with a representative from the DA's office, Gardner released us all on our own recognizance. Christine returned to the Renaissance to sleep. For good measure, C.J. left Linda to keep watch over her.

"How'd you know where Cooper was?" I asked the private investigator before he took off.

"We were staking out the hotel, thanks to your call," he said. "Linda spotted them in the lobby. She let me know, and I took it from there."

"That you did." I thought for a moment, then asked, "What are you doing for Christmas?"

"Neil, I don't do holidays anymore."

"Candace has been trying to call you."

"I know, she invited me down to her stables."

"Good, see you there. And Linda."

"I'll think about it," C.J. said reluctantly.

"I want to thank you for all your help," Grandpa told him.

"You ain't out of the woods, yet, Santa."

"Oh, but I am." He shook C.J.'s hand heartily.

"Marshalls ain't nothing but trouble." C.J. scratched Samson behind the collar. "I sure was wrong about you," he said to the dog. Jerry snored, sprawled on the end of the couch. "And about you," he told Grandpa as he trudged out the house.

"Merry Christmas, Mr. McDaniels," Grandpa responded.

"I'll send you a bill," he called back.

"Perhaps I'll pay it. We have to consider this Marshall tradition, after all."

C.J. laughed, and was gone.

"Come, Neil, we have much work to do," Grandpa said.

"I know. I have a big dinner tonight."

"Before then, we have more important things."

"Don't go *Miracle on 34th Street* on me," I said.

"Better," he replied with a grin.

The day was crisp and cold. Sunlight glistened like lemon candy. Grandpa opened his arms to the sky as if he were a child amazed at its magnificence. His energy was contagious.

"It's going to snow tonight," he declared.

"You're nuts." I laughed. "It's cold, but the clouds have broken."

"Yes, I am nuts. But that's part of my Christmas gift to you."

"If it snows, I'll believe you truly are the gent from the North Pole."

Suddenly he grabbed me and pulled me into a tremendous bear hug. "Thank you, Neil, thank you," he cried joyfully. The two of us hopped around. "I knew I was right to count on you."

I felt tears coming. "Aw, shut up. Like C.J. said, we're not out of the woods yet."

"Your Lieutenant Gardner believes us, the gun will match, and Cooper broke down. Perhaps we're not out of the woods, but I see the light." Then he stopped, and we broke apart. "Damn shame about Walter, though. He was a good friend for years."

I wasn't going to encourage that train of thought. "Come on, Gramps," I said. "Let's get dressed and go out for breakfast."

We had a wonderful meal at The Flower, and Grandpa flirted with Juanita, who was at work early as usual. From there we went to The Kitchen and proceeded to polish off what needed to be done for the Gilcrest party.

I prepared the rich and creamy crawfish bisque while Grandpa diligently cleaned the greens for the salad. He even peeled and sliced the jicama—a chore unto itself. As everyone arrived I noticed a bit more pep in their steps. It was Christmas Eve, I thought, and the work was ending. But then I noticed a certain anticipation.

Trisha was talking about the church service she was going to with friends as if it were the premiere of the greatest show on earth. Her New Age stuff was strange to me, but I couldn't deny the energy or excitement she brought to it.

Then there was Robbie, eagerly awaiting the arrival of his sister. Perry was a guest violin soloist at St. John the Divine for their midnight mass. Conrad talked about seeing his son for the first time on Christmas in five years, and the boy was only seven. And Mattie arrived with a black Lab puppy in her arms.

"You think J.J. will like him?" she asked.

"He'll adore him," Grandpa assured her. "He must have just been weaned."

"She. And, yes."

The pup trembled in Grandpa's huge hands until he held her close to his heart. Then her nervousness became physical.

"That's what you get for letting J.J. believe a dog was a possible gift," Mattie said ruefully, retrieving the pup.

Grandpa simply laughed, deep from the belly. "Worse has happened the last few days." He tossed off his apron.

"Come along, Neil," he called. "We have places to go and promises to keep."

"I'll be back," I announced, tearing off my own apron.

"You'd better be," Perry responded, and trotted out of the office, waving envelopes. "You won't get yours until you are." He proceeded to distribute the Christmas bonuses until he came to me.

"Okay, I guess," he finally said, winked, and handed over the envelope.

"Thanks. I've been a bit busy to do any shopping—" I started to say.

"No worry." Grandpa cut me off. "Their gifts are at Keely's with the rest of them."

"Their gifts? The rest of them?"

"I knew you had no time."

The phone rang, thankfully, and since I was standing beside it in the front room, I answered.

"Yes, hello," the woman said in a thick English accent, "this is Mrs. Porterhouse. Is my dinner ready yet?"

I was thrown for a loop. Mrs. Porterhouse, the British consul general's wife. Dinner? What did I forget?

"Ah, Mrs. Porterhouse," I said, "we don't have you down for dinner tonight."

"Oh, I'm sure you do."

Then it clicked. "Mrs. Porterhouse, you have your holidays confused. This is Christmas Eve, not April Fools' Day."

She laughed. "I put a scare into you, though, didn't I? Is the old codger there?"

"Yes, and yes."

"Well, Merry Christmas, Neil."

"And you, too, ma'am." I called Perry to the phone.

"Let's go," I told Grandpa. "Things just keep getting stranger and stranger."

At the door we bumped into Claudia.

"And where are you running off to?" she asked.

"Everything's ready for the Gilcrests." I felt like Bob Cratchit.

"I hope so." She reached into a paper bag and pulled out a present. It was unmistakably a book. "I've always favored Langston Hughes," she said.

Life for me ain't been no crystal stair, I thought. "I like him very much, too," I replied. "Thank you."

"Be at the Gilcrests' soon enough to take over for me. I got to see my grandbaby play an angel in her play."

"He'll be there," Grandpa promised.

We cruised through the busy streets over to Keely's. The masses of people bustling around—readying for trips, conducting last-minute shopping, filling grocery carts to stock up for their own feasts—should've irritated me because of the congestion. But it didn't. In fact, I felt a sort of weightlessness. A little tired, though it was a good tired— like after a strenuous physical workout. The only time a shot of anxiety kicked in was when we pulled to a stop in front of Keely's house and I recalled the possibility of her leaving.

"Not a bad little car, eh, Neil?" Grandpa commented, referring to the rented Camry we'd been driving.

"Not at all." I didn't have to slam the door to make sure it closed. And I clicked down the locks with the remote control. "I'm just getting used to it, but I suppose we should return it and pick up my Bug."

He smiled. "The Camry's yours."

I tugged on my ear, shook my head.

"You heard me right," Grandpa said.

"I can't accept—"

"Like hell you can't. I want to give you something you really need, and after riding around in that eggshell the last few days and freezing my butt off, I decided you need a new vehicle. I bet you roast in that VW in the summer."

"But, Grandpa—" Wind ruffled his beard and lifted a few strands of his long, gray hair that his cap failed to hold down. He squinted into the sun.

"Your VW will never make it up to Colorado, so I'll never see you. That's why I wanted to rent a car, to see how you'd feel about upgrading. And I believe you took to this machine right fine.

"Oh, you can still keep your Bug," he continued. "It's not worth anything as a trade-in, anyway. Neil, I want you to have the car. I'm old, I have enough money, and like millions of souls before me, I haven't figured out how I can take it with me."

I clutched the keys. I felt a little awkward accepting a gift of this magnitude, even from my own grandfather. The result of having been raised with a strong work ethic, I imagined. My family was supportive but not lavish. And this was lavish.

Still, it would be useless to argue. "Thanks," I acquiesced. "I appreciate your generosity, but let me tell you, after pulling through the last few days, it's just gravy. Pure and simple."

Grandpa patted my back. "Come on, I have some explaining to do."

"We should've called Keely first," I muttered.

"I did."

She met Grandpa and me at the door and exuberantly ushered us inside.

"Lovely sweater," Grandpa commented. It was a thick white fisherman's knit. She wore it with a long black skirt, and a pair of dangling red mini-ornament earrings completed the outfit.

"Thank you. I really don't get much of a chance to wear it here, but I love this old sweater. My mother made it years ago. But you didn't come to talk about my mother's craftsmanship. First, tell me what happened." She led us to the living room, where a coffee service was set up on the glass table. A tray of Christmas cookies accompanied it. "Stephen mentioned everything is all right now," Keely added, and poured out three cups.

"More or less," I began, and went into the drama of the early-morning showdown. Grandpa filled in a gap or two. Keely listened intently, her flats kicked off and feet curled under her skirt as she sat on the couch sipping coffee.

"Cooper's such a bitter man. But what happens if it's not his gun Walter was using?" she asked when I finished. "Seems a lot rides on that."

"Yes and no," I said. "Life will be easier if the murder weapon was in Walter's possession. If not, there'll be the slow process of piecing the events together with adequate proof."

"Which I believe we can do now," put in Grandpa. "They made us all sign statements; even Albright did. So if he starts acting psychotic later, there's his own words to throw back at him."

I smiled and thought Albright could fight the statement, claim he was under duress, but I saw no reason to go there at this point.

"Your coffee's getting cold, Neil," Keely pointed out.

"Oh, well—"

"I should've known better than to try to pass some froufrou blend off on you."

"Raspberry mocha, yum."

"I think the coffee's delightful," said Grandpa.

"You're just saying that because she wrapped all your presents," I teased him.

"Did what?" Grandpa asked.

I pointed to the two big plastic bags by the fireplace. "Those are yours, aren't they? Look gift-wrapped to me."

"My dear Keely, you didn't have to go to that effort," the old man said in surprise.

"It was fun. Reminded me of the big family get-togethers I had as a kid. Lots of wrapping, lots of gifts. I miss all the activity. That's what happens when you live so far away."

"What are you doing on Christmas day?" I asked.

"Mark's brother and sister-in-law are coming over."

"Where is Mark?" I asked, noting his absence.

"Last-minute business." Even her usual easy tone couldn't mask the edge of anger.

I paused. "What are you doing after Christmas?" I forced myself to ask.

A sadness came over her. "The powers that be at Berkeley agreed to let me teach a trial semester. See if they like me, if I like it out there, and how Mark deals with the situation. He is less than happy, but I have to give it a shot."

"Yes, you do," I agreed.

"I wasn't going to tell you until after the holidays."

"I suspected you'd go."

"It may only be for one semester, like Peter Winford's visit to Harvard," she offered, almost hopefully.

"And it could be for a long, long time," I said. "Good luck, Keely." I tried to sound upbeat, but I didn't think the words came out that way.

"Oh, Neil, I'm not gone yet."

"I know."

"But we need to be gone." Grandpa interrupted our sad conversation and rose. He set his cup and saucer down on the table.

"I had the suit pressed," Keely told him. "And our contact is Marsha Rivers."

"Suit?" I asked. "Contact?"

"We're taking a little trip over to the Medical Center," Grandpa informed me.

"The children's cancer center at M. D. Anderson Hospital," Keely added.

I glanced at the charcoal picture of her late daughter that hung over the fireplace. Now I understood what they had been up to.

Grandpa left the room and soon returned wearing full Santa Claus regalia.

"If I didn't know any better," I told him, "I'd swear you were the real McCoy."

"Very handsome," Keely complimented him, and slipped on her shoes.

Grandpa picked up the bags of gifts.

"You do this often?" I asked, and took one of the bags from him.

"Year-round and ever since my hair grayed. Those kids'

smiles fill me with joy and break my heart all at the same time." His voice fell. "The hardest is when I visit a ward in July and know some of them won't see the next Christmas."

Keely carried the coffee service through the swinging doors and into the kitchen. She returned carrying her purse and sporting dark glasses.

"You sure you're ready for this?" Grandpa asked her.

"Positive."

Outside, the wind was a cold drink from the north, and clouds, like snow-crested mountains, were beginning to pack together.

"There's a quick stop we need to make first," I announced to their surprise. I didn't explain, either, but they caught the meaning when I stopped at The Kitchen and ran in and grabbed a plate of Trisha's angel cookies. With the golden piped hair, blue robes, and minute detail, the tray was a good four hours' worth of work—which Trisha reminded me of and suggested I have a new batch ready for Perry in the morning. They were gifts for his choir friends.

As Keely and Grandpa talked I realized that this sojourn to the hospital was as much for them as for the kids. Keely had lost a daughter to cancer, and Grandpa had lost a son, my uncle. The old man was guiding her through a painful pilgrimage, a chance to honor young souls that had passed on, and to bring a moment of joy to those who, in many cases, would soon join them.

This was Grandpa's Christmas lecture in action, I thought as I drove them across town. Comfort the sick. Feed the needy with Christmas cheer. Perhaps lame beggars could walk and blind men see.

And maybe ill children, I prayed, really could get well.

Ashamed of my selfish melancholy, I knew I viewed life differently the instant we entered the hospital. The spark on the children's faces when Grandpa entered the room—even those feeling most poorly—mirrored the spirit of the season.

Keely, Santa's helper, was more beautiful than ever. I wished her only the best. God, I'd miss her, though.

This evening was a far cry from this morning. I hoped somewhere the ghost of Walter Pierce was watching, and repenting. Maybe evil died with the body, and maybe shedding that mortal waste brought understanding. Wouldn't that be a lovely thought?

A little girl took a cookie from the tray I offered.

"It's too pretty to eat," she said.

"You could hang the angel on your tree," I suggested.

"Then my brother might eat it," she objected.

I laughed, hugged the tiny child. "Perhaps you should just hold on to it." I recalled all the cookies my mother used to make, and how we complained if we didn't have enough extra frosting to eat while decorating. I was glad I had absconded with Trisha's angels. Grandpa would help me replace them.

Before we left, Keely kissed me on the cheek and squeezed my hand. I put my arm around her, smiling warmly.

She tried her best Schwarzenegger imitation. "Ah'll be back."

"Ah'll be here," I replied.

"Merry Christmas, Neil," she said.

"Merry Christmas, babe." I stared at Keely's eyes beneath her dark glasses. Her long lashes were moist.

And I swear, outside in Houston, Texas, large flakes of snow began to fall.

For a recipe
from Neil Marshall's Cookbook,
turn the page. . . .

Apple Strudel

Yield: Makes one three-to-four-foot strudel.

Filling:
8 Granny Smith apples, sliced
3/4 cup brown sugar
3/4 cup granulated sugar
1/2 cup raisins
1/4 cup dark rum
1 tablespoon vanilla extract
1/2 cup chopped walnuts
1/2 teaspoon cinnamon
Grated rind of one small lemon
Juice of one small lemon

Dough:
1 egg, slightly beaten
2/3 cup warm water
2 tablespoons melted butter
2 1/2–3/4 cups bread flour
1/2 teaspoon salt
1/4 teaspoon white vinegar
Melted butter to brush the dough with
1/2 cup yellow cake crumbs
Powdered sugar

Combine sliced apples with lemon juice. Add brown sugar, granulated sugar, raisins, rum, vanilla, walnuts, cinnamon, and lemon peel. Allow mixture to sit at room temperature while preparing the dough.

Sift 2 1/4 cups of the flour together with the salt. In a separate bowl, combine water, melted butter, and vinegar. Add to the flour mixture. Add egg and mix. Turn out onto a floured surface. Knead dough ten minutes, using the remaining 1/2 cup of flour as necessary. Set dough in a slightly greased bowl and cover with a cloth. Allow it to rest in a warm place for twenty minutes. Note: dough must be warm to the touch when stretching begins.

Cover kitchen table with a small tablecloth and lightly flour it. Roll dough with a rolling pin until it's approximately 1/4-inch thick, then carefully stretch the dough with the back of your hands until it is the thickness of tissue paper. Brush dough with melted butter and dust it with cake crumbs. Place filling on one end. Trim off thick edges then fold in. Using the tablecloth as a guide, roll the strudel the length of the dough. Lift it onto a baking pan. Brush with butter. Bake ten minutes at 400 degrees F. Again brush with butter, turning strudel around in the oven, and bake ten more minutes. Repeat, baking strudel for a final ten minutes or until golden brown. Allow strudel to cool. Top with sifted powdered sugar. Cut into two-to-three-inch slices.

NOTES:

This version of Austrian apple strudel was derived primarily from recipes found in the *Time-Life Austrian Cookbook* and the *Pennsylvania Dutch Cookbook—Fine Old Recipes*. As any cook knows, after working with a recipe over a long period, you tend to individualize it. I worked with this recipe for more than ten years.

Stretching the dough is the tricky part. Be sure to flour your hands before pulling the dough. Also, two people stretching and rotating the dough will be much more successful than one person going it alone. Procedure must be done quickly, as once the dough cools, stretching becomes close to impossible.

When adding the filling, use a slotted spoon or your hands—as I always did—in order to drain off excess liquid. I *do not* recommend draining the filling in a colander, as this will render it dry.

Finally, the strudel holds up very well served by itself. However, whipped cream, ice cream, or a hot rum sauce are tasty accompaniments. *Bon appétit.*

A CONVERSATION WITH TIM HEMLIN

Q. Aspiring authors are often advised, "Write about what you know." Since one might say you are intimately acquainted with the principal settings of If Wishes Were Horses . . . — *that is, Houston, the university, and gourmet catering—is that adage true for you? Did you purposely set out to "write what you know"?*

A. "Write what you know" is not only an adage—it's a battle cry, especially for aspiring writers. I even remember my father, a farmer, advising me that fifteen years ago. But writing "what you know" is not simply for aspiring writers. Look at Hemingway, for example. He traveled around the world and told us, in some form, about every step. In my case, I chose familiar settings because I'm able to draw from my university experiences as well as from being a gourmet chef. This dual training opened many interesting doors. Like Neil, I am a poet and had the great fortune to study under Pulitzer Prize–winning poet Charles Simic. Simic pulled my writing into the twentieth century and taught me the value of each word. As for my career as a chef—in my second Neil Marshall novel, *A Whisper of Rage*, I include a scene where Neil talks about preparing and serving a six-course dinner for former secretary of state Henry Kissinger. Well, that's something I drew from personal knowledge. And though I omit client names and change the setting, I record Dr. Kissinger's responses exactly.

Q. Beyond the obvious parallels of profession, how is Neil Marshall similar to you? And how do you and your hero differ?

A. Outside of profession, the most obvious similarity is that both Neil and I have suffered through divorces. Neil's, however, was less amicable. My ex-wife and I actually get along quite well. Other than that, my character and I tend to go our own ways. Neil is in search of love, though he guards his new independence carefully. In fact, the object of his affection, Keely Cohen, is very unobtainable. In contrast, I have ten years on Neil, am happily married, and have so many kids rampaging through the house you'll have to read the dedication in my second book to believe it.

Q. What drew you to the crime fiction form?

A. Raymond Chandler. Dashiell Hammett. Alfred Hitchcock. Ellery Queen. Jim Rockford, as embodied by James Garner. I grew up under these influences. Then in college I fell under the spell of Robert Parker.

A tremendous amount of credit has to go to my wife, Valerie, who is also a writer. When I first met her, she was working on a novel and I was just starting to dabble in fiction. Valerie's talent for creating vivid scenes and characters moved me to a deeper appreciation of novels. Well, the only genre writing for me was crime fiction. I subsequently wrote a partial first draft of *A Whisper of Rage* that ended up in the "brood box"—a place of mine where, over time, either diamonds in the rough or ashes develop. It wasn't until Valerie and I had been married for almost two years that she read the draft and ruled it a diamond in the rough.

She encouraged me to complete the manuscript, tighten it, and send the baby off. Fortunately, it landed in the lap of Ballantine Associate Publisher Joe Blades.

Q. Why did you decide to write about an amateur sleuth rather than a private eye? From your standpoint, what are the advantages (and disadvantages) of a protagonist who is an amateur investigator?

A. For me, this relates back to the experience factor. I know there are many writers of police procedurals who have never served in law enforcement. I say more power to them. I just didn't feel comfortable with that approach.

As homework background for my novels, I have taken courses at the Houston Police Department through their citizens' academy program—the shoot/don't shoot exercise was particularly exhilarating—and I have friends in law enforcement, so I'm able to tap reliable resources. However, I like the idea of an Everyman—Jimmy Stewart's Hitchcock roles come immediately to mind—in murderously unusual circumstances.

I shied away from the traditional private investigator roles, too, because you can't get much better than Rockford and Spenser.

Q. If Wishes Were Horses . . . is your first published novel. How long was the writing process? How difficult was it getting the novel published?

A. I've been writing for twenty years—it took me that long to find the right combination. Getting published these days is very difficult, and I give tons of thanks to Joe Blades for taking a chance on me. *If Wishes Were Horses . . .* was actually written after *A Whisper of Rage.* Joe read the original manuscript of *A Whisper of Rage* and liked its basic premise and characters but wanted a novel before it in order to strengthen and develop the characters. Thus, *If Wishes Were Horses . . .* was born. I wrote that novel over the summer of 1995, and I'm very proud of the way it turned out. *If Wishes Were Horses . . .* not only captures Neil, the university, and the catering firm as I desired, but it also presents Texas (especially Houston) from my perspective.

Q. What's the pertinence of the title?

A. Beyond the general fact that the victim is a man who began a horse-breeding ranch, the title comes from something my mother used to tell me when I was a child. If there was ever anything I wanted that she wouldn't, or couldn't, provide for me, she'd say, "If wishes were horses, then beggars could ride." She was a schoolteacher, as I am now, and she had a maxim for every occasion. Some, like this one, stuck with me. Hated it then. Guess I owe her now.

Q. Since A Whisper of Rage, *Neil Marshall has appeared in* People in Glass Houses *and in a new mystery,* A Catered Christmas. *Will you continue to write mysteries featuring Neil?*

A. Yes, Neil will be in the next book, and the next and the next . . . We're bonded, and though I move on to middle age, he's just riding out of his twenties with a great future. At the moment I'm writing the fifth novel about Neil—and I hope to be able to chronicle his adventures for a long time to come.

—This interview originally appeared
in a slightly different form in *Murder on the Internet.*

TIM HEMLIN

"Tim Hemlin is a welcome new voice
in the mystery field."
—EARL EMERSON

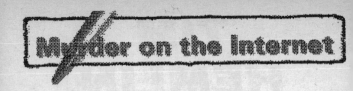